# THE MERGER

## THE KELLER FAMILY ~ BOOK NINE

## BERNADETTE MARIE

5 PRINCE PUBLISHING

The Merger, Bernadette Marie

Copyright Bernadette Marie 2014

Published by 5 Prince Publishing

ISBN Digital: 978-1-63112-083-1

ISBN Print: 978-1-63112-084-8


First Edition/First Printing December 2014 Printed U.S.A.

4th Edition January 2022

12-8

*For Stan,*
*Our Merger has made for one amazing adventure!*
*Thanks for being my partner in business and in life!*

# ACKNOWLEDGMENTS

For Stan who has backed my wild adventures 100% since the minute I met him.

For my Fab 5 who are my greatest successes to date!

For Mom, Dad, and Anni who have given me those shoves up the ladders I was climbing when I needed it.

For Connie, Clare, and Marie who have helped me build (what is in my head) an empire to making dreams come true.

For Cate and Connie who polished my contractual commitment so that it shined.

For all men and women who dream big!

Date for Hire

# THE MERGER

# CHAPTER 1

*O*regon was a fine place. Perhaps, Spencer Benson
thought, he'd like to come back someday and visit as a
tourist. However he was into his fifth month of merger negotiations with Pacific Line Lumber, and his desire to ever fly out to
the Pacific coast again was waning.

He pressed his head to the back of the boardroom chair as he
listened to the eighty-year-old owner of the company reminisce,
again, about the day his father had taken down the first tree to
build their family house—and an empire was born.

Spencer had a great appreciation for family business. He was
part of one. His great-grandfather had started Benson, Benson,
and Hart. His grandfather took over, followed by his father. His
cousin Ed had been holding the CEO position for years now. It
was time for him to rise to the position. However, taking five
months to close a deal wasn't making him shine.

A moment later, the door opened, and Spencer felt the twinge
in his chest start as it did every time that bitch of a lawyer walked
in the door. Julie Jacobson had found a million little flaws in the
proposal. He'd like to not see her face again.

Okay, he thought, it wasn't a bad face. She wore her blonde

hair back in a ponytail most times. Her eyes were brown. He'd noticed that as she'd burned holes through him for the past five months with them.

Today she hurried into the boardroom dropping a stack of paper on the table. It toppled over, slid to the floor, and she scrambled to pick it up as every man in the room watched.

Okay, he'd later admit he'd rather have watched her fume over the papers and thought it was just, but he wasn't that kind of man. Spencer rose from his seat and walked across the room to help the frazzled lawyer with the mess she'd created.

When everything was stacked back on the table, she turned those brown eyes on him. They were bloodshot and full of sadness.

"Thank you," she said very softly as if not to let the rest of the room hear her.

"My pleasure," he lied and walked back to his seat.

The meeting continued with interludes from the owner as he reminisced about this or that. A brief five hours later, they finally broke and Spencer gathered his things and headed back to his hotel.

As he walked through the lobby, his phone rang. It was his father and he toyed with the idea of not answering it. However, that wasn't like him either.

"Hey, Dad."

"Make any progress?"

Spencer blew out a breath. "You know that lawyer is making me crazy. We're up to replanting. How many trees and seedlings will we replant each year to replace everything we use. We've gone over that."

His father laughed. "And how many will we?"

"I don't know," he said pushing the button to the elevator. "I have a lot of math to do tonight."

"This is your project. You'll do fine with it."

"Sure, you just don't get what a piece of work this woman is," he said just as he noticed that very woman step into the elevator as the doors closed. He let out a grunt. "Dad, I'll talk to you later."

He disconnected the call and shoved his phone back into his pocket.

Julie Jacobson didn't turn to look at him. She didn't say a word to him. But there was something going on inside of her. Something was wrong. Why was she in the hotel elevator?

Was she crying?

Oh, who cared? She deserved to cry. She was costing him time and money each time she opened her damn mouth in that boardroom, and he was tired of her. Let her cry.

The elevator opened again and another man walked in, looked her up and down, then he pushed a button. The elevator rose a mere two floors before the man got off. Spencer watched as Julie literally stomped her foot in aggravation for the stop.

They rode in silence for a few more floors, and then the doors opened. Spencer began to step off, but the blood that ran through him wouldn't let a woman suffer. He lodged his hand in the door and looked at her. She was indeed crying.

"Ms. Jacobson, are you okay?"

She lifted her head. The woman with the attitude didn't seem to be looking back at him. This was a broken woman with troubles. He could see that. She only nodded and he accepted her answer.

"Okay, then, have a pleasant night." He stepped back again, but when her head lifted again, and the sadness burned through him, he couldn't handle it. He tucked his foot back into the door forcing it open.

"Mr. Benson, what are you doing? I'd like to get to my room, please."

Ah, there she was, he thought as he stepped back into the elevator and the door closed behind him.

"You don't look okay. I mean something's going on and I just want to be here if you need someone."

She let out a grunt. "You hate me. I know you hate me. I'm costing you time and money." So, she was a mind reader. "My private life, on the other hand, isn't any of your business."

He nodded. He could accept that.

She lifted her hands to wipe away the tears and he noticed the sign of a wedding ring having recently been taken off. There was an indent in her finger, and a white line where it must have been worn for years.

"Would you be interested in having a drink?"

She turned to him and those brown eyes bore right through him. "Are you kidding me? You want to take me out for a drink? I'm the lawyer for the company you're trying to buy. I don't think that would look very good, do you?"

He hadn't thought of that. "No. You're right. I just…"

He only had a moment to catch his breath before the woman lunged at him and pushed him up against the wall of the elevator. Spencer was ready for the knee to the groin, but her mouth coming down on his, her tongue pressing into his mouth, her hands in his hair—none of that he'd expected.

Spencer was gripping the bar on the wall, but the man in him decided that a woman throwing herself at him would be better to hold. He placed his hands on her hips and pulled her to him even tighter. Heat rose between them. The moan from her throat was enough to make him go light headed as the blood traveled away from his brain.

When the door opened, Julie stood straight and stepped away from him. As Spencer moved to her, she held up her hand and straightened her shoulders.

Her breath was coming in great big gasps. Pink colored her cheeks and those brown eyes didn't hold fire.

"Good night, Mr. Benson," she said as she stepped out of the elevator.

Goodnight? What in the hell? His body wasn't quick enough

to chase after her before the doors closed and she was out of his sight.

The blood was rushing back to his head and he thought he might need a very cold shower when he got back to his room.

What was that all about? Bitch one moment—panting horny woman the next?

Who needed it? This was just the force and fire he needed to walk into that meeting tomorrow and say take it or leave it. He'd had enough of Pacific Line Lumber and their legal staff.

He pushed the button for his floor.

As the door opened, Spencer stepped out onto his floor and went straight to his room. He slid the keycard into the lock, and then again, and again. He hated these stupid pieces of plastic. Finally, the door beeped and he pushed it open.

The lightness in his head took over. He was going to need to sit down.

He knew this feeling. He'd had it before. Crap! That woman had kissed him senseless. That's what it was.

Something was up with the blonde with those dark, burning eyes. Never before would he have imagined a woman like her in tears. No, something was hurting her—or someone. He'd make sure to take the time tomorrow and find out what was going on.

Spencer sat down on his bed and lay back. He closed his eyes. The heat of that kiss swam in his head again. Her hips under his hands. Her body pressed to his.

Oh, hell, she'd messed with his mind.

Tomorrow, she'd finally see his fire. She wasn't going to mess with him like this. All hell was going to break loose tomorrow.

For now, though, he was going to take a very long, very cold shower.

# CHAPTER 2

*O*nce again, Spencer sat in the boardroom at Pacific Line Lumber, and once again he waited for the moment that bitch of a lawyer, with those amazing lips, walked through the door.

They'd already started breaking ground on the first Benson, Benson, and Hart residential neighborhood project, which he'd made happen. Since he hadn't locked down the merger with the lumber company, costs were already going to go over budget, which meant they'd have to raise the cost of the houses. Every day she opened her mouth it cost him more and more.

When the door opened, Steven McDaniels, another lawyer, walked through the door and set his briefcase on the table.

"I'm very sorry to keep you waiting. I'll be wrapping things up here." His dark suit was pristine. His salt and pepper shaded hair gave him some distinguished credibility, but the man had never spoken during the negotiations when he was in the room. Now he was wrapping things up?

He began to pull out papers and pens from his leather case while Spencer kept his eye on the door. It never opened again, and the meeting began with, "Congratulations. We have finally decided to accept all of your terms."

Papers were set in front of Spencer, and all the while the eighty-year-old man at the head of the table talked about hard times and how this would be a new start for the company.

"I'm sorry," Spencer interrupted not even having listened to the man. "Where is Ms. Jacobson?"

The man in the suit pushed his shoulders back. There was a flash of something in his eyes. Anger? Sadness? Spencer wasn't sure. "She's no longer with the company. I'll be handling the final portion of the merger."

Spencer sat back in his seat as Steven McDaniels began to explain the paperwork. Spencer had merged more than one company with Benson, Benson, and Hart. He knew what the paperwork said. He wondered if this man was the reason Julie Jacobson was crying in the elevator last night before she jumped on him and landed that mind-blowing kiss. Had he taken over her position on this merger?

"Mr. Benson?"

Spencer looked up at the man and realized he'd zoned out, his mind wandering back to the night in the elevator.

"Sorry."

"I was asking if you had any objections to the new clause wording in the contract."

Spencer rubbed his eyes. He needed to pay some damn attention before this guy suddenly owned Benson, Benson, and Hart and Spencer walked away with nothing but Julie Jacobson on his mind.

\* \* \*

FRIDAY MORNINGS WERE USUALLY QUIETER around the office, and that suited Spencer just fine.

He'd taken the red eye out of Portland just to get the hell

home. If it rained in Nashville, he was going to be pissed. He'd had enough with the cloudy skies and mist on his face to last a very long time.

His mood further soured when he saw his brother's car parked in his parking space. Tyler didn't even work for their father's company. Why was he there and parked in Spencer's space?

With more force than necessary, he pushed open the door to his BMW, stepped out, and slammed it. He needed to get a freaking grip on his mood. His brother was forcing him to walk an extra car space, not walk around the whole damn building.

He slid his key into the private elevator, stepped inside, and rode it to his father's office.

When the door opened, he heard them all cheering. He didn't have to see their faces. He knew exactly who stood there.

His mother ran to him and enveloped him in her arms. "Oh, I missed you."

He wrapped his arms around her. "I missed you too."

His father was there to pat him on the back. "Thought maybe you'd bitten off more than you could chew."

Spencer gave him a chuckle and accepted the jab.

As he stepped into the office, his brother Tyler stood there with his wife, Courtney. He hadn't even seen them since the wedding. Things had become so hectic for him that he'd neglected his family. He was sure that was why they'd all joined him on this fine Friday morning.

"You parked in my space," Spencer said as he held out his hand to Tyler.

"Couldn't help myself," he said with a laugh pulling his brother in for a hard hug.

Spencer looked at Courtney who kept a proper smile on her face as she took in everything with her ears. If anyone knew he wore a mask of happiness it was his vision-impaired sister-in-law.

"It's nice to see you, Courtney." He kissed her on the cheek.

"Been a few days since you shaved, huh?"

That was just like her. "I didn't think I needed to impress anyone. I should have thought about you. I should always try harder to impress you."

She giggled and touched his arm. He tensed under her fingers and she nodded, but kept her smile. He'd been caught and she'd corner him later.

"You always impress me, Spencer," she said sweetly.

His cousin Ed and Spencer's half-sister Darcy stood near the window. Darcy was leaned up against the credenza rubbing her pregnant stomach while Ed bounced their little girl Emily in his arms.

"Well done, cuz," Ed shot him a smile, "You almost went over budget."

That made Spencer laugh. "No Benson, Benson, and Hart job goes over on time or budget."

"We taught you right."

Spencer walked to his sister and gave her a kiss on the cheek. "How are you holding up?"

"I'm a pro," she said with a groan. "Six more weeks. I can do anything for six more weeks."

Spencer laughed as he ran a hand over Emily's thick dark hair. They'd adopted their daughter eight months ago and became pregnant a moment later. They were about to have their hands full.

"We have bagels and coffee in the boardroom. I got your favorite schmear," his mother said as she took his hand and began to lead him there.

Spencer might have been annoyed as he drove into work, but his family always had a way of making things better. Always.

# CHAPTER 3

The rest of Spencer's day was spent catching up on work. He'd spent so many hours, days, weeks even, working on getting the merger to go through. He was behind on everything else.

The first Benson, Benson, and Hart community was his brainchild. The houses were being sold. Model homes were going up. School districts were restructuring for the influx of new families, and now the cost of the homes could stay in the affordable range due to the merger with the lumber manufacturer.

His assistant had kept him abreast of everything going on in the office and on his sites. They'd assembled a good team at BBH, and he had perfected it, he thought.

His father and Ed had carried on the old way of doing business, but Spencer was bringing it into the twenty-first century. Yeah, he was good at what he did.

Tyler wasn't interested in the family business. He didn't care if a building went up at all. He was heading up their aunt Simone's *Diamond Gift* non-profit. Tyler's heart was certainly in a different place.

Spencer liked the spoils that success brought. He didn't live in the old house his aunt Arianna had owned and nearly every Keller and Benson had lived in. No, he lived high above Nashville in the penthouse that his own father had designed years earlier for himself, but instead had married Spencer's mother and moved out into the country before the project was ever finished. BBH had kept ownership of the penthouse for all those years, but now it was Spencer's.

It had been decorated with the very best of everything—he had dated the decorator. It had some of the most exquisite art hanging on the walls—the artist had been a love affair one hot summer.

Spencer Benson had it good for his mere twenty-five years. Money wasn't everything, though he enjoyed it a hell of a lot.

He'd seen the world, and he'd fallen in love in every country he'd traveled to. He wouldn't say he was a player— mostly because no one wanted to think of themselves that way—but he enjoyed the company of beautiful, intelligent women.

Spencer knew he wasn't the only one in his family that hadn't settled down with the first person he'd met. His uncle Curtis had a lot of *friends* before he'd fallen in love and married his aunt. Curtis was refined enough know not to talk about it, but it was there. There were a few stories lingering.

Not that it mattered. Spencer loved his family and cherished the business he was helping to build. As long as it had perks, he was going to enjoy those too.

Of course, the whole reason the perks were even on his mind was because of that bitchy lawyer in Oregon.

He scrubbed his hand over his face. Where the hell had she gone the next day? Did they fire her because of what had happened in the elevator? Surely no one knew about that, unless she told them. Honestly, he wasn't sure why he cared. She was old news in another state. He was home and had already solidified a date for the evening, and he was fairly sure his date would still be around by Sunday morning. He deserved that after having put up with that lawyer and her attitude.

But she kept gnawing at his brain, which she always did. Over the past five months, she'd crept into his consciousness more than once. There had been many late night discussions over the contracts—or arguments might be a better term. They'd walked away from each other at least a hundred times in disagreement. Oh, she made his blood boil in anger, but then she'd creep into his thoughts again.

She was married, and it made him mad that she'd be on his mind. He wasn't that kind of man. He shouldn't care where she went on that last day, but the problem was, he did care what happened to her. Something had her crying in the hotel, and what about that ring—or lack thereof—on her finger. She was hurt. Perhaps not physically, but emotionally.

Spencer might like to move from woman to woman, but he never broke their spirit. If they thought something was going on, he nixed it. There was no forever with him. He didn't want it. But he wouldn't hurt a woman over it either.

Then that kiss crept into his mind. If a woman was crying in the elevator over something, why would she kiss a man that made her as crazy as Spencer was sure he did? None of it made sense.

He sat up in his desk chair and rolled back his shoulders.

He didn't need to be thinking about it. Julie Jacobson been a thorn in his side. She had cost him thousands of dollars with her questions and her demands. Good riddance to her. If he never saw her again, it would be too soon.

Someone moved past his office door and it caught his attention. He looked up to see them backtrack and stand in his doorway.

Spencer's shoulders dropped. What-in-the-hell was she doing there, he asked himself as that very thorn in his side looked at him from the hallway.

# CHAPTER 4

*J*ulie stood there as if she'd been frozen in place. She was the last person Spencer thought he'd ever see in his office, that was evident by the wide-eyed, jaw-dropped look he was giving her.

Every part of Julie was shaking. The entire trip to Nashville had been a mistake. This man hated her. Most men hated her. Okay, that wasn't fair, but it seemed to be a current trend.

She was opinionated. She was stubborn. And now she was alone, homeless, and jobless in a town she knew nothing about. Worse, she was still staring at the man she'd kissed in an elevator and then run off.

Was he going to say anything? Should she just keep walking? Where was she going to go?

Yes, she'd just walk on.

Julie turned away from his office door and continued down the hall. She heard his chair, then his footsteps. Julie sucked back a breath of courage and turned around to go back toward the office just as he rounded the corner.

Spencer Benson plowed right into her, and her shaky legs

simply couldn't hold up. Julie fell backward and landed right on her ass.

Damn that hurt! She sat on the floor, every part of her body aching from the collision. Spencer stood above her looking down at her. His eyes were dark and his lips were tight, just as they'd get when he was mad. She'd seen that part of him even if he wasn't the kind of man who lashed out. No, he grew silent mad, and there had been many she'd many times caused it.

A moment later, she remembered she had on a skirt and it had nearly crawled to the top of her thighs. She wasn't helping his impression of her. Julie fixed her skirt and looked back up at him. He'd held out a hand to help her up, but still he hadn't said anything to her.

Swallowing her pride she reached for his hand. Graceful wasn't happening as she tried to pull her legs under herself to gain leverage. Why had she worn shoes with heels too high? Why had she come at all was more like it.

Finally, she managed to get her ass off the floor, and as he pulled, she found the leverage needed to get up, and ended up slamming her body right into his.

Julie let out a grunt as her chest pressed right into Spencers, and his eyes—those dark eyes—were staring right at her.

His hands were on her hips, and the stupid thought of kissing him flashed into her mind again. But she couldn't do that. Doing it the first time was bad enough.

"Why are you here?" He spoke through gritted teeth while he still held her.

"I—well…"

"Spencer?" A woman's strained voice broke through the awkwardness of the moment.

Spencer's hands dropped, and he turned from Julie, and faced the redhead standing behind him.

Her eyebrow was raised and her hands were fisted on her hips. "What are you doing?"

Spencer gave a grunt. "Picking lawyers up off their asses when they fall on them," he said snidely as he moved to the redhead and put his hands on her hips. "Sorry."

She slid her hands up his chest and then shot a look Julie's way before looking back at Spencer. "Where are we going tonight?"

"Thought we could order in Chinese and stay at my place."

The redhead's painted red lips curled into a devious smile. "I packed a bag, just in case you were going to say that.

"Did you?" His shoulders dropped slightly. "I have at least another hour or two of work."

She nodded with a pout. "I could meet you there."

Spencer pulled his keys from his pocket and removed one from the ring. "You remember how to get up there?" He obviously teased with a smile that had the redhead puckering up her lips.

"I remember," she said, her voice airy.

"I'll see you then."

She slid Julie another look before pressing her red lips to Spencer's and pulling him closer to her.

Julie thought she might be sick, but she stood there and watched as if it were some kind of show.

The redhead gave him a seductive grin as she strolled away with a sway in her hips and Spencer's eyes glued to her ass.

Once she was out of sight, with both of them watching her walk away, Spencer turned back to Julie and narrowed his eyes on her again.

"What are you doing here?"

Julie's mouth had gone dry and she wanted to rub her thumb over his lips to wipe away the red lipstick that still stained his bottom lip.

She didn't reach out. Instead, she took a deep breath and acknowledged, mentally, the pain in her butt from where she'd fallen.

"I came to talk to you."

He moved toward her, and Julie pushed back her shoulders hoping she seemed to be in control.

"You're in Nashville because you need to talk to me?"

"Yes."

"A phone call, text, or even email wouldn't work?"

"No."

He nodded slowly and moved in even closer. "Did you get fired?" he whispered.

She hadn't noticed the number of people in offices and behind cubicles when she'd fallen on her ass. In fact, even when the redhead was seducing Spencer, she hadn't heard the noise she did now.

She looked around, but no one was watching them. Obviously, they were as oblivious to her as she had been to them.

"Can we talk in your office?"

His eyes sparked and softened. His mouth turned up into a grin—with red lipstick on it. "Can I trust you?"

Was he serious? He had some hot redhead ready to jump him in the hallway of his office, and he was grinning at her asking her that?

Spencer turned and walked back into his office.

Julie turned and picked up her purse from the floor. She rubbed her hands down her skirt, looked around to see if there were any eyes on her, and followed him into the office.

As she walked in, the door closed behind her. She spun to see him standing there with his back pressed to it.

"Okay, why are you here?" He asked again, his voice had lost its playfulness again.

Looking at him in his white button down shirt, only wrinkled from having sat in his desk chair, and his tie loosened around his neck, made her stomach jumpy. There had been a good reason she'd pounced on him and kissed him the way she had in that elevator. To be honest there were a few reasons she'd done that.

Just the sight of him did things to her body she couldn't control. For the past five months, she had controlled it. That's what a married woman did—controlled it. Well, she wasn't married anymore. It should matter that smeared on his mouth was the lipstick of a voluptuous redhead, but it didn't seem to.

"Can we sit down?"

"You need business formal? I get it. Fine," he said motioning to the chairs in front of the desk. "Have a seat."

That was better, she thought as she walked to the chair. Her butt, back, and shoulders aching from their collision in the hallway, but she did everything she could not to let him see that.

Sitting down in the chair, she tucked her purse into the seat with her, and then looked back toward the door. Spencer was still standing there with his hand wrapped around the knob. Was he going to run?

"Are you going to sit?" she asked.

"I don't know."

She gave him a nod. "Okay, fine."

"Let's do this again. Why are you…"

"I'm here to apologize." His hand released the knob on the door. That was better. "I acted spontaneously the other day, and well, I'm sorry."

Now he took a few steps toward his desk. "You flew all the way out here to tell me you were sorry? I assume you're sorry for the elevator?"

Her chest clenched when he said it. "Oh, that. I'm sorry for that too. I hadn't given any thought to the fact you probably had someone back home." She motioned toward the door to indicate where the redhead had kissed him. "And I drove out here. Flying is too expensive."

Spencer didn't sit behind his desk. No, that would have made things easier on her. Instead, he walked right in front of her and leaned against his desk.

This wasn't helping her thought process at all. She could smell his cologne. He was only inches from hers. She could stand and kiss him again. Was that what he was egging her to do?

Spencer gripped his hands on the side of the desk. He had nice hands, she thought. God, she needed to stop this. Julie wasn't like this. She wasn't some sex-crazed woman who threw herself at a man, but this man seemed to have a different effect on her than others. The last thing she ever should have done was kiss him. But in that moment, back in the elevator, she had needed validation.

It would have been better had he pushed her back but he hadn't. No, he'd given into her kiss and gripped her body next to his. Instead of discarding her, which she was sure he'd have done, he held on tight.

Julie pushed it all down into her gut. There was a reason she was there, and he kept asking, so she needed to get to the point.

# CHAPTER 5

*S*pencer was gripping the desk trying to keep himself in control. Julie, that annoyance of a lawyer, was in his office. He needed to keep reminding himself that he didn't like her, because it had become harder to remember after she'd kissed him.

She looked broken, and Spencer had been raised to help those who needed him, no matter the circumstance. The only problem was he didn't know her circumstance yet.

What he did know was how his body felt pressed to hers in a hot kiss. He knew what those pink pouty lips felt like against his, and now he knew what those legs looked like all the way to the top.

"You have a little..." she wiped her thumb over her lips only drawing more attention to them.

Spencer lifted his hand to his lips and wiped. On his finger was Tiffany's lipstick.

"Thanks."

His heart ached thinking about the sexy redhead on her way to his house. When he'd called her up, she was all he could think of. She wasn't anything serious, and never had been, but he was her go-to man and she was his go-to woman. They hadn't been serious since they were nineteen years old. She'd been engaged to two men, married a different one, and called Spencer on the day after the divorce was final. Three weeks ago he'd driven all the way to Memphis to pick her up at some bar when the musician she'd gone with had hooked up with someone else.

They'd had sex on and off for the last five years when one of them needed it. He wouldn't be surprised if he got home tonight and she was in her yoga pants, her hair pulled up onto a knot on her head, and a big glass of wine in her hands. That's how they were. They were friends first.

Oh, he'd had every intention of having sex with Tiffany tonight. Some of that mind blowing, body numbing sex to forget about women kissing him in elevators. But looking at Julie Jacobson, with her hands gripped so tightly in her lap that her knuckles were white, he wondered if he could even wrap his mind around sex with Tiffany.

"I'm sorry I showed up here. I know you probably never wanted to see me again," Julie began as she wrung her hands together.

"I didn't expect to see you is more like it."

She gave him the slightest smile, but it disappeared again. "With the merger between Pacific Line Lumber and Benson, Benson, and Hart my legal position was in jeopardy."

Spencer nodded. That must have been why she drew the process out so long.

"We agreed not to let any of the original staff go until an evaluation a year into the merger."

"I know."

"Then why was your position in jeopardy?"

"First of all, I'm a very thorough lawyer. All T's crossed all I's dotted."

"I know that."

"The granddaughter of the owner had been hounding me. She

wanted you to pay more for the company. Initially, she wanted me to draw it out until your offer went up."

"Oh, in all that stalling you were supposed to be making it sound more appealing?"

Her eyes were sad and she shrugged. "You made a wonderful purchase."

"I'm not feeling it."

"No, you really did get a good company. The family built a wonderful business. Unfortunately, they have a greedy heir."

"The deal is done, so now what's the problem?"

The first tear fell and she quickly wiped it away.

"What happened that night?" he asked.

She swiped at her eyes again before looking into his.

"The morning I came in late and dropped all my papers—well I'd been up all night." She let out a hard breath. "The day before, my divorce had gone through. Judgment said I got nothing. All I had rights to was my car."

"I can see where someone would be distraught over that."

She nodded. "I'd found out just prior to the merger that my husband was having another affair, so I'd filed for divorce."

"Another affair?"

She puckered her lips to obviously try and push back her emotion. "This was the third time."

Spencer's shoulders dropped. That was inexcusable, no matter what he'd thought of the woman.

"That was when I found my husband in bed with the owner's granddaughter. In my bed. In the house I would later lose in the divorce," she bit out the words.

"Oh, Julie."

"That's why I was late and was such a wreck when I walked in that morning, and you helped me when no one else would."

He couldn't help himself now. Spencer pulled her from the chair and to him, wrapping her in his arms.

She sobbed against his shoulder, and her body began to ease

against him. Spencer closed his eyes and inhaled her. There were a lot of things going on in his body making him forget that he didn't like this woman.

JULIE FELT his large hands on her back rubbing, holding, and soothing her. This wasn't why she was here, but she couldn't back away from him either. At this point, it would be easier to look up into those dark eyes and kiss him again. She needed to push away.

"I'm sorry. I didn't mean to cry on your shoulder either," she apologized.

"It's okay."

She stepped away from him and stood behind the chair she'd earlier occupied. "I was staying at the hotel because I had nowhere else to go."

"And your job?"

She let her shoulders drop. "When I walked in the next day, my desk had been packed up. I was given severance and that was it. They concluded the merger I'd worked so hard on without me."

"That's just not right. I'd ask why you were telling me that, but I'd assume since I was now the new boss that…"

"No. Oh, no. I don't plan to take legal action or anything."

"I'm glad to hear that."

"I need a job. I can't be there with them having their little affair. I needed to move on. I needed to…" She wiped her eyes again. "I need a job."

Spencer tucked his hands into his pockets and rocked back on his heels until he rested, again, against the desk.

"You're here for a job?"

"I'm a good lawyer. I'm very thorough."

"Yes, you are."

She swallowed hard. Guilt was swimming in her stomach. "I lost you a lot of money."

"Yes you did."

She winced. "I'm sorry. I was only trying to be thorough."

"You said that was your style, and you were."

"I know this industry. I was raised in it. My father—well I know the industry." It was those connections that had landed her the position at PLL, and that was strictly between her and Mr. Grayson.

"So was I," he confirmed his relation to the industry.

She nodded. She'd known his history as well.

Spencer studied her. "I just don't understand why you're in Nashville. You could have called me. I could have arranged your job back."

"I needed to leave. I'm going to find somewhere in Nashville to live. And I'd like to work for BBH because I believe in the company. But if there isn't any room for me in your legal department, perhaps you can give me a good reference, since you're familiar with my work, and I'll be on my way."

Now Spencer crossed his arms and his brows drew in. "You want to apply at BBH?"

"I know the business."

"You said that."

"I don't mean to seem desperate, but I am."

"It's Friday afternoon. I don't have anyone I can call to get you a job."

"I have enough to stay in town for a week, maybe two. Will you help me?"

Spencer stood and moved toward her. "Why me? Why did you come here?"

"You're a decent man."

"I'm sure there are a few of us in Oregon."

She nodded. He wasn't going to help her. She could feel it.

"I've taken too much of your time. I appreciate you talking to me."

Julie picked up her purse, hoisted it onto her shoulder, and turned for the door when Spencer reached for her arm.

"Where are you going?"

"I've been enough of a burden to you. I need to go. This was a mistake."

His hand slipped down her arm to her hand and he gently tugged her back in the office.

"Let's talk."

# CHAPTER 6

*S*pencer drove slowly down the familiar street with Julie following closely behind in her car. They'd spent the better part of the afternoon in his office making arrangements.

He understood her a little better now. All that time she'd been making his life miserable, it was her that was suffering. He couldn't imagine such betrayal.

She'd driven straight through from Oregon to Nashville to ask him for a job. He still wasn't sure why she wanted one with BBH, but he did know she needed a place to start over with her life. For some reason, she thought this was the place. He'd still have to see what he could do about that.

Spencer made a few phone calls to his connections within the lumber company. It seemed that he'd just bought a family company with one bad seed, and Libby Grayson was that bad seed."

It appeared that Julie's husband wasn't the first one Libby had sunk her teeth into.

In the past year alone, they'd had three executives leave the company because of her. How was it that he hadn't heard about that when he'd spent the better part of the past five months there?

What was done was done. The family was going to help BBH transition into the company for the next year. Spencer's team would just need to be warned about the granddaughter.

But now he was taking Julie to the one place he could offer her a brand new start.

* * *

JULIE FOLLOWED Spencer down the residential street. He'd been more than gracious, she thought. Especially since she was a whiny, crying, pathetic woman who showed up in his office groveling for a job after having made his past five months hell, then kissing him unexpectedly.

Yes, running off to Nashville was extreme, but she knew it was the right thing to do.

She had a good reputation back in Oregon—not to mention she was licensed in Oregon. That didn't matter. She could be licensed in Nashville soon too, and it would be a fresh start.

Julie could feel tears begin to sting her eyes. How had she been so stupid to marry a man who could so easily be enticed by a pretty face? She'd thought that by marrying a man who was fifteen years older he'd have been mature. Nothing was further from the truth. He was easily persuaded and ruthless when he wanted to be.

It would have been one thing if this were the first time she'd caught the lying bastard in bed with a woman, but it wasn't. It had been nearly a year that she'd been the laughing stock of PLL. Well, now who was laughing? She was following the new CEO of PLL to a house. That lying, cheating, idiot of an ex-husband of hers could have his cheap and sleazy little…

She stopped that line of thought when Spencer pulled up in front of a house on the street. He seriously wasn't bringing her to someone's house. He said he had a place for her to live—a rental —but there were lights on in this house. She wasn't going to live with some friend or relative of his. What had she gotten herself into now?

Julie pulled up behind Spencer's BMW. He'd stepped out looking glorious in the streetlight. She put her car in park, turned it off, and jumped when she noticed he was standing at her window.

He pulled open the door and held out his hand to her to help her from the car.

Who was this man? He didn't freak out when she'd kissed him in the elevator, but was put off when she'd shown up at his office. He'd held her when she cried then told her he knew of a rental she could move into right away. He hadn't exactly offered her a job, but he'd promised he'd help her.

She knew who he was. He was the decent man she'd needed and that was why she was in Nashville.

Julie took his hand and stepped out of her car.

"This isn't what I had in mind when you said you knew of a rental."

His teeth shone white in the dark. "It's a nice place."

"I can't afford a house and I'm not keen on renting someone's room."

He laughed easily. "Then you're in luck. It's a basement apartment. Fully furnished. And the upstairs tenant is a nice lady."

She nodded. "Okay, that sounds more doable."

"C'mon, I'll show it to you."

He started up the drive and an automatic light came on illuminating the driveway and the alley behind the house. There was another fancy car parked out back. By the look of it, she'd assume it was a Mercedes.

Spencer turned and started down the steps to the basement entrance. Another motion light turned on.

"Well lit," she mentioned.

"This has to be one of the best kept up houses you'll ever find."

"How do you know about this?"

He took the keys out of his pocket and slid them into the door. "My aunt has owned this house for nearly thirty years. She rented it to my mom when my mom moved back to Nashville and my aunt moved to New York to perform on Broadway."

"Your aunt is an actress?"

He nodded as he pushed in the door. "She was. She runs a theater now."

He turned on the lights.

"Oh, this is nice," she said as she poked her head in and looked around.

"You can come in," he laughed.

Julie stepped in and she knew she was home—if they didn't want an arm and a leg for the rent.

Spencer walked in and turned on the kitchen light. "My half-sister lived here when she came to Nashville and that's when they furnished it."

"Where does she live now?"

His face contorted and then he grinned. "This is going to sound a bit backwoodsy, so give me time to explain."

"O-kay." She drew out the word.

"My half-sister Darcy came to Nashville after her adoptive mother died. She came in search of her birth parents. All she knew was a private investigator led her to BBH."

"Scandal in the ranks." She grinned, but he lost his smile when she'd said it. "I'm sorry. I joke when I'm uncomfortable."

"I understand." He ran his fingers through his hair. "Long story short, she fell in love with my cousin Ed. Later we found out my mother was her mother. Something I didn't know—that she'd had other children other than my brother and I."

He tucked his hands into his pockets. "My mom had been in an abusive relationship and the man tried to kill her. She gave away the baby to protect her," he said as if he were making sure she understood his mother wouldn't just give away her children.

"That must be a very hard decision to make."

"I think it was. Anyway, she fell in love with Ed and now they're married with a beautiful daughter they adopted and one on the way."

"It does sound backwoodsy. Your sister is married to your cousin?"

His grin widened as he brushed past her to close the door. "I'll make it a little better. My mom is adopted. My uncle is adopted. My half-sister isn't my dad's child, so…" he drew out the word. "They in essence aren't related at all."

That caused her to laugh. Realizing that might have been rude, she covered her mouth with her hand. "Sorry."

"No, it's part of the charm of my family. My mom and aunt are full sisters. They were adopted by my grandparents when my mother was only a baby. My uncle is adopted. And now my sister and Ed have adopted to give a baby a good home too. It's just how they roll on that side of the family."

"And on your dad's side?"

"He's an only child."

She nodded taking it in. "It's hard to be an only. I know."

"No brothers or sisters?"

She shook her head. "No. I was born to older parents. They both passed before I was twenty-one."

He reached for her and touched her arm. The very simple movement sent a charge through her.

"I'm sorry."

She shrugged. "I think you grow up knowing you'll always be alone."

Spencer shook his head. "Not if you're woven into this family."

He grinned again, revealing a dimple in his cheek, before he moved further into the apartment.

Julie stood there unable to move. Had he even realized what he'd said? *Not if you're woven into this family.*

She took a deep breath and followed him.

# CHAPTER 7

$S$pencer noticed how Julie kept her distance from him now. Tiffany had really done a job on this one. That was fine. He was raised to help people out when they needed, it and that was what he was doing.

She was freshly divorced, recently fired, and new in town. And again, he needed to remind himself she'd cost him a lot of money and he didn't like her—really—or so he'd thought.

But those brown eyes and their contrast with her blonde hair did something to him. Not to mention that he'd felt her in his arms. He'd tasted her kisses.

Spencer coughed when he realized he'd sighed aloud and she'd turned to look at him.

"Do you really think I can afford this?" she asked looking around the apartment.

"We keep the rent very reasonable."

She looked around. "I'll need a job first."

"Right." He tucked his hands in his back pockets and leaned back against the wall. "I don't have any openings in my legal department."

"I understand. That would be an area you'd want to have staffed at all times, and I would need to pass the bar here first anyway. I'll go looking tomorrow. If I could have a week…"

He pulled a hand out of his pocket and rested his fingers against her full pouty lips to stop her from talking.

"The reason I wanted PLL was because I opened up our first residential project." He lowered his hand. "I have an assistant that is harried right now trying to keep up with the four high-rise projects Ed and I have going too. I could use someone to help me with the community project."

Her lips parted and her eyes widened. "You want me to work with you?"

"I've seen how thorough you are and how organized," he said, but the flash of her dropping all of her papers on the floor burst into his mind. "I've seen you in action."

"Wow. I didn't expect that."

"I'd understand if you wanted to work on the bar and would rather look for a law job. I just thought…"

This time she raised her dainty fingers to his lips and pressed to stop him from talking.

"Thank you. I'd like the opportunity to be your assistant."

Her eyes locked with his as her fingers slipped from his lips.

Spencer fisted his hands to his side. Every muscle in his body tensed, wanting to pull her in and press his mouth to hers again. She was too vulnerable, which was probably what had her kissing him in the first place. He didn't need that complication in his life right now.

"Why don't we go upstairs and I'll introduce you to Avery."

Julie stepped back. "Avery?"

"She lives upstairs. Also a cousin," he said smiling. "You're going to learn it's hard to not find a member of my family intertwined in your daily life."

She took a deep breath. "Okay. Let's go meet your cousin."

. . .

SPENCER PASSED by Julie in the hall and walked through the kitchen to another door. He gave it a solid bang with his fist before unlocking it with his key.

The door opened to another staircase that went upstairs, but inside of the house.

"Hey, I'm coming up," Spencer yelled.

"I'm decent," a woman's voice yelled back.

Spencer started up the steps and Julie followed. At the top of the stairs, they came out into a kitchen. It was femininely decorated in pink and black, which instantly gave it girly charm. There were flowers in a vase and candles lit on the stove. A wine rack was on the counter filled with beautiful bottles of wine.

Julie realized couldn't wait to meet Avery. She had to be some brilliantly beautiful woman with taste.

As they passed through the kitchen and into the living room, Julie got her first glance at Avery.

Her taste absolutely matched the woman.

She was in the middle of a yoga workout, but even so, Julie's breath was taken by looking at her.

Slim with long limbs in a warrior pose and long black hair pulled into a silky ponytail on the back of her head—she was stunning.

Avery paused the video and turned toward them. Her skin glowed from the sweat that slicked her skin, but it only made her more beautiful.

"As if you need to do that yoga stuff," Spencer joked.

"I do if I want my wine." She smiled back with a brilliant set of white, straight, beautiful teeth.

Had Julie not known this was his cousin, she'd have been instantly and insanely jealous.

"I wanted to introduce you to your new basement tenant. Julie Jacobson, this is Avery Keller."

She shifted her eyes to Julie, but didn't do the head to toe scan that most people did to judge another. "It's very nice to meet you. I'd shake your hand, but…" She wiped them down her thighs.

"It's okay. It's nice to meet you."

"I'm leaving her here. She has the key. Are you only parking out back?"

"Yeah. Easier for me," Avery said.

Spencer turned toward Julie. "You can park in the driveway then. You can pull right up to the door almost."

"You both have been very generous. I appreciate it," Julie said sincerely.

"Do you do yoga?" Avery asked Julie.

"I've taken a few classes. I've never really done much."

"Well, I'm right here doing it every day at eight o'clock. You are more than welcome to come up. I also run in the morning if you're interested."

This woman was insane.

"I don't run, but I might join you for yoga someday."

"You get settled. I'll knock tomorrow and we can at least have some wine. Do you drink wine?"

"I do drink wine."

"Good. It was nice to meet you."

Julie hadn't expected that the beauty would be so gracious, but she found herself falling in love with her as someone she'd want to be friends with.

Spencer turned to lead her back to the stairs.

"Hey, Spence," Avery shouted after him. "I ordered our cake."

"Please tell me it's not pink and black."

Avery was silent, except for an evil laugh. Spencer just shook his head as he led Julie down the steps back to her new apartment.

"Why is she ordering a cake for you?"

"We share the same birthday. Our family is throwing us a big birthday party dinner. Although, all dinners with my family are big."

"You were born on the same day."

"Literally. We're less than an hour apart."

"That's really cool."

"It is until my birthday cake is covered in pink and black."

Julie gave a little laugh, even though jealousy ripped right through her. It had been years since she'd had a birthday cake and a dinner with her family. Spencer Benson was a lucky man.

When they returned through the door at the bottom of the steps, Spencer locked the door. "It locks from both sides."

"Good to know."

"So, are you interested?"

"Very," she said, though she thought the word came out much too airy.

Spencer held out the keys to her and she held open her hand.

"Welcome home, Ms. Jacobson."

"Thank you, Mr. Benson." She took the keys from him letting her fingers brush his and looked back up into his smiling eyes. "I guess you'd better be heading home. Don't you have a date?"

His eyes lost their glimmer. "Right. I have a date." He looked down at his watch. "Hmm, guess I'd better get going. My two or three hours turned into nearly five."

"I didn't mean to take you away from your evening. I should have..."

Spencer pressed his fingers to her lips again. "She'll understand. I'll see you on Monday. Eight o'clock. In my office." He hesitated a moment before dropping his hand.

"Thank you."

"You're welcome." He walked to the door and disappeared through it.

Julie closed the door and locked it. She turned and looked around the small basement apartment. She smiled. This wasn't what she'd expected when she'd driven all day and all night heading to Nashville. She wasn't sure what she'd really expected.

All she knew was she needed to get away from her ex-husband and Libby Grayson. She figured she'd done that.

Now she needed to stop thinking about Spencer Benson because that was making moving on much harder.

# CHAPTER 8

Spencer rubbed his hands over his face as he watched the numbers on the elevator climb. Twelve hours earlier he'd been looking forward to stepping off that elevator where Tiffany would be standing on the other side.

Sometimes she'd be cooking. Sometimes she'd be stark naked. Tonight he just didn't know what he was hoping for.

When the elevator reached the penthouse, he stepped off and it was quiet. His shoes echoed on the marble floor. He noticed the key he'd given her laying on the kitchen counter.

He walked through to the kitchen. She'd ordered a pizza, which amused him. Tiffany loved pizza and she loved having someone come up the elevator to deliver it to her. It had always given her some satisfaction to have someone see her in his place.

He looked around at the pretentiousness of it. Sometimes it surprised him that his own father could have designed it.

The home Spencer was brought up in wasn't pretentious. It was big and roomy, and sat on acres of land. It wasn't flashy like the penthouse. The penthouse was for show.

For the past few years, he'd enjoyed that. He had the fancy car, the fancy house, even the designer suits. But he was never sure it fit him.

It fit his cousin Avery, and even she was living in his Aunt Arianna's old house—with Julie.

Her name rattled in his brain. He didn't even like the woman —really. He'd spent nearly a half a year cursing her.

But it was different now.

The very moment she began to cry in the elevator, it became different. And the moment she'd pressed her lips to his, and they'd taken the kiss further than just a crazy, spontaneous kiss— it was all different.

There was a bottle of wine open on the counter. The patio door was open and Spencer heard the unmistakable sound of Tiffany's laugh. The one with the flirty undertones.

He looked in the pizza box. There were two slices of cheese pizza. Yep, she'd ordered. She was fancy about everything but her pizza.

He took a slice from the box. It was cold enough that he knew she'd ordered it a long time ago. He opened the fridge and pulled out a beer, twisted off the top, and headed out to the patio.

"Oh, Spencer! I thought you gave up on me." She laughed again. "Have you met your neighbor?"

The man seated at the small glass table on his patio stood up. The lights of Nashville were his backdrop. In the shadows, he towered over Spencer as he held out his hand for Spencer to shake.

Spencer rearranged the pizza into the hand holding the beer and shook the man's hand.

"Clark Dwyer," the man said in a deep voice with a British accent.

"Spencer Benson."

"Beautiful flat you have here. Tiffany was kind enough to invite me up for a bite."

"Was she?" He turned toward her and she was grinning.

"Clark is staying a few floors down in that corporate apartment."

Spencer nodded. "Right. The telecommunications company out of London."

Clark nodded. "Correct. Here for a few months setting up the U.S. office."

Feeling like a third wheel in his own home, Spencer took a bite of the cold pizza.

"I think I'll go get out of this suit. You two enjoy the view."

He excused himself and headed down the hallway to his bedroom.

As he pulled his tie from around his neck, he thought of the small basement apartment he'd just set Julie up in. The entire apartment might be as big as the bedroom he was standing in.

The wood paneling that had been painted over and the queen sized bed that took up nearly the whole room made the basement apartment bedroom charming.

His room overlooked Nashville.

Walking to the window, he began to unbutton his shirt.

He could see the cars drive up and down Broadway. Perhaps his cousin Clara's husband was playing tonight in one of the bars that lined the famous street. Perhaps in the bar he'd just opened with his partners.

They made up the popular duo The Wrights, until Clara became pregnant and now Warner was solo. Though he toured with some of the biggest names in the music industry, he still liked to play in the smaller bars where he'd gotten his start.

Somewhere down there, among the streets of Nashville, was his aunt's theater. They were running The Phantom of the Opera now and it was amazing. She and her husband John had really outdone themselves on producing that one.

The Riverside Building hovered over the skyline. There was some comfort in knowing he could see his office from home and his home from his office. Inevitably though, he turned to look at the outskirts of town and he knew, that on a residential street, not too far away, was the house his aunt owned. Tonight it became Julie's house—Julie's home.

He pulled off his shirt and walked toward the enormous mirrored doors of his closet. When he opened it, hangers of neatly hung suit pants and coats met him. He tossed the shirt into the laundry bag for the cleaners, hung up the tie, and began to unbutton his pants.

"Hey sexy."

He looked up to see Tiffany standing in the doorway. "I'm taking the key. I'm going to ride down with Clark, but I'm coming back up. I want to talk."

She gave him a little wave before he could tell her he thought he'd like to just go to bed—alone.

Spencer pulled off his shoes, slipped out of his pants, and hung them up. He found an old pair of running shorts and his University of Tennessee shirt, which he put on.

He walked back to the kitchen, took out the last piece of pizza from the box, and warmed it in the microwave before he heard the elevator open up and Tiffany walked through to the kitchen.

"Is that the last piece?" She asked as Spencer took a bite.

"Yes."

"Will you share it?"

"Are you kidding me? Didn't you eat?"

She grinned. "I had one piece. I didn't want to seem like a pig in front of my guest."

"Oh, that would be horrible."

She walked over next to him and opened her mouth. He moved the pizza so she could take a bite. "Thank you."

"I thought we were going to order Chinese."

"And I thought you were going to be home hours ago."

"I got caught up."

"In the lawyer?" she asked with the side of her mouth turning up into a grin.

He took an enormous bite from the pizza. "With."

"She's cute."

Spencer nodded slowly. "I suppose."

"You suppose? You're going to act as if you didn't notice she was cute?"

He took another bite while she stared at the slice. "She's got a lot on her plate right now."

"Like?"

"A cheating husband which led to him being an ex-husband."

"Bastard."

That made him smile and he offered her another bite of the pizza.

Tiffany leaned in close enough he could feel her pressed against him in all the right places.

"She's free game," she said looking up into his eyes as she chewed.

"Remember the bitch lawyer?"

That made her step back a bit. "From Oregon?"

"Yep."

"That's her?"

"Yep."

"Oh, screw her." Now she moved in and pushed her body tightly to his. "I thought this was something for me to keep my hands off you for."

She reached her hands behind him and gave his ass a squeeze as she worked her mouth against his.

A moment later she pulled back. "Crap, Spencer!"

He just looked her in the eye as she stepped back from him.

"You're off the market for a while," she whined.

He picked up his beer from the counter and took a long pull. It had gone warm and he held it in his mouth for a beat before swallowing hard.

"I didn't say that."

"You didn't have to. That was like kissing my brother."

He chuckled. "You've kissed your brother?"

She slapped him on the arm. "You know what I mean."

He sipped from the bottle again and as he swallowed, he walked the beer to the sink and poured it down the drain.

"I don't see any future with the lawyer, so don't get bent out of shape."

"Oh, good. You just want to sleep with her too?"

He turned and narrowed his gaze on her. "That's not fair."

"I know. You and I aren't heading anywhere either and that's always been the case. It's nice to have a sure thing once in a while. Not just for sex, but also for hanging out, weddings we don't want to go to, or pizza in a nice place. Sometimes I just want to be around family, and you have the best one for that."

Spencer couldn't agree more. He walked toward her and pulled her into his arms. She rested her head on his shoulder.

"You and I have something that no affair, marriage, or divorce can break apart."

"Kinda nice isn't it?" Her voice resonated in his chest.

"Yeah." He kissed the top of her head. "What about this Clark guy?"

She snapped back and was grinning. "Isn't he yummy?"

"I don't want to answer that."

"I'm going to happen to be around tomorrow when he comes home. I think that there could be something for us while he's here."

"Don't get hurt."

She moved to him and cupped his face in her hands. "You either," she said as she pressed her lips to his again and then pulled back. "You like her more than you're letting on. I can't get a good kiss out of you."

"I don't want to like her."

Tiffany patted his face. "Problem is you were born and raised to give everyone a chance." She stepped back and gathered her purse from the counter. "It's one of your biggest faults."

She pressed her lips to her fingers and blew a kiss his way. "I'll see you tomorrow. If you need consoling, I'll bring ice cream. It looks like you and I are on a hiatus from the bedroom."

With that, she was gone and he was alone in his pretentious penthouse with Tiffany's kisses on his lips and Julie on his mind.

# CHAPTER 9

*I*t had been a long time since Julie enjoyed the pleasures of a Saturday morning of leisure.

With the merger between PLL and BBH, she'd been working overtime for months. Of course, she was as she'd told Spencer, just being thorough.

Except for Libby Grayson, the entire Grayson family had been nothing but generous and kind to her. When her parents died, they'd covered her law school tuition so that she could continue doing what she'd had a passion for. Mr. Grayson had given her a job, and she'd done right by them for years.

Finding out the same family had fired her—that was a blow.

She knew there was more to it, and she knew Steven's involvement with Libby had something to do with it. It had been the most stressful year of her life, that was for sure. Surpassing even the years she'd lost her parents and all of her inheritance had trickled away as she took care of her ex-husband's bills.

For that reason alone, she was going to enjoy her Saturday to herself in her new town and her new apartment.

Julie pulled up in front of the grocery store and parked at the end of the lot. She didn't know if she'd get the chance to join

Avery for yoga or not, so she'd better get in as much walking as possible.

Funds were limited for a few weeks so groceries would be equally limited, she decided.

Food that was affordable was unquestionably less healthy, but it would have to do until she'd secured a few paychecks. Then she could find an organic, whole food kind of grocery store and eat better. She was sure that from the look of her, Avery would be able to help her with that.

As she strolled down the cereal aisle, she contemplated her choices. Usually she didn't eat cereal, but this week it would be a staple. She settled on a wheat cereal and moved on. When she turned her cart, she noticed the butcher block. She was going to need at least one decent meal, and maybe she could stretch it out. She began to look at the selection, but a conversation just beyond her had her turning her head.

"I think you're crazy. Steak?"

The redhead laughed easily. "I want a sure thing."

Julie's heart caught in her throat. It was Spencer and the redhead shopping for groceries. How much more intimate could that be?

She lowered her head. Her hair was pulled back in a ponytail and looped through a Star Wars baseball cap. The last thing she needed was them noticing...

"Hey," his voice came through softly and she realized he was standing right next to her.

She turned her head. "Hey."

"You should get a few veggies to go with all that boxed food," he commented and she narrowed her eyes on him.

"When I have a paycheck I'll do that. Right now, it's survival."

"I could loan you..."

She shook her head. "You've done more than I ever could have expected. I won't be taking a loan too."

"Too bad my mom's garden hasn't started to produce yet. I could have loaded you up. Give it a month or so."

She nodded. "Thanks." She looked over at the redhead who was leaned over the counter speaking very seductively to the man in the white jacket. "Planning a nice dinner?"

"I don't know what she's doing. She's lost her mind," he said loud enough that the woman turned and smiled.

"I'm sure you'll enjoy it. I'd better get going."

She turned and walked as quickly as she could to the front to pay, and then out of the store.

SPENCER WATCHED her nearly run from him. What was that all about, he wondered.

"Okay. What should I make to go with it?"

He turned back to Tiffany. "Does the guy even like steak?"

"What guy doesn't like steak?"

"A vegetarian."

Tiffany's eyes widened. "Oh. I don't know."

"This is why you don't cook for someone you spent an hour with."

"You do if he's as sexy as Clark."

"I think you're insane," he laughed as he pulled the cart from her. "Are you almost done?"

"Yes. I need some pasta and some salad. I'll just cover my bases."

"I can't believe I'm going to let you use my place for cheap sex."

"Well, you're too preoccupied to let me have sex with you. I'm going after the accent."

He laughed. He loved Tiffany because she was just like one of the guys, only with perks.

# CHAPTER 10

*T*iffany had, in fact, scored the date with the accent. All Spencer could hope for was that she'd either go back to his place or she'd wash the sheets when she was done.

She was very sure they were going to stay at Spencer's place since the corporate apartment Clark was staying in had two tenants.

Usually, Spencer would call up his brother and hang out with him and his wife, but he knew Courtney was going to ask questions.

He'd tensed under her touch yesterday. He'd never known a blind woman could see so much, but she did.

Spencer wasn't ready to explore what he was feeling. He'd wait to see his brother another day.

So, the question remained, what was he going to do for the night since his place was otherwise occupied?

As he drove through the streets of Nashville, he thought about calling Clara and seeing if her husband was performing. But, Clara was pregnant too. She wouldn't want to go out. Ed and Darcy had their hands too full to entertain him and so did his other cousin Christian. He let out a grunt. When did everyone grow up?

They were all married and having babies. Well, everyone but him and Avery.

That settled it. He'd go to Avery's and hang out. Maybe he could convince her to not have a pink and black cake for their birthday.

Since he hadn't gotten his Chinese food the night before, he stopped and picked up carryout. Oh, Avery would squawk over it. It would make her ankles swell and she'd have to do another few hours of yoga to combat the sodium, but he was confident she'd still eat it.

He parked out back next to her Mercedes and walked up the back porch to the back door. Julie's car wasn't in the drive. That was probably better. He didn't need to have her there, or even as near as the basement.

Spencer knocked on the door before pushing it opened. He really wished she'd keep it locked.

"Hey, you here?" He called out.

"I'm upstairs. I'll be down in a few."

He set the bag on the table and retrieved two plates.

When Avery walked into the kitchen, still putting on her earring, she wasn't dressed in the usual yoga gear he'd expected. Her long black hair was curled and her makeup was fresh.

"Ah, are you going out?"

She adjusted her necklace. "Yes. What are you doing here? What is this? You brought Chinese food? You know I don't eat that and I can't stay away from it."

She sniffed at it.

"I need a place to hang for a while. Tiffany is using my apartment."

She scrunched up her face. "Yuck."

Spencer shrugged. "Where are you going?"

"Pete has an engagement at work. His date canceled last minute and I'm his escort."

"Escort." He laughed. "You two are a riot."

"Meaning?"

"The guy is in love with you, has been since childhood, and you just string him along."

She reached into the takeout bag and pulled out a fortune cookie. Breaking it open she said, "What about you and Tiffany?"

"What about us?"

"Don't you just string her along?"

He pulled out an eggroll and took a bite. "No. We did date and we know it doesn't work. We have sex when it's convenient, but I don't string her along."

Avery looked down at the fortune in her hand. "I think this relates more to you."

She handed him the fortune and he read it. *Love is coming for you. Open your eyes.*

He crumpled up the paper and threw it at her. "Funny."

"Hey, I have to go. Stay and eat. You can use the spare room if you need a place for the night. I'll be in late."

"Do you have protection in your purse?" He called out as she walked through the back door.

"Shut up, Spencer. I hate you."

"I know you do." He laughed as the door closed and he was alone in her house.

His life was pathetic, he decided, as he took out another container of food and dished it out on a plate. They'd only given him chopsticks, which wouldn't work for him. He simply had never mastered the art of them.

Spencer stood and walked to the drawer for a fork. It was then he heard the sound of someone stomping up the back steps of the porch. A moment later the door flew open and there stood Julie with two enormous cups of coffee in her hands.

"Oh, hi," she said kicking the door shut behind her. "I didn't know you'd be here. I could have brought more coffee."

"I didn't know I'd be here either and Avery just left."

Julie's eyes opened wide. "She left? We just did yoga and decided to splurge on fancy coffee. She bought, I flew. You know how that is."

"Her friend Pete needed a date for a work thing. She just left."

"Date for work." She laughed just as he had. "He came by this morning and I met him. He's absolutely in love with her and she has no idea."

"I told her that too. He's been in love with her since the second grade and she's been in denial that long."

Julie set down the coffees. "You're having dinner?"

"I brought it thinking I could convince Avery to have dinner with me."

"I guess she left us both hanging."

"Looks like it. Join me then? I have plenty and could use the company."

She smiled easily. "I'll trade you a French vanilla latte for dinner then. On Avery."

"Deal."

# CHAPTER 11

*J*ulie sat down at the table in her yoga pants and a snug exercise top that showed off a soft set of shoulders that led to toned arms. Her blonde hair was in a ponytail high on the top of her head.

With chopsticks woven between her fingers, she began diving into the sweet and sour pork.

"Oh, this is fabulous," she said with a moan. "Much better than my soup I'd been planning."

He smiled as he watched her take another bite. He'd never seen anyone eat with such enjoyment. It was nearly erotic to watch her.

"Eggroll?"

She nodded and he slid the small white bag toward her. "You'll have to tell me where to get this. I enjoy Chinese food."

He figured, by the way she dug in with those damn chopsticks. Spencer looked down at his fork full of noodles and thought he was pathetic sitting there eating like that.

"Trade?"

She nodded and passed him the box in her hand and took the noodles.

Spencer stabbed a sweet and sour pork piece and lifted it to his mouth, just as he caught sight of her sucking in a noodle through her lips.

Certainly he wasn't going to be able to eat with her anymore. His mind wasn't on food.

His eyes were on her lips. Those lips, which had taken him off guard the night in the elevator. Her fingers, which wrapped around the chopsticks, had pressed to his lips when they'd toured the apartment in the basement. With her hair pulled back, he could see the very delicate skin of her neck and the gentle pulse on the side of it.

Spencer bit down on his fork. Why hadn't Tiffany just had sex with him? He could have gotten all this pent up frustration out and he wouldn't be sitting at his cousin's kitchen table dissecting the delectable parts of the lawyer he'd thought he didn't like.

When Julie raised her eyes to him, a strand of hair fell over those dark wonderous eyes, he realized he'd been staring. She wasn't so much a bitch, he thought as she sucked in a noodle, and he wasn't so afraid of her.

"Is something wrong with the pork?" she asked before she covered her mouth and finished her mouthful.

Spencer shook his head. "No. I just have a few things on my mind."

Julie set her chopsticks on the table and picked up her coffee cup. "I've always been told I have a good ear. If you just want to get something off your chest, I'm here."

What he wanted was to scoop her up, and he didn't like that he wanted that at all. He was much more comfortable before he liked her.

There had been some deep satisfaction when she'd fallen on her ass yesterday.

"It's nothing really. You know in this industry there is always something going on."

She sat back in her seat and studied him. "Why are you here having Chinese?"

He shrugged. "I was hungry for it."

"I thought you were having steak for dinner."

Confusion took over as he considered what she'd said, and then he realized what she'd been thinking that morning at the store.

"Oh, no. That wasn't for me. Tiffany is trying to hook up with the British guy a few floors below my apartment."

Cautiously, she lifted her cup to her lips and studied him. "She's trying to hook up with another guy? I thought you were an item."

"Me and Tiffany? No."

She nodded slowly and her dark eyes narrowed on him. "So what was that scene in the office yesterday? The kissing and touching?"

Spencer set his fork down and took a sip of the coffee. He winced at the taste. "Oh, Lord. Avery drinks this?"

"She ordered it."

"Our tastes are very different." He set down the cup and realized Julie was still staring at him. He hadn't answered her question. "Me and Tiffany."

"Let me guess. It's complicated."

Maybe she did, or would, understand him. "Yes. It's complicated."

"Open relationship?"

"No. No." He stood and walked to the refrigerator to grab a bottle of water and wash down that nasty taste from the coffee, which didn't go with Chinese food at all.

Julie was still staring at him over the rim of her coffee cup. Why did he have to answer her? He didn't owe it to her. What he and Tiffany had was good, when it was anything. Besides, had Julie ever come clean with why she'd kissed him in the elevator?

Spencer reminded himself that he was her boss. Maybe he should be asking the questions.

Her eyes grew wider and he squirmed where he stood next to the counter. "Why are you glaring at me?"

"You're not answering my question."

"Do I need to?"

"No. It's just a politeness factor. But your love life is your own business. I was just making small talk. I can stop." She took another long sip of that nasty coffee and smiled. "I should probably leave you alone. I don't think either of us expected to spend the evening together and we probably don't have a real good basis for a friendship."

"You don't think we're friends?" he asked.

Now she narrowed her eyes on him again. "We're friends?"

"Well, we're not not friends."

Now she nodded and stood. "I know how you feel about me. I can read people. I spent the better part of five months knowing how you felt about me. Everyone in that room hated me. I was just trying to do my job."

"Now that's not fair," he said taking a single step toward her. "I never said I hated you."

"Not to my face. I'll bet somewhere in your vocabulary when talking about me you used the word bitch a time or two," she said sharply.

He took a breath to argue the fact, but then stopped. He had, in fact, more than a dozen times, at least, called her a bitch aloud to others. He'd even used the term when speaking to his father.

Julie's pained look let him know she had her answer. "I'm very grateful you even considered giving me a job that will work so closely with you. I'm even more grateful you found me a place to live. I'll look for something that isn't so close to your family. I think that would be easier."

She stood and started for the back door, but he had to stop her. He set his water on the counter and cut off her exit.

"Don't go looking for a new place to live. I can tell Avery has already taken to you."

She wasn't looking at him now. "Then I'll find a new job. There is no reason for you to have to work with me."

He reached for her arm and rested his hand against her skin. "I offered you the job. I wouldn't have if I thought it was a bad idea."

"You're uncomfortable around me. I don't like people to be uncomfortable unless I'm trying to make them uncomfortable."

He stepped even closer. "I'm not uncomfortable around you. In fact, I seem to be too comfortable."

Again, her eyes dulled in confusion. "I need to go." She reached for the door handle.

"Why did you kiss me?" He blurted the question out there.

"Is that what all this is about?"

"I know why you were in the hotel now, but the kiss..."

"I will talk to you on Monday."

She pushed past him, hurried down the steps of the back porch, and disappeared down the steps to her apartment.

Spencer bit back an oath. He wanted to go after her. He wanted an answer. The angrier he got, the more he wanted another kiss.

# CHAPTER 12

*J*ulie paced the floor, finally ripping out the tie that held back her hair just so she could run her fingers through it.

How come that man could spark both love and hate in her? Okay, not love, but strong attraction. With that dark wavy hair and those shimmering brown eyes. Then the thought about his lips made her body throb.

She cursed. She didn't need to think of him that way. She didn't need to think of him at all.

Julie set her coffee cup on the end table and picked up the remote control, only to set it back down again.

Her mind was buzzing. So asking if he had some open relationship with the redhead he was kissing was wrong? Yet he needed to know why she kissed him?

Well, she didn't have an answer for that. Maybe she had too many answers for that.

He was handsome.

He was nice.

He was right there.

Weren't those good enough reasons to kiss him?

Of course, she was hurt.

She was desperate.

She needed validation that she was every bit as desirable as Libby Grayson.

Had Spencer Benson pushed her away the moment their lips touched, she'd have known that there was a reason no man wanted her. But he hadn't pushed her away. He'd deepened the kiss. He'd pulled her in. He'd pressed his body right to hers.

Julie's breath caught.

It was vivid in her mind. Less than a week had passed since their mouths had melded. Now she would work in his office and live in his aunt's home. This was crazy.

What had possessed her to drive across country to his doorstep? She had connections in the industry. There were other jobs. But for some reason this had been her choice when she realized she had nothing left in Oregon.

Her mind drifted back to Spencer, which it did so often. So what really was the story with him and the redhead? Should she just forget about it?

The answer to that was yes. Attraction wasn't a reason to pack up and move, but she had. The moment she'd been released from PLL, all she had was emotion to guide her because she had nothing left.

No job. No house. No family. No husband. She was pathetic.

No wonder her ex-husband was making his move with Libby. Julie had nothing to offer anyone. From the day they'd met, he'd done nothing but belittle her. She wasn't a good lawyer, a good cook, or any good in bed. That must have been why he'd been caught in more than one indiscretion.

The very thought made her sick to her stomach. There never should have been an opportunity for more than one. She should have left him the first time.

Julie slid to the floor and sobbed.

This was what she wanted wasn't it? After all, if she didn't have the position she'd worked for and earned, she didn't want to be in Oregon anymore. She didn't want to miss it either.

Fresh starts were supposed to be enjoyable. But she was miserable and she'd only been in town two days. It would get better.

Benson, Benson, and Hart was an enormous firm. She'd be working with a lot of people, not just Spencer Benson. Assisting on his new community build could mean a lot of things. She'd be working with architects and land developers. Construction foremen and accountants would filter into her day to day. There was a whole new world to open up to her, even if she'd been in the construction world most of her life, in one capacity or another.

But the pain of being absolutely alone gnawed at her and made her heart ache. It was a slow and squeezing pain that some-times made her lose her breath. No brothers or sisters. No cousins that she personally knew. All she'd had for years was a husband and even he couldn't be faithful to her.

She was twenty-seven-years-old. Being alone wasn't the end of the world. Lots of people started over before they were thirty. She'd just keep that in mind. And when she turned thirty she could reevaluate.

For now, she'd become exhausted at the thought of every-thing. And just to keep her sanity, she promised herself she wouldn't even leave the small basement apartment tomorrow. There wasn't any need to. That would ensure she wouldn't run into any other of Spencer's family or friends.

Julie pulled off her yoga clothes, ran a hot shower, and washed away the pain.

Pulling on a pair of shorts and tank top, she crawled into bed. If she were lucky, sleep would take her away from all those feel-ings that were bundling up in her mind and body. And maybe sleep would erase Spencer Benson from her mind for a few hours.

# CHAPTER 13

*S*pencer tossed and turned all night long. He didn't know if it was because the spare bedroom in Avery's house was hot, or if it was knowing that Julie was only feet away.

He'd heard Pete and Avery stumble in around two in the morning. He could only assume Avery had indulged in too much wine and Pete, being the diligent friend he was, brought her home and tucked her in.

Why they didn't hook up was beyond him. The guy would do anything for her. He was simple though, and Avery was anything but simple.

She'd been brought up by an oil heiress and a doctor. Although, Spencer had never seen a snooty side to his uncle, his aunt Simone's rich upbringing showed through once in awhile.

Avery had been the mend between Simone and her father. So Avery had tasted the heiress life. She'd been on the yachts and flown on the private jets. Her tastes were big, and her desires for fine things, even bigger.

She had a taste for wines and wasn't it interesting that her grandfather had just purchased a vineyard outside of Paris?

Poor Pete. He'd been in all of their lives for as long as Spencer could remember, and yet Avery was still looking for Mr. Right. Spencer was sure Mr. Right was the one who had tucked her in and quietly let himself out the back door.

But what did he know? He'd been so involved with the lawyer, he'd thought he despised, that he'd ruined what was supposed to be a sure thing. Now, he was sleeping in his cousin's spare bedroom so that sure thing could be someone else's sure thing.

He pounded the pillow into a different position and flopped back against it.

The question remained, he decided as he folded his hands over his chest and lay there looking at the moonlight on the ceiling, why had she kissed him in the first place and then driven to Nashville for a job?

Spencer would get his answer. In fact, he didn't have anything going on Sunday. He'd just wait her out.

That's right, he'd stay at Avery's and just wait until Julie emerged. He'd corner her, and they'd try that conversation thing again. Spencer closed his eyes. Now he just needed some damn sleep.


SPENCER WOKE the next morning to Metallica blaring from the living room. What in the hell was Avery doing?

He rolled out of the bed, nearly wrapping himself up in the sheets and falling on his face. He threw his clothes on and started down the stairs.

When he saw Avery, he wanted to break out into laughter, but Avery dancing in the living room in her pink pajamas was exactly what he needed to perk him up.

When she saw him, she gave him a grin. Her hair was in a mess piled atop her head and she held in her hand a black coffee mug.

"C'mon dance with me."

"Why?"

"Because I need to wake up and this is how I do it."

He laughed. "And what does your neighbor think of your morning ritual?"

Her eyes flew open wide and she ran to the stereo and turned down the volume.

"Damn! I forgot all about her."

Spencer shook his head. He figured that was some of Julie's bitchy problem too—nobody paid her much attention.

"I thought you two were hitting it off," Spencer reminded her.

"We are. We did yoga and she was bringing coffee yesterday," she winced when she'd remembered. "I left."

"I drank your coffee. I don't know how you drink that crap."

"I have taste," she rebutted. "God, she must think I'm horrible. I just ran out."

"I think she'll be okay."

"I should go talk to her. Apologize for being such a twit and making so much noise." She headed toward the kitchen and pulled down a coffee mug. "I'll take her some coffee too."

"What time is it?" He realized he hadn't even looked at a clock.

"Ten."

"Really?" When was the last time he'd slept in that late? That's right—not since college. If he wasn't in Oregon the past year, he was on that community site making sure everything was running smoothly. The thought crossed his mind again. That's where he probably should be now too.

He started back up the stairs. "Hey, if you talk to her, see if she has dinner plans."

"Really? You're asking her out? Isn't this the lawyer you didn't like?"

He backtracked down the stairs. "Don't ever tell her that."

"Do you think I'm so thoughtless?"

"She's not that bad. She has a lot going on in her life. I didn't know that."

Avery narrowed her eyes on him. "Interesting. Look at you with a soft spot."

"Shut up. Just ask her for me, okay?"

She nodded. "Where are you going?"

"To kick Tiffany and the accent out of my bed so I can get down to the site."

"Work. Work. Work. Be careful or you'll have a heart attack like your grandfather did."

"Never," he called back down as he raced up to the bedroom to get his shoes.

# CHAPTER 14

Sunday mornings were for lazing around, Julie had decided. She hadn't enjoyed a lazy Sunday in a long time. The merger with BBH had taken a lot of her time over the past year.

She sunk down deeper into the chair. What a waste of time that had been. She'd put her heart into that work, and they dismissed her as if she'd done something wrong. Okay, so she'd dragged out the process longer than necessary, but she was thorough, hadn't she told Spencer that? Why had she been fired? And why had it been Mr. Grayson who signed the papers, but never spoke to her about it? Perhaps he'd reconsidered the reason he'd hired her. When it came down to it, she shouldn't have been dismissed just because her husband—ex-husband—was screwing his granddaughter. The very thought made her sick.

Maybe that's why he was so willing to merge with Benson, Benson, and Hart. It would have been heartbreaking to work that hard to build an empire, as he had with PLL, and to have his granddaughter inherit it all in the end. Of course, they'd taken care of that, her and Mr. Grayson. But now PLL was in good hands and not in Libby Grayson's hands. Spencer Benson would take good care of Pacific Line Lumber.

Trying to be relaxed and enjoy the lazy day, she picked up the remote to the TV. Barricading herself into the basement apartment had her bored out of her mind. It was silly to coop up inside just so she wouldn't run into Spencer, but that's what she was doing.

Nashville was an enormous city, and one she wanted to explore. Looking at the clock, she realized it was much too early for a drink down on Broadway, but she was sure she could find a decent meal there.

Quickly, she calculated what she might have in her wallet. Maybe she'd better just eat the few groceries in her refrigerator.

She sunk down even further in her chair.

The moment she heard the knocking on her door, Julie stiffened. Who would be knocking on her door? Only two people knew she lived there. It had to be one of them—or she hoped it was one of them.

Slowly, at the second knock, she rose to look out the small peephole. There stood Avery with two coffee mugs in her hands.

Julie pulled open the door and smiled at the woman who still looked absolutely beautiful in her pajamas and her hair piled on her head.

"I realize it is much too late to still be in pajamas, but it's never too late for sharing coffee, right?"

Julie nodded. "Come in."

Avery handed her a mug and stepped into the apartment. "I swear it never changes down here. Well, when tenants add their own personal effects. Are yours coming?"

Julie looked down into the coffee mug. "No. I left with what I could carry. Nothing else seemed very important."

Avery's eyes went wide. "Oh, I'm sorry."

"You do what you have to do," Julie said. "Please, have a seat."

"I'm sorry about my loud music this morning. Spencer

reminded me I can't do things like that anymore," she said sitting down on the couch.

"It's okay. It startled me at first, but it doesn't bother me."

Avery toed off her flip-flops, curled her legs under her, and sipped at her coffee as Julie sat in the big recliner.

"So I'm told I can be a little straight forward. So I'll ask, can I be nosy?" Avery asked as she settled in. "Why did you come to Nashville after you were done with the merger?"

Julie wondered if she really needed to answer that. Hadn't Spencer told her all about the bitchy lawyer Julie Jacobson?

What did she have to lose? "They fired me before the merger was complete. I got divorced after I found out my husband was sleeping with the granddaughter of the owner of PLL. And I needed a change."

Avery's eyes widened. "Are you kidding me? He was sleeping with someone else?"

Julie shook her head. "The worst part is, this isn't the first time he's had an indiscretion during our marriage."

"Indiscretion? Look at you with the polite words. What a prick!"

Julie tried to swallow back her smile, but decided it would be hidden behind her coffee mug.

She sipped, let the smile fade, and lowered the mug. "That's what happens when you marry for companionship."

"I can't imagine you needing companionship. You're beautiful and very nice to be around, no matter what..." She stopped and pursed her lips.

"No matter what Spencer told you?" Julie set her coffee on the small end table next to her chair.

"I didn't mean that. I really didn't. I just get to talking so fast sometimes that I..."

"It's okay. He has every right to think what he thinks. I cost him a lot of time and money while I was doing my job."

"Money isn't anything to them."

"Well, it is to me. I thought I was doing the right thing."

Avery watched her for a moment and then smiled a brilliant, model kind of smile. "Do you want to go down to Broadway and get a drink?"

Julie let out a snort of a laugh. "It's not even noon. And I'm extremely short on cash. I think I'd better take a rain check."

"Let's just say I'm not short on cash. Today it's my treat."

"Are you sure? I certainly don't want to impose."

"Trust me. I could use some good ole' girl time. I also happen to know that Warner Wright is rehearsing and we could get in."

Julie stared at her. Was she for real? "You know Warner Wright?"

Avery grinned. "He happens to be married to my cousin."

"Of course he does. Are you guys not related to anyone?"

Avery gave her a shrug. "You and I aren't related, yet."

"We will have to remain friends. I don't see me getting married to anyone in the near future. Unless you have some other unmarried cousins you want to introduce me to."

"Nope, only Spencer. He's the last of the single men."

"No."

"I guess we'll just be friends then," she said swinging her legs over the couch and standing up. "I'll go get ready and call Clara. She can get us in."

"Clara? Another cousin?"

"Yep," she said heading toward the door. "You know, if you just hang out with us, you'll never need to marry for companionship again. You'll probably have too much of it."

Avery opened the door, gave her a little wave, and walked out.

Julie already knew that even being introduced to Avery's family had given her a job, a home, and an opportunity to meet a reality TV personality and one of the most famous country artists in the country. Knowing the Bensons and their cousins certainly couldn't hurt anyone—especially someone who could use some companionship.

# CHAPTER 15

*I*t was a sight, Spencer thought as he drove up to the neighborhood—or what would be a neighborhood.

From the street, it looked like a dream from his childhood. A sandbox filled with big yellow machines that would move the earth into piles and then smooth it all out again.

Roads were beginning to take shape. One day there would be sidewalks in front of houses. People would walk on those walks while their children rode bikes. Couples would hold hands and would walk dogs on leashes.

He could almost see the people running under the shade of the trees on the path that would circle the neighborhood park. If he closed his eyes, which he did, he could hear children playing on that playground at the park.

When he opened his eyes again, he saw the dream being built right in front of him and he grinned.

This was his dream, just as high-rises had been his great-grandfather's. Families would call this home for generations to come, and he'd envisioned it and drawn it out on the back of a napkin the day he'd thought of it. He'd been sitting in his car, just as he was now, looking over a tree farm, which had gone out of business, and the land was a mess. But Spencer had seen a vision and in a few years that vision would be complete.

He continued on, passing the sign that read HART ESTATES, A NEW COMMUNITY FROM BENSON, BENSON, AND HART.

He'd chosen the name to honor his great-grandfather who had started it all. Back then, it had been Hart Construction. Spencer smiled as he pulled into the spot they reserved for him in front of the trailer that housed the offices.

Under Hart Construction, his great-grandfather had helped build most of Nashville and other cities including New York. When Spencer's grandmother had married the first Tyler Benson, and he then became part of the company, his great-grandfather changed the name to Hart and Son, but after a few years they changed it again to Hart and Benson Construction.

Spencer picked up his leather portfolio and stepped out of the car. Dust kicked up under his feet and he breathed in the scents. Right now the area smelled of dirt, mud, and water. But in time it would have floral notes from gardens and the smell of fresh cut lawns.

On the door of the trailer were the initials BBH. The company had come a long way since his grandfather joined his great-grandfather's company. They'd changed the name again when Spencer's father joined the company as a young man. Under Zachary Benson's lead, the company had flourished.

Spencer opened the door to the air-conditioned trailer. That felt better, he thought. He set his portfolio on the old metal desk and looked at the plans on the wall.

His cousin Ed had added some key elements to the community, including the park placement.

Ed had held the reins of BBH for years, now it was Spencer's turn to make his mark, and that was what he was doing with Hart Estates.

The door opened, letting in a wave of heat from outside. Ed

slid through the door and gave a sigh when the cool air of the trailer washed over him.

"That's better," he said.

"What are you doing here?" Spencer asked as he pulled out a checklist he'd made from his portfolio.

"I could ask you the same thing, but I know we both have the same answer. We have a problem, you know. We're workaholics."

Spencer chuckled with a nod. "I just came down to check…"

"You came to check on your baby. There isn't anything that Chuck doesn't have under control and you and I are both in the way."

"You're right."

"I know I am." Ed scratched at his day worth of whiskers. "What do you say we check on Chuck and get out of here and have some lunch? Clara said Warner is rehearsing today so we could go get a beer and eat."

Spencer agreed with a nod. "I guess that is a perk of this town, those hotshot musicians using local establishments to practice their new music before they go back out on the road or record. You get a fine meal, a cold beer, and good entertainment."

Ed laughed as he opened the door to walk back out into the heat. "Doesn't hurt when you're a partner in the establishment either." He beamed. "I have all afternoon. My mom, your mom, and Darcy all went for pedicures."

"Where's Emily?"

A different smile formed on Ed's lips. "She's spending the day with my dad. What that means is they will both need a nap when I get back to them. She has him wrapped around her finger."

"That's how it should be," Spencer joked knowing his father was wrapped around Emily's little finger too. He followed his cousin outside.

"Absolutely."

As they headed toward the area where they knew they'd find Chuck, their foreman, Spencer's phone rang.

He shook his head as the ringtone screamed *Call Me Maybe* and Tiffany's picture popped up on the screen. He had to stop giving her his passwords to things since she found it necessary to change everything including ringtones.

"Well, good morning sleepy head," he gave her the vocal jab through the phone.

"What the hell are you so cheery for? And how come you came home, changed your clothes and left me here?"

"Honey, you were sawing logs and were all alone in my big bed. I thought I'd just leave you there."

She let out a loud grunt. "I don't snore."

"Whatever you say."

"I'm starving," Tiffany whined. "Are you coming back home soon?"

"Ed and I are on site then headed down to Broadway to listen to Warner rehearse. We're going to eat down there. Feel like heading down?"

He heard the familiar sounds of a hungover moan escape.

"Or I could pick you up," he offered.

"I'd love that. I'll clean up."

"Oh, and Tiff, take my sheets off the bed and dump my trash before I come home."

"Ha-ha. I slept in this bed alone you saw."

He held back a step and let Ed go on. "Everything okay?"

"Yeah, I'll tell you about it later. I'll be ready when you get here."

Spencer disconnected the phone call and slid his phone back into his pocket. He knew the sound of her voice after a night of drinking. He sincerely hoped she'd drowned her sorrows in a bottle of wine, but he'd been in the apartment. There were two plates from dinner. Two glasses of wine, a few beer bottles, and some Jack to go with the Coke cans. She had to be feeling like crap, but where had the British accent gone? He didn't take advantage of her when she was drunk did he?

Spencer's temper began to fuel. He'd kill the bastard if he…

"You coming?" Ed shouted.

Spencer looked up and saw Ed and Chuck looking over plans. He nodded and headed their way.

He'd been too worked up over Julie all night and now he was worried about Tiffany.

They'd be done in a few minutes and he'd pick up Tiffany and take her to lunch. They could discuss what had happened the night before over a beer for him and a club soda for her.

As he walked toward the other men, he thought a day with his girl was exactly what he needed. She could always make him feel better. And for a few hours, he could forget about work and the next week when Julie would be right there with him—every day.

im-Tim-Tom's was the name on the door. Julie laughed as she followed Avery inside the extremely small bar on lower Broadway, which appeared to be tucked between two bigger bars. She couldn't imagine Warner Wright was actually inside, but a moment later she heard the familiar sound of his music.

Though Julie wasn't really familiar with country music, she was familiar with reality TV. That's where she'd known Warner Wright from.

"I've never heard of this place," she said as they weaved their way around the empty tables that were crammed into the small area.

"No. You probably haven't. It's new. It's small. And it's kind of a secret so far. Warner and Ed are some of the partners."

"Who are Tim, Tim, and Tom? The other partners?"

Avery sat down at a high four top. "Would you believe it if I told you they had us all throw names into a hat and they picked three."

"And that's what they came up with?"

"I think it's catchy."

Julie agreed with a nod.

"I'll go up and order for us. They don't have much in the food department yet, just your basic bar food, but the nachos are killer."

"That sounds good."

"How about a beer?"

"I could go for that."

Avery started for the bar. "We'll do yoga and take a walk later to combat this."

She watched her wave to the man on stage and Julie turned to see Warner Wright and another man on stage.

The surreal moment washed over her. She was sitting only feet from a famous person. Panic flowed through her. Chances were she was going to meet that famous people.

Her stomach began to slowly twist into a knot.

She looked toward the bar where Avery stood with a woman who was very pregnant. They laughed and both turned toward the stage before they walked back to the table.

"Julie, this is my cousin Clara," Avery said setting two beers on the table.

Clara held out her hand to shake Julie's and it was then she got a good look at the woman with the dark hair and familiar face.

No words came out. She was meeting Clara Wright. Warner Wright's wife. Half of the duo of The Wrights.

Clara smiled warmly. "It's nice to meet you. Avery says you're the newest tenant in the basement."

Julie could only nod and then she pushed that lawyer's gut into place and took back her calm. "It's very nice to meet you. Yes, I'm living in the basement."

Clara sat down and placed the bottle of water she carried on the table.

"I love to watch those two perform," Clara said watching her husband with dreamy eyes. "They work well together."

"And here I always thought you'd end up with Randy." Avery said of the other man on the stage with Warner before she lifted her bottle to her lips and sipped.

"I had as much chance with Randy as you do with Pete." She considered for a moment. "I had less. I still think you and Pete will figure it out."

Avery nearly choked on her beer. "What I have with Pete is exactly what my mother had with Uncle Zach. Nothing. All I can hope for someday is he will marry someone with a nice brother and set me up. It worked for my parents."

Julie sat and listened to the two women banter. What an interesting web this family had woven. She tried to put all the pieces together.

"So your dads are brothers, right?" Julie asked.

Both women turned toward her and nodded.

Julie pointed toward Clara. "Your dad is the adopted one?"

"You've been getting a Keller family run down."

Julie shrugged. "I thought it was a Benson run down."

Both women laughed. "It all ties together," Clara confirmed. "But yes, my father was adopted by the Kellers when he was seven. Avery's dad is the only biological son of my grandparents."

"That's awesome," Julie said with quite a bit of enthusiasm. Being an only child she couldn't even imagine what it would be like to have a bounty of cousins and siblings.

Clara rolled her bottle between her hands. "My parents were high school sweethearts. Got married. Had kids. Got divorced and married other people—then got married again. To each other."

Julie realized her mouth had fallen open. "They're married now? To each other?"

"Have been for nearly twenty-five years this time."

"Why did they divorce?"

"Times were hard. They just forgot their way. But you can't mess with fate. When it's meant to be, it's meant to be."

Julie turned to Avery. "Your uncle Zach, is that Spencer's dad?"

Avery grinned. "Yep."

Julie picked up her beer and motioned to Avery. "Your mom had a thing for his dad?"

Avery's shoulders straightened as she crossed one slender leg over the other. "They grew up together. His dad was shipped off to France to boarding school. My mother is French."

That explained the beauty of Avery, Julie thought. The dark hair, the fine, nearly fragile features of her face—she was model perfect.

Avery tossed her hair over her shoulder. "My mother fell in love as a small girl and chased Spencer's dad until he married Spencer's mom, Regan. Then at Clara's dad's wedding to…" she looked at Clara for confirmation.

"Kathy." Clara looked at Julie. "He married a woman named Kathy. They were married about eight hours."

Julie nodded as if she had kept up, but she might need a refresher course later.

"Right," Avery said. "Kathy. Anyway, my dad was set up as my mother's date for the wedding. They ran off and had this quick affair. Jetted off to my grandfather's yacht where my mother stranded him."

Julie swallowed hard. Who was this woman?

"You *know* they had some affair?" she asked.

"It was a big deal because I came from that lustful week."

Clara laughed and her cheeks filled with color. "Her family is a lot more open about this stuff than mine would have been."

Avery shrugged. "Sex is sex. Love is love. My mother doesn't hide that she had sex with a lot of different men. She was in a position to have whatever she wanted. My dad was a young, and handsome doctor with his own list of go to nurses."

Julie had to remind herself to blink. "You know all of this?"

"I know all of this. It's no big deal."

It sure would have been to her, Julie thought. Then again, her parents were in their late forties when she was born. She didn't really know anything about their younger lives. She'd missed out on grandparents and everything these girls seemed to have.

"Anyway," Avery continued as she picked up her beer. "Mom got pregnant, moved to Nashville and did what she could to prove to my dad she could be more than some rich snob. She could be a good mother and she wanted him to fall in love with her."

"Rich snob?"

Avery's eyes lit. "Pierpont Oil ring a bell?"

"Are you kidding me?" Julie's voice rose in pitch and volume.

"That's my grandfather."

Clara shook her head. "Tell her about the vineyard. You're going to want to."

Avery grinned. "He just purchased a vineyard in France and it's going to be mine. I'm going to be producing my own line of wines."

That would explain the extensive collection in her kitchen, Julie thought.

"Wow. And here I am without two nickels to rub together." She reconsidered her comment. "I'm sorry. That was very rude."

"Don't worry about it." Avery brushed off the comment with her hand. "I'm excited for the opportunity. My grandfather and mother only recently began speaking again, so this is all new to me, but I certainly can embrace the vineyard and château," she said with a hint of an accent. "It won't change who I am."

"No, because she'll have Pete right there to remind her that she's a Tennessee girl not some Parisian princess," Clara joked with a thick Southern accent.

"He's my rock," Avery said and Julie noted the darkness that shifted in her eyes when she thought of him.

"Well, look what walked in," Avery said.

Julie and Clara turned their heads toward the door.

A man walked in and gave them a wave as he stopped by the bar and collected a beer. He had the same dark complexion as Clara and Julie was sure she'd seen him before.

"Hey, they sound good." The man looked toward the stage and lifted his beer in salute.

"Of course they do," Clara agreed. "Where's your family?"

"Mom took Darcy for a pedicure with Aunt Regan. Dad has Emily," he said as he sat down next to her.

Clara laughed. "Who'd have thought she'd be a grandpa's girl."

The man looked toward Julie. His dark eyes smiled before his mouth did. He reached his hand across the table. "I'm Ed. Clara's brother."

Julie shook his hand. "Julie Jacobson."

Now his eyes widened. The smile remained, but it had a strain to it. "Lawyer."

"Yes."

He nodded as he retracted his hand. "Very nice to meet you." He eased back in his seat. "I didn't know you guys would be here."

"I'd rather be here than sitting at home with my feet up," Clara said giving her stomach a rub. "It won't be long until backstage and loud bars aren't going to fit into my schedule."

Ed rubbed her back. "That baby will fit in just fine here."

Julie thought the tenderness between them might just make her cry. She'd longed her whole life for something like that—compassion from someone. Wasn't that why she'd gotten married? And still she longed for it.

She took her beer from the table and noticed her hand shaking. Quickly, she lifted the bottle to her lips and took a sip to calm her nerves. These people who surrounded her already treated her with compassion as she'd never known. Regardless of what came from showing up in Nashville, she decided she'd made the right choice. And she was extremely grateful that Spencer had set her up in Avery's house.

Julie felt the panic slide away and she took another sip of her beer.

"Oh, hey! It's a party!" Avery waved again at someone walking in the door.

Julie looked up and the panic set back in as she saw Spencer and Tiffany walk in, hand in hand.

# CHAPTER 17

Spencer reminded himself to breathe when he saw his cousins sitting at the table with Julie. He certainly hadn't expected to see her there. And he didn't like what it did to him when he saw her.

He stopped at the bar. "I'll take a Bud and she'll have a Blue Moon," he said nodding toward Tiffany.

"No, I'll have a glass of water, please."

"Pansy," he joked.

"My head hurts so bad I can't see."

"You shouldn't get drunk with strangers in my apartment."

Tiffany closed her eyes, but he could see them roll at what he said. "I'll get him. I'll just try it sober next time."

"You're lucky he tucked your sorry ass into bed and left without touching you or stealing anything."

"Don't lecture me," she warned.

"Someone has to. I don't want to come home and find you dead in my apartment or yours. Or raped. Or drugged. Or…"

"I get it." She rested her hands on both sides of her head. "Maybe I should just go home."

"No," he said softly covering her hand with his. "Stay a while."

"Afraid to be alone with her?"

They both looked toward the table. "Maybe just a little."

The bartender handed him his beer and Tiffany a glass of water. He took her hand, as much to steady himself as to balance her, and walked toward the table where his cousins and Julie sat.

Julie had turned to watch Warner and Randy. Her blonde hair was pulled up and he noted the dainty little earrings she wore on her ears. Were they butterflies? They were cute.

He shook his head. That was about the most stupid thought he could ever have. They were cute. Who the hell was he? Someone's grandfather?

"Hey, guys," he said as warmly as he could as they approached the table.

That caused her to turn and force a smile so strained it made his own cheeks hurt.

"Pull that table over," Ed said as Avery scooted her chair closer toward Julie to make room for the tables to push together. "Hey, Tiff."

"Hi," her voice was low.

"Don't mind her she's a little hungover from a date," Spencer shifted his eyes toward Julie as he sipped his beer. She darted her gaze in another direction. He made her uncomfortable when Tiffany was around. He wondered if he'd always make her this uncomfortable.

Tiffany had her head down and he knew it had been a mistake to bring her. It was too loud. This little relaxing trip downtown was about to be cut short. But that wasn't what he wanted. He had an urge to talk to Julie more. This wasn't as intimate as his office, Avery's kitchen table, or the basement where she was living. Maybe she'd relax a little around Ed, Clara, and Avery, but having Tiffany there wasn't helping.

Nachos arrived at the table and Spencer ordered another, noticing that all six hands dove into the platter.

Tiffany moaned as she ate. "I don't think this is going to help either." She slowly sipped her water.

Spencer knew he needed to get her home. He should probably stay with her for a few hours too and make sure she was okay, but Ed had said something to Julie and she'd actually thrown her head back in laughter. The sound of it was electrifying, sending a jolt through his veins.

Warner and Randy finished their set and the volume in the room lowered. People moved to the bar, a few cornered Warner for autographs before he made it to the table.

Randy passed by the bar, collected a glass of water and headed toward them.

Ed stood and held out his hand to him. Spencer watched the greeting and the introduction to Julie. Her eyes were wide and he'd seen enough women flirt to notice that when she tucked a loose strand of hair behind her ear she was certainly attracted to the musician.

"You're grinding your teeth," Tiffany leaned in close and whispered in his ear.

"Am not."

"She's being friendly. Don't read into it."

He shifted his eyes to Tiffany and she narrowed her gaze at him. She knew him well enough to know when he had an interest. Julie seemed to strike that nerve. Hadn't Tiffany said that when she'd kissed him in his kitchen?

Warner joined them and they all moved to accommodate two more chairs as the second platter of nachos arrived. He kept Tiffany's groans stirring in his ear as he watched Julie lean in on her elbows and intently listen to Randy talk as she twisted that damn butterfly in her ear.

To his left, Avery pulled her ringing phone from her purse and put it to her ear as she covered the other with her hand.

Her frustration with the phone call caused Spencer to shift his attention from Julie to his cousin.

"Okay. I need an hour. Tyler, I said I'd help. But just one more time. Okay? I don't want to do this." She finished the discussion and ended the call.

"My brother?" Spencer asked.

"They swore I wouldn't have to help with the *Diamond Gift* gala this year. But it seems that big sponsor I brought in last year only wants to talk to me."

She tucked her phone back into her designer purse with big bangles that jingled on the strap.

Tiffany looked up at her. "Are you leaving?"

"Yes. Tyler and Courtney need me to help them with the gala."

"Can I bum a ride home on your way? Please," Tiffany moaned.

"Sure, let's go."

Avery stood and swung that jingly purse over her shoulder and gave her hair a push back. Tiffany slid off the stool next to him and then gave him a kiss on the cheek. "Make your move, slick." She winked.

"Give my girl a ride home, okay?" Avery nodded toward Julie, who was nearly forehead to forehead with Randy as he showed her something on his phone. "She's occupied and having a good time." She patted him on the shoulder and walked out of the bar with Tiffany, leaving him at the end of the table watching Warner run his hand over Clara's stomach, Ed texting on his phone, and Randy flirting with Julie.

# CHAPTER 18

*S*pencer swallowed hard. He could use another beer and then maybe another. First he'd better finish the one in his hand, so he downed it and let it swim in his head.

He signaled the waitress for another as Ed lifted his head and gave him a nod before he hopped down from his stool and walked toward Spencer.

"Where'd your date go?" Ed joked as he sat where Tiffany had been.

"Avery had to go and she took Tiffany home."

"Looks like Julie is hitting it off with Randy."

Spencer bit the inside of his cheek. "Looks that way." He took the beer when the waitress arrived with it and set it on the table. He wrapped his hands around it. "I hired her," he admitted in a low, quiet voice.

"You did?"

"She came to Nashville looking for a job."

Ed nodded slowly. "Why did she leave PLL? Don't we need her there? She's an intricate part of the structure."

"Was. They fired her the morning the merger went through."

"So send her back. They all work for us now."

Spencer nodded. He actually hadn't thought about that. Why hadn't he thought about that? He'd spent the past five months damning her name and then she shows up and he gives her a local job.

He drank again. He knew why he did it. It was just that he wasn't sure he wanted to admit it yet.

Ed lifted his beer to his lips and sipped. "What's her job title here?" He kept his voice low as another act took to the stage.

"She's going to assist me on the neighborhood build. At least until she passes the bar in Tennessee."

Ed ran his fingers across his chin. "Family? Husband? What's her story?"

She twisted that butterfly on her ear again and placed a hand on Randy's shoulder as she laughed.

Spencer took another long, purposeful pull from his beer. "Newly divorced. Looking for a new start somewhere else."

"Are you sure you want her this close to you? She made you miserable for the past five months. I've never heard her name and anything pleasant come out of your mouth."

Spencer felt the regret sink in his stomach. He wished he'd known her better before he'd said all those things about her.

"She's been dealing with a lot this year. She's not who I thought she was," he admitted.

"I figured. Avery wouldn't have taken to her so quickly if she wasn't a good person."

That was true enough. Spencer finished off his second beer and assessed how he felt. He could drive home now, but one more he'd need a ride. He needed to consider that she'd need a ride home. Avery had asked him to get her home. Maybe if he needed a ride she could take him home. He could invite her inside. Show her the view from the top floor. Maybe they could...

Randy and Julie both stood from their stools. Julie assessed the table. "Where did Avery go?"

"She had to leave. She took Tiffany home on her way," Spencer explained.

"Oh, good. Randy and I are headed to get some barbecue for lunch. I'll catch up with her at home."

She threw her purse over her shoulder and gave them a wave as she said goodbye to Clara and Warner before she walked out of the building with Randy.

Spencer could only assume Avery didn't get around to asking Julie if she had dinner plans or not. He let out a regretful breath, ordered up that third beer after securing a ride with Ed, and had every intention of following it with a fourth.

* * *

JULIE HAD no idea the music industry could be so temperamental. She and Randy hadn't even made it to the restaurant when his phone rang. They needed him in the studio because something somewhere had been lost and they needed it now.

He must have apologized a thousand times, she thought as she built herself a turkey sandwich in her kitchen.

At least he'd been gentleman enough to take her home before hurrying off. There weren't any sparks between them, but she did like how heat had burned in Spencer's eyes when he'd seen her get up to leave with him. It was priceless.

It made up for him kissing Tiffany in the office—or so she told herself. No matter what he said about Tiffany, Julie still wasn't comfortable when they were both around. What man cared that much for a woman and wasn't in love with her? That meant he just used them. Well, she certainly didn't need more of those kinds of men in her life.

There was no doubt he'd be an attentive boss. That was something she could handle. Even though, many times, he'd been the youngest person in the room, she'd seen him in action with his team and his lawyers. Spencer Benson treated people with kindness—but was ruthless enough to hold his ground and get what he was after, but he was willing to listen to ideas as well.

What she needed to remember was that she'd need to listen too. Her instinct was to argue everything. That was what had made her a successful lawyer, even if it was in the boardroom and not in court.

She'd single handily stalled the merger for nearly five months making sure the Grayson family was selling their company to the right people. Likewise, she knew that because of her thoroughness, the Bensons were equally getting the best deal.

Adding the top slice of bread to her sandwich, she carried the plate to the small table and sat down.

With more thought, she decided that stalling wasn't something to be proud of. Libby had asked her to stall. She'd told her it was so that she was sure her grandfather got everything he deserved.

Julie took a hard bite of her sandwich.

The thought of Libby sitting on the edge of her desk making a list of things she wanted to see happen during the merger just made her sick now. She'd thought they were a good team. She thought, even though Libby wasn't involved in the day to day running of PLL, she had wanted what was best for her grandfather. How could she have been such an idiot to even believe one word that woman said?

It was her husband that should have been fired. Not her. She'd been ethical in her dealings with Spencer. They'd had plenty late nights alone in her office arguing over the merger. They'd had many decent conversations too, as they worked together to make the best deal. None of that had been easy as she watched her husband's affair continue while she worked with him during their divorce. Julie should have gotten a raise for remaining so professional.

All she could think was, Ha! Now he was stuck with Libby. Sooner or later he too would be out of a job. Spencer had promised to keep the employees as long as the jobs they were doing were beneficial to Benson, Benson, and Hart. Her ex-husband was certainly not beneficial.

She took another bite of her sandwich.

He'd screw up. He always did. Only this time he wouldn't have his wife there to fix his mistakes. He'd only have Libby Grayson, and she'd be moving on to the next conquest—that was for sure.

What Julie needed to do was figure out how she was going to keep it all together until she could pass the bar in Tennessee. One wrong step and Spencer could fire her and she'd never get a legal job in construction again.

But she thought about the kiss she'd planted on him in the elevator. She closed her eyes and rested her head in her hands. She'd wondered for nearly a week if he'd felt the earth move beneath his feet—and not the rise of the elevator. It had been impulse just to feel like a woman, but it had turned into something so much more.

She feared she'd do it again and make a mess out of everything. But that was what happened to her when she was around Spencer Benson. And on Monday they'd be working closely—perhaps alone.

Julie knew she had two sides—fun loving and bitch. It would be imperative that she find a middle ground.

# CHAPTER 19

*S*tress had Spencer in the office at six-damned-thirty on
Monday morning.

He'd had calls from Oregon on Sunday saying loads were
going to be late getting to Tennessee. That was just a sticky mess.
Spencer made a few more phone calls and lumber was on its way.

Chuck had called and let him know of a concrete shortage for
the next week. Been there done that. Again, a few Sunday phone
calls and that section of concrete they needed to pour would be
filled.

What had him pacing the damn floor all day yesterday, and
now in his office as the sun was bright in his window, was Julie
leaving with Randy from the bar and Avery commenting that she
hadn't seen her since.

He'd driven by the house. Her car was still parked where she'd
left it.

It wasn't so much her leaving, and God only knowing what
went on, it was that no one would tell him anything.

Avery said she hadn't seen her or talked to her, but then she'd
been busy.

When he'd called Clara she let him have it.

"It's none of your business what they did or didn't do. I'm not telling you crap."

He'd sighed into the phone and she'd continued her rant.

"You hang on to Tiffany like she's some prize to keep around and you want another woman to not assume you're involved and not go out with someone as amazing, and sweet, and gentle, and considerate as Randy? She's just an employee. Why do you care what she did all weekend? That's not even fair to her. I should hire her away from you. I don't know what I'd do with her, but if you're going to be checking in on her all the time, you don't deserve her."

The conversation had lasted nearly twenty minutes, though it wasn't much of a conversation. It was Clara yelling at him and then crying because she was just so emotional because of the baby.

Clara had been right. It wasn't any of his business.

So why did he care?

Spencer sat down in his plush leather chair yawning as he kicked up his feet and leaned back. He tucked his hands behind his head and let his heavy eyes shut for a moment. What did his father ever get done in the office this early, he wondered.

The smell of coffee began to tingle in his nose and wake up his brain. The sound of someone moving about in his office made him quickly pry his eyes open and put his feet on the ground.

His back ached and the room was much brighter.

"What time did you get here?" Amber asked as she set his mail on his desk.

"What time is it now?"

"Seven-thirty."

He groaned as he worked his head from side to side. Had he really just fallen asleep in his chair for an hour?

When Amber moved from in front of his desk and he spun his chair forward, he saw Julie seated in one of the large chairs before him. She held a mug of coffee in her hands and a tight smile on her lips.

Her hair was knotted at the base of her neck and she wore one of those uptight navy blue suits he'd seen her in for months. This sure was a change from the girl at the bar on Saturday, who twisted that butterfly earring—which had been replaced with a sensible little hoop, he'd noted.

Spencer pressed his fingertips to his eyes. When he opened them again, she just stared at him. That she'd done for five months too. That was more comfortable.

"I see you met Amber," he said cutting through the silence.

"I did. She's been showing me around," she said coolly.

Amber threw down a report on his desk. "You know if you hire someone else to help out around here, it's nice to know before Monday morning."

"Right. Hey, I'm sorry."

Amber shrugged. "Thank God you did. I'm tired of running multiple projects. At least with her here now, you don't have to call and tell me how miserable she's making you in Oregon." She gave him a curt grin before leaving the room, and him alone with Julie.

Julie's eyes had lowered to look at her coffee. Her lips twitched and he wondered if she was going to cry in his office again.

"I'm sorry about that. She…"

Julie lifted her head and he could see those chocolate eyes mist. "She's threatened. She's feeling replaced. Unprepared."

"She told you that?"

"Didn't have to." Julie gripped the coffee mug tighter. "It was a mistake for me to come here and ask for a job. It already looks like I'll be causing problems here. I should just go before I even get started." She stood and set her mug on the desk. "Randy told me that his label has some opportunities in legal. I could consult until I…"

"You're not leaving here to get another job," he cut her off. "I hired you to help me and that's what you're here to do."

"I don't want to upset someone who has been with you a long time."

"And she'll continue to be with me a long time."

Julie nodded, picked back up her cup, and sat down. "She's actually very nice."

"That was uncharacteristic of her."

"She's protective of you. I'm someone who obviously brought you a great deal of anguish," her voice dropped as she said it.

This wasn't how he wanted to start their first day working together in his office.

Spencer walked around his desk and leaned up against it. He pulled a tissue from the box on the corner and handed it to her. "Maybe you need a few more days to adjust to being here."

"I need work. I told you, I left with nothing."

He nodded and then sat down in the chair next to her. Her eyes remained averted.

"Let's get this out of the way," he said and she lifted her sad eyes to meet his. "You're going to run into more than one person who may or may not have heard me refer to you unkindly."

Her shoulders dropped and her gaze moved back down to her mug. In his chest, his heart ached to see anyone look so crushed. Worse, he'd caused it.

"I was wrong," he said as he placed his hand on her forearm and rested it there. "I didn't take time to understand you or realize there was more to you than just some…"

"Bitch behind all the stalling?"

The ache in his chest sharpened. "Julie, I'm sorry."

"I get it. I do." She sucked in a deep breath and let it out slowly. "Let's just get to work. I'll get a few days under my belt and then we can decide if I need to move on."

He certainly hoped they could move past this. He'd been so wrong about her being the horrible human being he'd told everyone she was. This woman was nothing more than lonely and misunderstood.

Julie lifted her fingers to the small hoop in her ear and twisted it. A tell, he thought. When she was nervous, she touched her earring. It was cute.

Spencer shook his head. Again with the cute.

The intercom on his phone buzzed and Amber's voice rang through the room.

"Chuck is on line one."

"Thank you," he said walking around his desk.

"I'll wait outside," Julie said as she stood from her seat.

Spencer shook his head as he picked up the phone. "No need. I'll be one moment."

# CHAPTER 20

*J*ulie sipped her bitter and cold coffee as Spencer took his call. He was jotting down notes and replying with grunts. When he was finished, he stood still until she looked up at him.

He was casual today in a pair of dark Dockers and a button up shirt, already rolled at the sleeves. She was used to him in a suit, but casual suited him just fine too, she thought.

The day hadn't warranted his fingers through that dark hair yet, but she knew what that looked like too. She'd studied him for months. He did that when he was thinking too hard about a certain task. When he was stressed, as he was now, his eyes were dark. When he was enjoying himself, they sparkled with hints of gold. When she'd caught him off guard and kissed him in the elevator, they were rich, and dark, and wide.

She swallowed hard as he studied her.

"We need to head over to the site. Chuck, the foreman," he clarified, "says the wiring is done on the model home. I want to do a walk through before we close up the walls."

"You want me to go with you?"

"This is your project. You might as well get to know it and see your desk."

She bit down on her bottom lip. "I'm not working here?"

"You will be expected in both locations. For a recently unemployed woman, you're about to be extremely busy."

Quietly, she let out a little breath. For being someone the man certainly didn't like, it seemed he was about to give her a lot of responsibility. That she could handle. She wasn't afraid of a challenge. Obviously she'd proven to him she could be thorough and organized. Her only hope was that Spencer Benson was a decent man and not just trying to seek revenge on her for being such a bitch.

"I have a bag in the employee lounge, in my locker. I brought some different shoes, but I didn't think to bring different clothes."

"You'll be fine today in what you have on. Don't feel as though you have to wear your lawyer attire unless we're in meetings with big clients."

She nodded. A shopping trip might be in order. She had business attire and almost too casual. There needed to be a middle ground in her wardrobe, just as she was having to find one with her attitude as well.

"I'll meet you back in here in ten. I'm going to head up and talk to my dad and Ed."

Her stomach tightened when he mentioned his family. It was as if she'd forgotten they would be in the same building. What had they heard about her, she wondered as she left his office and headed toward the employee lounge.

Eyes followed her as she walked down the hall. Had they all heard about her? Had they seen her fall on her ass on Friday before Spencer pulled her to her feet and then groped all over Tiffany?

The nagging question kept running through her head, why had she come here?

As she opened her locker and pulled out her bag, she remembered why.

Because her ex-husband was still working at PLL and Libby Grayson was pulling his strings. They were in Oregon and she wasn't. However, they we're still embedded in the same company now and she could keep an eye on what he was doing.

Her hope was he wasn't doing anything that would cause Spencer more grief. Her ex-husband was a stupid man, but he wasn't mean.

She'd keep her eyes on him through channels. As far as she knew, Spencer wouldn't know who her ex-husband was. She'd never taken his name.

There would be no need for her to run into him either. He was embedded in a merged company on the coast. She was embedded in a single project through the main company, many miles away.

THE FLASHY BMW was as nice on the inside as it was on the outside, Julie thought as she took in its ambiance. The black leather seats and faux wood trim was beautiful. She wondered what a car like this would set someone back.

One thing was for sure, she'd never own one. She'd be lucky if her little Toyota Corolla, which was nearly as old as she was, would hold out another ten years and another one hundred thousand miles. Maybe by then she could afford a car payment again on a much smaller scale than a BMW.

Spencer had on the radio and *Home Sweet Home* played and comforted her.

"You don't listen to country music?"

He shot her a look and from behind his sunglasses his eyebrows rose. "This is country music."

She laughed. "This is Mötley Crüe."

He chuckled with a shake of his head, diverting his attention back to the road. "No, this is Jason Aldean and Vince Neil. Trust me. In ten minutes, you'll have me turning up Blake Shelton nice and loud."

"The guy from The Voice?"

He was still humored. "You knew who Warner Wright was, but you don't know Blake Shelton?"

"Warner Wright was on reality TV."

Spencer let out a grunt. "That was crap TV. And I wouldn't mention it to him."

"It was intriguing."

"I don't know what anyone sees in that junk. But I know Clara used to watch it."

Julie shrugged. "I guess it makes you feel normal."

"Doesn't it make you wish you were a Kardashian?"

Julie shook her head. "Oh, I could never fit into that life. I'm not that pretty."

He turned toward her again, but he wasn't laughing—he wasn't even smiling.

"You're prettier than all of them combined."

Her breath caught in her lungs, but somehow she managed to say, "Thank you," between loud heartbeats pumping in her ears.

# CHAPTER 21

*T*hankfully Spencer pulled up to the lot where two different construction trailers sat. One was landscaped with a parking lot and banners waving to draw attention into the development. The other was a few feet away, in the dirt, with a beat up old Ford pickup parked in front of it.

"So this is it huh? The future Hart Estates?" She looked at the mounds of dirt and machines that moved it.

"It's going to be amazing."

She felt the smile settle on her lips. "My mom used to talk about building a house in one of these communities. But they'd lived in their home since they'd been married. Actually, my mother had lived there her whole life. It had been her parents' home before that."

Spencer turned off the car. "Ed and Darcy live in my grandparents' home. It's very sentimental."

"Did he move in when they passed?"

Again his brows moved, but this time into a confused V beneath the rim of his glasses. "Passed." They rose. "Oh, they haven't died. They moved to a retirement community. They're both in their nineties, but I think they have a few good years left."

"Really?"

"You can't take down a Keller."

"That's your mom's side of the family, right?"

He nodded. "You'll have to meet all of them some day." He opened his door and she did the same, stepping out onto the paved lot where he'd parked in front of the sales trailer.

"I've already met three of your cousins. How many more are there?"

"You haven't met Chris and his family or my brother and his wife. Then aunts, uncles, parents."

Her chest tightened. "I'm feeling a bit overwhelmed already," she said as she shut the door to the car.

"You won't when you meet them."

"And why would I meet them? Are they all involved in the business," she asked as she skirted the front of the car.

"No. But if you're with me, you'll meet them."

He started toward the sales trailer, but she fell back a step.

What exactly did he mean by if you're with me?

Spencer opened the door to the sales center and a very familiar face smiled up at them.

"Hey guys!" Tiffany stood from behind the desk. Though she worked on a construction site, she was dressed to impress.

Her deep blue dress fit the lovely curves of her body and the top of the dress nicely V'd right to the swells of her breasts.

Julie caught herself looking and she was sure Spencer's gaze was stuck there too. But when she looked at him she noticed he'd picked up a stack of mail and was thumbing through it.

"First day and he has you out here in his sandbox, huh?" Tiffany leaned a hip against her desk.

"Yeah, he wanted me to see it."

"He's pretty proud of all this. Come here, I'll show you what it will look like."

Tiffany moved from behind the desk and walked toward a

display in the center of the room which had the development mapped out and tiny pins sporadically around the map.

"This is what the development will look like," she said leaning over the display.

Julie noted just how tall she was and then noticed her footwear.

"I like your shoes," she complimented.

"I got a bonus last quarter. Splurged."

"Aren't you worried they'll get ruined out here?"

Tiffany looked at Julie's athletic clad feet. "I have a pair just like that under my desk. Most people understand when I switch them out to go look at lots."

Julie didn't want to, but she smiled. "So what are the pins?" she asked directing her attention back to the display.

"Those are the lots we've sold already."

"So the first houses to go up?"

"You got it. You want to see the designs?"

Julie nodded enthusiastically and Tiffany walked her to the other end of the trailer where large posters lined the walls.

"It'll have everything from the ranch style homes with two bedrooms, perfect for your retired couple, to six bedroom homes for big families."

"That has to be immense."

"They are all roomy and beautiful." Tiffany lowered her head toward Julie. "Nothing in my taste mind you. I like efficient and small. Easier to clean."

Julie let her eyes wander over the designs. They seemed to focus on the four bedrooms, three and a half bath, with the master suite on the main floor. She walked closer to it.

Beneath the poster were design options for everything from the trim around the house, the shingles on the roof of the house, and the floor in the kitchen.

"People can choose all of this?"

"Yep. Custom home really, but with the options we give you."

"Perfect for your new families with the park right in the middle of the development."

Tiffany nodded. "That's what Spencer had in mind. Ed designed the park."

Julie looked around and noticed Spencer wasn't there. She wasn't sure when he'd snuck out, but it had to be between her mentally driving the streets on the display and picking out countertops looking at the design posters.

"So you work here? With Spencer?" Julie swallowed hard waiting for her answer.

"Temporary job. Well, until the development is done. I'm a jewelry designer, but it's more of a hobby." She tucked those red curls that swayed at her shoulders behind her ears to flash a set of ornate hoops encrusted with what looked like small sapphires.

"You made those?"

"I did. Not a cheap hobby," she said running her fingers through her hair to bring it back to place.

"I thought you meant wire and beads."

Tiffany laughed. "Why bother then? If you're going to do it, go for the real good stuff." She too looked around. "Where did he go?"

Julie shrugged. "Didn't see him leave."

"Typical. He's like some superhero who can disappear through walls. C'mon, I'll introduce you to Chuck and show you where you'll be working."

Tiffany headed toward the back door of the trailer to a small path between the two mobile offices.

"Aren't you going to change your shoes?" Julie asked.

"Chuck likes it when I wear these. Watch him fall all over himself."

"That's sexist isn't it?"

"Man has been married for twenty-five years. Wife is a gem. He has four kids, but he's still a man. He will be tongue tied for about ninety seconds. Maybe a whole two minutes when he sees you too."

"I don't know if I want to work around a man like that."

Tiffany slowed and turned toward her. "You do. He appreciates the look of a woman, but he is a solid man, in a solid relationship. He'll have your back, but he'll never touch you or say a word to you that isn't strictly polite. Of course, the words not said to you are all curse words," she said on a laugh.

Tiffany gently walked up the two wooden steps to the door of the trailer on her toes and yanked it open.

Julie watched the man standing next to Spencer take a sweeping look at Tiffany from head to toe and back again.

"Hey, Chuck," she said in an airy voice. "Brought your work companion to meet you."

Julie watched as he gave her the same head to toe glance and his mouth opened slightly.

Julie waited for him to say something, anything, but Tiffany had been right. He'd been rendered speechless.

She shifted her gaze to Spencer and was surprised to find his eyes meet hers. The corner of his mouth lifted in a grin.

Quickly, Julie pushed her shoulders back and approached the dumbstricken Chuck. "Hello. I'm Julie Jacobson."

Chuck's hand reached for hers, but it still took a few more seconds before he could say, "Nice to meet you. Chuck."

Spencer cleared his throat. "C'mon, Chuck. Let's go look at these walls. Tiff, get her settled in," he said as he picked up a clipboard and slid his sunglasses off his head and onto his face, then walked out with Chuck in tow.

When the door closed behind them Tiffany burst into laughter. "I told you."

"How am I supposed to work in here with that man?"

"He'll get used to you. Wait until he cusses and then backtracks to make it go away. You'll enjoy him."

Julie wasn't sure what she'd gotten herself into, but she was glad that she'd finally gotten past her insecurity around Tiffany. Hadn't Spencer told her they weren't an item? They were casual friends. Well, she was a casual friend too. They'd both kissed him, though she was very sure Tiffany had done quite a bit of that with him and more.

So why was it that she wasn't jealous?

# CHAPTER 22

Tiffany had set Julie up in the construction trailer, on the side of a mobile wall. It would give her as much privacy as possible. There had been an open invitation that when Julie needed a more comfortable space, she could visit the sales trailer if no one was house shopping.

In a few weeks the model house, which was still bare, would be ready for them to move their offices into. At that time, Julie would work in the house with Tiffany, and Chuck could have his space back.

Spencer had promised to come back for Julie and give her a ride back downtown to the Riverside Building office. He had an offsite meeting first.

Now that she was comfortable in her surroundings, it didn't matter if he picked her up or not. She was sure either Tiffany or Chuck would have given her a ride into town to pick up her car. Though she wasn't sure that Chuck wouldn't have a heart attack doing so.

The thought made her laugh when her phone buzzed on her desk with a text message from Spencer.

*I'll be a little after five-thirty, don't leave. Need help on a design.*

She absolutely had no idea what that meant, but she'd wait for him. She had the urge to dig deeper into his relationship with Tiffany, especially now that she'd spent most the day with the woman in the custom made jewelry and beautiful shoes.

Chuck had said his goodbyes nearly an hour earlier and now as it inched toward six-fifteen Julie was getting worried that Spencer had forgotten her.

Tiffany had brought her a set of keys and had offered to drive her home, but Julie told her about Spencer's text.

"That man," she'd said as she took her phone out of her purse and pushed a button. "Where the hell are you? You can't leave her sitting here all night." She paused. "Fine. I'm calling her in ten minutes, and if you're not here, I'm turning around and coming for her." Tiffany disconnected the call. "He's just down the road."

"What does he want help with?"

Tiffany shrugged, turned the camera on her phone to face her, and fixed her lipstick. "This will only be late night number one. You're in for a million of these. The man's head doesn't work nine to five." She tucked her phone back into her purse.

"I've spent many nights working late with him. When he gets something in his head, he wants to talk about it until he's satisfied with it."

Tiffany nodded. "I guess his moods aren't new to you."

No, they certainly weren't. But now, his late nights wouldn't be working against her.

"Will you be okay here until he gets here?" Tiffany asked.

"Yeah. I'm almost sorted out with everything. A few more minutes would be good."

Tiffany looked around the little space she'd set up for Julie. "You are very organized aren't you?"

"As a lawyer you have to be detail oriented."

Tiffany nodded. "Remind me to never invite you over to my place. You'd have an aneurism."

Julie laughed. "I doubt that."

Tiffany only grunted. "Okay, I'm out of here. Lock the door."

Julie nodded, but when Tiffany opened the door, she saw Spencer drive up.

"About time," Tiffany's voice faded away as the door closed.

Curious, Julie moved to the window to watch them.

Spencer climbed out of his car on the gravel patch and gave her a long, lingering hug. Then giving her an arm to balance against, he walked her to her car behind the other trailer.

Julie moved to another window to watch.

Spencer opened the car door for Tiffany, and she leaned in and pressed a kiss to his lips then gave his cheek a playful slap.

Julie let out a breath as he started back toward the trailer. She sat down at her desk and flipped open a book full of countertop colors.

She wanted it to seem as though she was perfectly normal in her surroundings.

The kiss he'd given Tiffany played in her mind as she heard his steps on the gravel. It wasn't intimate.


SPENCER PULLED OPEN THE DOOR. He didn't see Julie immediately, but he heard the sounds from behind the little wall.

She was sitting at her neatly organized desk looking at a design book. Eleven hours after he'd seen her the first time that day, she still looked as fresh and nice as she had when he'd opened his eyes from his little nap.

"Studying?" he asked as he walked toward her.

"I suppose. I think this will be fun. I can't believe how simple some of these clients are and how fussy others are in their taste. I mean one of the files I put together today had a thirty thousand dollar kitchen," her voice rose as she said the figure aloud. "The next one had your run of the mill, basic kitchen for ten thousand. It's fascinating to think they will be next door neighbors."

He loved her enthusiasm. He hadn't been sure that she had anything like that buried down under that lawyer skin.

"Now, I particularly like Mr. and Mrs. Svenson's choices on their flooring. Look at this," she said as she opened the file to their build. "That is going to be one marvelous entry way, don't you think?"

"I do," he said smiling and wondering why she'd ever taken up law. It didn't fit her now that he'd seen this side to her. "So do you know anything about kitchen cabinets or countertops?"

"Only what I've been looking at in books today."

"Sky's the limit. What would you choose?"

She was studying him now with those rich, dark eyes, assumably working up an answer, he thought.

Spencer pulled out the chair across from her and sat down. "Go on. Show me."

She waited a moment and pulled out a book which had a sticky note attached to it. Julie opened it, and laid it in front of him, facing him.

"You do have good taste," he said looking at the dark granite countertops and cherry cabinets. "Stainless steel appliances?"

Her lips puckered as she thought. "Yes, but the brushed kind that don't take fingerprints."

"Flooring?"

"I was going for wood, but I changed my mind." She pulled out another book with another sticky note. "With the dark cherry and the granite I think a stone floor." She pointed to the tiles that had warm tones and nothing too dominant in color.

His gaze moved from the book and up into her eyes that were wide with the wonder of it all. "This is fun, isn't it?"

"I suppose if I were paying for it, it would be a different story. Laminate counters, light cabinets, subway tile backsplash." She grimaced.

Spencer stood and took a set of keys from his pocket. "C'mon, I want to show you something."

He moved toward the door as she slowly walked around the wall. "It's getting late. I should be getting back to my car."

He stopped with his hand on the doorknob. "It's only six-thirty."

"I realize that. When do you go home? You don't work twelve hours a day every day do you?"

He considered for a moment then rubbed his hand over the back of his neck. "Yes."

"That's not healthy. Do you take off weekends?"

He ran his fingers through his hair. "Sometimes."

"I thought being a lawyer was bad," she said moving toward the door. "That was why I chose to work internally in a big company. I didn't want to be in court. Of course, the merger took a lot of time, but…" She stopped as she neared him. "What?"

"You're being chatty."

"I'm sorry."

"For being chatty? Why?"

"I thought it was bothering you."

He shook his head. "No. It means you're warming up to me. I'd prefer that," he said opening the door and letting her walk through.

"Where are we going?" she asked as he locked the door behind him.

"Just over to the model house. I want you to see it."

# CHAPTER 23

Julie looked across the street where the house under construction stood. "And that's where I'll be working?"

"In a few weeks. The garage is made into offices."

"What do you do when the community is done?"

He started across the street with her next to him. "We convert the offices into garages and sell the house."

"Someone will live here?"

He slid the key into the door where the offices would be and unlocked the lock.

"Yep. Some family will make their home here, but first you and Tiffany will work here. You'll probably have a few more people join you in the office when it's done."

She nodded as she stepped through the door.

"Seems odd that this will be done in a few weeks," she said looking around at the bare walls with wires and pipes running through them. "Is it safe to walk around?"

Spencer walked over to a worktable and picked up two hard hats. He handed her one. "Safer with this."

"This will do wonders for my hair." She placed the hat on her head as he retrieved a flashlight from the table.

"It gets shady in the evening."

He held out his hand to her and she studied it for a moment and then looked up at him.

"I'm not making a pass at you," he promised. "I know my way around here."

"There is still enough light," she countered.

He withdrew his hand. "Fine. I want to show you the kitchen."

He walked up a small set of three steps and into a mudroom. Through the next door, it opened up to an entry. To the right was a vaulted ceiling entry and front door, which opened to the staircase to the second level. An office was to the left and a family room right in front of them. On the back side of the staircase, hidden from view, or would be, was the kitchen.

Spencer led her through the room and to the framed out kitchen. "There will be an island here," he demonstrated with his hands. "Sink under the window. Stove. Fridge. Dishwasher," he said all while pointing to areas that were bare.

"Spacious."

"Families like their space."

"I suppose they would," she said softly and it reminded him of how lonely she seemed.

"I want you to design it. Fill it with whatever you want."

She turned to look at him fully. "Me? You want me to pick what goes in here?"

"Sky's the limit."

"Oh, no. No. No. I'm not cut out for this. This isn't what I'm doing."

"You're the assistant on the job. That's what I need assistance on."

"I'm the woman who filed all the paperwork for all the other builds. I'm the woman who will follow up with the clients when

Tiffany can't. I'm not the one to pick and choose things and spend other people's money."

"It's my money."

"That's worse. I've cost you too much money as it is."

Even in the evening light, he could see the skin on her neck grow red. Usually that was a sign of anxiety. He hadn't meant to do that to her.

"Fine, I'll…"

"Wood floors. What kind of woodwork is in the house?" She scrubbed the thought with her hands. "Doesn't matter. Don't paint the wood. Keep it stained. Floor darker."

Spencer smiled as she walked into the kitchen.

"Do that glass tile on the backsplash. Cabinets a shade lighter than the floor. Very neutral, but warm." She walked around the island that had already been framed. "Dark granite," she said shaking her head. "I'll have to look again. Not black, but," she sighed. "Brown?"


WHEN JULIE LOOKED up at him, Spencer was leaned against a framed out wall. His arms were crossed and his feet crossed at the ankles. His smile had widened when she looked at him.

"What?" Her voice cracked as she spoke.

"You did just fine designing this."

She shook her head. "I didn't design it."

He stood and walked toward her, taking the hard hat off of his head. "You didn't even break the bank. You went for warmth."

"A family home should have warmth." She gulped back the buzz she was feeling from seeing the space in her head, and him looking at her.

"I like seeing this softer side of you."

Julie pursed her lips. "Are we done here? Will you take me back now?"

She turned to walk back out of the house, but he caught her

arm. For a moment she hesitated before turning to look back at him.

"Why did you kiss me?" he asked.

This again? Was it going to be like this every day? She wasn't really sure she had an answer to his question anymore.

"It was a mistake," she said as he took the hat from her head. The inside of the hat caught strands of her hair and worked them loose from the knot at the back of her head.

Julie took her free hand and tucked them behind her ear, but his hand had moved from her arm to the base of her neck. He pulled the band from her hair and let it fall.

"That's better," he said freeing the hair with his fingers.

"Spencer," her voice sounded weak. She didn't want to be weak.

He set the hats on the floor and looked down at her again, this time without touching her.

"Why?"

"Why is it important?"

He took a small step toward her closing the gap between them. "Because I can't sleep."

"I'm sorry."

"You say that too much," he said as he lifted his fingers to her hair again and let them slip through the strands. "I'm not good company either."

"Who told you that?" She forced herself to keep her eyes open as his other hand lifted to her hair.

"Tiffany."

"Oh." This wasn't good. He was her boss now and he didn't even like her. Was this a test? Was she supposed to knee him in the balls and run? Did he want her out of his life and he was using some reverse psychology on her? She'd heard what he'd said to his father on the phone in the hotel. He hated her. Wasn't that the reason she'd actually come to Nashville? Perhaps if she didn't have a job built on favors she wouldn't be used as she had been in Oregon.

The kiss was a mistake—a need—a spontaneous moment of weakness when her world had fallen apart.

So what was he doing now? He was playing with her head and she didn't like it—but even her own mind was playing games now.

Julie hated that having him touch her excited her—just like that night she gambled everything and kissed him in the elevator.

"Maybe we should try this. I know why I'm going to kiss you," he said a beat before he cupped her face in his hands and pressed his warm lips to hers.

His eyes closed and a moment later so did hers. This was crazy, but she couldn't stop herself. His mouth moved against hers and she wanted to take—to taste—to feel.

Julie's hands came to his chest as his tongue slipped through her lips to find hers and entangle it in a hot dance that ignited the senses down to her belly.

Spencer's hands slid over her shoulders and down her back pulling her even closer.

A moan escaped her as he pulled her even closer yet so that she could feel his heart pounding against her fingertips.

This was wrong. This was so wrong. But still, she didn't have the power to move away. She wanted to take until there was nothing left. She just wanted to feel desired, and Spencer made her feel that way.

When his lips moved from hers, she was still wrapped tightly in his arms. His forehead pressed to hers.

"I kissed you because I couldn't stand not to anymore," he said with his breath escaping him as quickly as hers was.

"We can't do this."

"Why did you kiss me?" he asked again brushing his lips over hers.

"I needed to feel."

He brought his hand to her cheek and brushed his thumb across her skin. "Feel what?"

"Wanted."

Spencer brought his mouth to hers again, and this time she wrapped her arms around his neck and let herself feel —everything.

Perhaps it was that Julie had her eyes closed so tightly, but the house seemed darker now as she let Spencer hold her in the dusty frame of the kitchen—in the diffused light of the day.

"This isn't safe," she said and her voice shook.

"Safe?" He pulled her back at arms length. "What do you mean?"

She broke from him, pushing her hair back behind her shoulders.

"You're my boss."

He laughed easily.

Julie gritted her teeth and wrapped her arms around herself. "Why are you laughing? This isn't funny."

He reached for her hands and held them in his, raising them to his lips to kiss her fingers. "My dad married his assistant and so did Ed."

Julie shook her head and pulled away. "I'm not marrying you."

"I didn't say you were." He picked up the hard hats. "I didn't mean to push you. I just…"

"You didn't." She looked up at him. "I've been thinking of that since I kissed you in the elevator and you didn't push me away."

"Why would I?"

"Because you detest me." She pulled in a breath and locked eyes with him. "I heard your phone conversation with your father that day at the hotel. I know what you think about me."

Spencer stepped back and raked his fingers through his hair. She knew he was frustrated, that was one of his tells.

The only problem was, the more tunneled his hair was, the more appealing he became to her.

"Oh, Julie…"

"It's just better if we learn to work together and not do this. It was a mistake for me to ever kiss you."

She headed toward the door and he followed.

Spencer set the hats on the workbench and locked the door behind them.

They were silent walking back to the trailer. He unlocked the trailer door, she gathered her things, and he locked it back up. He opened the car door for her and she slid into his car, her hands trembling around the strap of her bag.

# CHAPTER 24

Spencer took a few moments to make his way around the car, cursing at himself for—well, for everything. Why did he even think she didn't know how he talked about her? He was honest about it, but to know she'd heard him, that was worse.

Of course, she'd still come to Nashville looking to him for a job. Why would she have done that if...

He pulled open his door and climbed in.

Before starting the car he gripped the steering wheel tightly. "There is no way to take back what I said. I wasn't raised like that." He sighed. "You deserve so much better."

"Take me home," her voice quivered on the edge of breaking.

"One more question." He saw her shoulders drop so he started the engine. "If you heard me say that, why did you come here looking for a job? Why would you want to?" The words echoed the disappointment he felt in himself.

"I don't want to talk. I just want to go home."

Now he heard the tears that strained in her voice.

Spencer pulled away from the site and drove her home without another word.

. . .

WHEN SPENCER PULLED up in front of Julie's house, he turned off the car and got out before she could gather her bag.

Spencer opened her door and held out his hand.

Reluctantly, she took it and then let out a long breath.

"My car is in town. How did I forget that?" Her voice was soft, sad, and full of regret.

"I'll pick you up in the morning."

She shook her head. "I'll take the bus."

"I could send a car," he bargained and her eyes finally lifted.

"I'll wait for you, but then never again."

She started past him, but he couldn't let her go like that.

"Julie," he called and she stopped, but she didn't turn. He'd take what she gave. "I never meant to hurt you. And for what it's worth, I care about you."

She swung her bag over her shoulder and walked toward the side of the house and disappeared.

Spencer waited a few more moments before getting into his car and driving home.

IT HAD NEVER OCCURRED to him that she'd overheard his conversation, but then again, a week ago he didn't care. Given the opportunity he wasn't so sure he wouldn't have told her to her face. Hadn't he even contemplated making her one of the first people he laid off in a year?

Now he cared as he rode the elevator up to his lonely penthouse suite.

As he stepped inside the penthouse, the coldness of it swept over him. White marble floors. White walls with Art Deco pieces adorning it. He stepped into the kitchen with its shiny black countertops and set down his keys.

Spencer opened the refrigerator, pushed the bottle of beer to the side, and reached for a bottle of water. He opened it and chugged it down.

The sky was orange outside his window. He walked toward the balcony that looked out over the east side of Nashville. The streetlights had turned on, and the neon blazed on familiar landmarks, and the hue of the sunset blanketed the city.

Julie was out there missing the sight. Buried in her basement apartment, she was missing Nashville being tucked in for the evening.

Spencer sipped his water again and tried to clear his mind. Julie wouldn't be in Nashville if she hadn't wanted to be with him. There was no good logic behind why she'd make such a trip and ask for a job. She could have buried herself away in another job in Oregon where she could have still practiced law. Why hadn't she gone for the warm sands of Southern California?

No, she'd driven straight to Nashville without anything and landed in his office. *His office.*

He walked through the apartment to his bedroom and stopped. The flat paint of the gray walls dimmed the room. The mirrors on the wall of closets only made the dim look larger.

Even the comforter on his bed was gray and white to accent the glass top and metal on the handles of his dresser where he set down his bottle of water.

Suddenly the penthouse wasn't so appealing. What was appealing were Julie's eyes when she spoke of countertops and flooring. How she told him one thing in the trailer when the budget was skies the limit and then changed when she stepped into a house that a family would someday own.

She had an eye for comfort.

The thought struck him.

He'd been her comfort.

Spencer sat down on the edge of his bed and untied his shoes, which he'd usually have left by the door since he'd walked on site with them. The dust and sand dulled them he'd noticed as he set them on the cold floor.

For five months, he had been her focus. For five months, he had been the one in discussions with her every day. On the last day she walked into the boardroom, he had moved to help her pick up the papers she'd dropped when no one else in that room had moved. And it had been him who rode the elevator that night to make sure she was okay, passing his floor and taking his time to focus on her.

He scrubbed his hands over his face, now whiskered under his fingers. Pressing his lips together, he thought of their kiss. That deep, warm, pressing of tender skin kiss that even now made his head swim and body ache for her.

This wasn't over, he thought as he stood to pull a set of lounge pants from the drawer in the dresser. For as long as Spencer Benson could remember, he got what he wanted.

He wanted Julie Jacobson and she wouldn't be in Nashville if she didn't want him—no matter how much she was pushing in the opposite direction. He wanted her in his business, in his life, in his apartment—he sucked in the air to fill his lungs and steady his head and heart—he wanted her.

# CHAPTER 25

*J*ulie had packed, unpacked, repacked, and was unpacking her suitcase again. It had been a mistake to run to Nashville. What had she been thinking?

She sat on her bed and buried her face in her hands.

She hadn't been thinking—not clearly.

Pain had ripped through her when she'd seen Steven and Libby together tangled in *her* sheets in *her* bed. Anger had coursed through her when Libby confronted her about it. Mourning the loss of her marriage had her toppling over papers in that boardroom and acting foolish in the elevator when she'd kissed Spencer.

But she couldn't help herself.

In the five months she dragged out those negotiations, it had been his steely look at her that made her know there was a place for her. Sure, she'd stalled, but in the end, he bought a strong company and the Grayson family knew their company was in good hands.

Something still didn't add up, but she'd never been able to put her finger on it. Sure she'd stalled at the original request of Libby

Grayson, before she'd found her in her bed, but then things began to happen at PLL that she couldn't explain.

She knew someone had been messing with her files and her computer, but nothing more than her over organized gut feeling. She wasn't known for misplacing things and yet since the beginning of negotiations with BBH she misplaced a handful of documents and even files in her computer. She had to make sure both Spencer and the Graysons were equally protected.

Seriously she thought she'd lost her mind a time or two.

Perhaps in the back of her head she knew something was going on with her husband and it made her lose focus. The late nights, when they worked in the same office. The phone calls he'd dismiss himself for. The missed birthday she'd never mentioned, but that hurt most of all.

Why she was blindsided by his infidelity, again, was beyond her. Perhaps she thought if they were in the same office it wouldn't happen again.

How stupid was that? If it happened once, twice, it was going to happen again. She'd been the fool to stick around any longer than she needed. The past five months with her husband near her, while they worked through their divorce, and Spencer there fighting her all the way, had been a mix of hell and passion for what she did well.

What did it matter? She was now seated in the BBH family. She could protect the Bensons if something was happening.

She just hadn't thought she'd fall for the man who hated her. That truly hadn't been the plan. He was supposed to be her safe haven. He was a chance at a new start in the industry away from the favor granting Graysons, who had stabbed her in the back. Away from her ex-husband and his greed.

Julie fell backward on the bed and closed her eyes.

She replayed his hands in her hair—on her skin. Even the memory of his kiss swam in her head like a cloud of pure pleasure.

Was it so bad that he'd had a change of heart?

Was it horrible to wish she hadn't stopped him?

Julie rolled over and let a muffled scream fly into the mattress. It was all so frustrating.

She rested her forehead on her hands and lay silent and still for a moment considering everything from the past five months to the past week.

Opportunity lay at her feet in a new way. Law consumed so much of her, but the simple task of setting up her desk and just keeping track of the builds was calming. Sure, she knew issues would arise. After all, it had only been one day. But she was in love with her minimal space on the other side of the movable wall from Chuck—who burped when he thought no one could hear and cursed like a sailor under his breath when he went over plans by himself.

Every job came with the hesitation that she'd fail at it. What if Tiffany wasn't as nice as she seemed to be? And that too—what if Tiffany didn't like Julie kissing Spencer? That was a tangled web she should stay away from, but she couldn't help it.

Now her biggest fear was that she was falling for the man out of desperation to be wanted. However, no kiss from her husband had ever sizzled in her or tasted so good. She'd kissed Spencer Benson in that elevator because she'd needed to and now no amount of talking herself out of what she'd done could take it away. She'd fallen for him. She just didn't want to hurt him by making him a rebound for her broken heart.

# CHAPTER 26

The house looked quiet, Spencer thought as he pulled up to the curb early Tuesday morning. He had assumed he'd see Avery dancing in the front window, but he didn't.

He'd bought her one of those damn vanilla lattes she liked so he'd be waking her up.

With the cardboard tray, and three coffees, he walked up the front steps and started his assault on the doorbell.

From inside he could hear her stumbling over things and he laughed. Served her right for not getting up like a normal person.

When the door swung open, Pete stood there in rumpled clothes. He rubbed his hand over hair and then ran his hand over his unshaven cheeks.

"Spence, hi," he said with his voice groggy.

"You're not who I expected. Sorry for the rude awakening."

"Right. Right." He shook his head to obviously try and wake himself. "Come in. Sorry." He stepped back and Spencer walked through.

From the look of the couch, that was where Pete had slept. Not unusual, he thought. Avery was too stupid and stubborn to let him sleep with her. The man was a saint to just hang around and wait for her to come to her senses.

The thought humored him, and caught him off guard. Maybe they weren't meant for each other. After all, Avery's mother chased Spencer's father from the time they were seven until Spencer's father married his mother. It was only then, Simone fell in love with Avery's father—Spencer's mother's brother.

"What's so funny?" Pete asked as he shut the door and walked toward the couch. He picked up the blanket and began to fold it.

"Just thinking. So where is Avery?"

"Paris."

"Excuse me?" His voice had risen in a slight panic and the humor he'd been enjoying was wiped away. "She didn't tell me she was going anywhere."

Pete shrugged. "All I know is she called me at nine o'clock last night and asked for a ride to the airport. Her grandpa had sent a jet for her. She said she'd be gone until next week." He tossed the folded blanket back on the couch. "But she did say she'd be back in time for your birthday."

"Which means she isn't changing the cake," Spencer moaned.

"Pink and Black?"

"So she says."

Pete laughed. "To think she's been torturing you since day one."

Spencer chuckles. "Do you like vanilla lattes?"

"Hell, no."

"Of course not. Strong and black?"

"That's more my style."

Spencer took the coffee he'd earmarked for himself and handed it to Pete. "Guess I'd better go down and get Julie."

"She's not down there," Pete said lifting the coffee cup to his lips.

"Where is she?"

"At work. That's where I dropped her off about an hour ago, before I came back to get more sleep. She said she'd texted you."

Spencer took his phone out of his pocket and sure enough there was a message. "Guess it's on silent."

Pete nodded. "Avery says I need an Avery setting so I never miss her calls. Mine is always on silent."

"I suppose I'll head in then." He turned for the door.

"Hey, what kind of food does Julie like?"

Spencer turned around. "Food?"

"Yeah, we were talking on the ride downtown about maybe going out."

"You and Julie?" His voice actually cracked when he said it.

Pete's eyes grew wide. "Oh," he let the word ride on the air. "You and Julie?"

Spencer shrugged. "I don't think she's too interested in me."

"Pretend I didn't say anything then. You let me know if things don't work out. But I'll let you try first."

Spencer only nodded and walked out of the house and headed back to his car.

He set the coffees on the top of the car and opened his door. Carefully, he took the coffees off the roof and set them in the passenger seat as he climbed in behind the wheel, and closed the door.

When the car purred to start, he pulled away from the house, and headed into town with Julie on his mind.

In one week she'd finalized her divorce to her cheating ex-husband, moved to Nashville, and now had three men vying for her attention.

Spencer knew he should step away from it. He wasn't wanting a competition for her attention—he wanted all of it.

JULIE SAT with Amber in the small boardroom across the hall from Spencer's office. Yesterday Julie wasn't sure she and Amber were going to be allies, but today, she was helpful and kind. Perhaps it was that Julie was taking the stress out of her job. The high-rise builds were enough to obviously make anyone stressed. Add a community build with one hundred and fifty custom jobs, and any sane assistant would want to walk off the job.

But Julie was sure Amber would never leave Spencer. She was very loyal to the man who was at least twenty years younger than she was.

"I have two luke-warm vanilla lattes for the taking," his voice broke through their conversation and both women looked up to see him standing in the doorway.

"A Starbucks in the lobby and you bring luke-warm lattes?" Amber joked reaching for the tray he offered.

"Bought them an hour ago for my cousin and my passenger. Only to find my cousin gone and my passenger hitched another ride to work."

Amber turned and Julie could feel her eyes on her. "I texted."

"I didn't get it," Spencer replied with a shrug.

"I'm very sorry for that." She took the cup Amber offered. "Thank you for the coffee."

He nodded his head slowly and backed out of the room.

Amber sat back in her chair and held the cup to her lips. "Past five months must have been interesting," she said.

No doubt Amber had been on the receiving end of whatever Spencer had to say about the merger and her. It was a wonder the woman was speaking to her at all. But she'd take the bait to her comment. "Why?"

"I've known that man for years. He doesn't bring coffee."

Julie swallowed hard and picked up her coffee. "Guess he was feeling generous."

"I suppose. How many dinners did you have in Oregon?"

The inquisition wasn't welcome, but Julie had nothing to hide. "Never ate a meal with the man that wasn't catered by the Grayson family."

"No quick bites out?"

"No."

"No late nights alone in the office?"

"Negotiations only."

Amber let out a hum. "You caused those few gray hairs at his temples," she said, but when Julie turned to look at her, she was grinning.

"I don't think that was all me. It was a big buy for him. There is a lot of responsibility that goes into buying a family company like PLL."

"Sure." Amber sat forward and set her coffee on the table. "And you made it harder."

Julie's defenses were starting to build. This was the part of her own attitude she didn't like. If she felt attacked, she went into attack mode herself. But, she was a lawyer. She could keep calm if she had to and continue the conversation without ripping the woman's hair out.

"I hope I didn't cause too much work for you while he was away."

Amber shrugged. "Nothing more than I'd expected."

"Good. Then I assume this is old business," Julie said as she began to put the files Amber had given her into a bank box on the chair beside her.

"Hey," Amber said softly touching Julie's arm. "I didn't mean to get you upset."

Julie pushed her shoulders back and turned toward Amber. "I am very aware that Mr. Benson was very vocal about detesting me. I know it seems odd I am here now working for him, but I'd like the chance to prove myself before everyone decides to hate me on merit."

Amber nodded slowly. "If it's any consolation, I like you just fine. I never bought into the bitch story anyway." She stood and collected her files.

"Why?"

Amber smiled. "You made him mad, no question. Yes, he called you the bitch lawyer often. But there was something in the delivery of it."

She left the room and Julie watched her walk away, still smiling.

# CHAPTER 27

*T*he erratic beating of her heart had Julie nearly gasping for air. Was it what she wanted? Did she want to throw in the towel and give into the feelings she was having for Spencer? It was stupid. That hadn't been the purpose of her coming to Nashville.

She needed to weigh her options. If it didn't work then what? If it did work...

Oh, she didn't even know what to do with that.

Hell, if it didn't work out she had options. Randy had asked her out and told her of a job. Even Pete was flirtatious and inter-ested, though she was damn sure he was more interested in Avery. But she had options.

So if she kissed Spencer a few more times, and felt it out it, that would be good—enjoyable. If they had a few meals together and spent some time together, it would be fun. And—the heat was rising in the room, she thought—if it went further, well...

"Are you okay?" Spencer's voice broke the silence in the room.

Julie looked up to see Spencer standing with both hands on the doorjamb looking at her.

"Fine."

"You're beet red and breathing hard. Are you mad? Did Amber say something out of line? I'll talk to her. I can…"

"No. I'm fine."

"Julie, I…"

She stood up cutting him off. Her breath was rapid now looking at him in his polo shirt with those tunnels already etched into that dark, thick hair that she'd like to tangle her own fingers in.

Blinking hard, and deciding that she'd panic over it later, she walked past him and straight into his office.


SPENCER LOOKED around the boardroom and wondered what could have gone on to set her off in such a way. He hadn't heard any arguing or shouting.

He turned and walked back to his office.

The moment he walked through the door it closed behind him causing him to spin around.

There she was, pressed with her back to the door. Her skin was still red and her chest heaved with breath. But it was her eyes —those dark tell-tale eyes—that told him exactly what she was thinking.

It was a risk to step toward her, but he was damn sure that was the point of all this.

He moved closer and she quickly pulled his arm and had him with his back flat to the door.

The air rushed from his lungs and she swiftly moved against him, her body pressed hard to his. Her fingers tangled in his hair and her mouth—her glorious mouth—crushed down on his.

Jesus, could he have wanted this any more than he did right now?

His hands came to her hips and gripped tightly as she feverishly sucked the very last ethic out of him with her kiss.

When Julie's hands skimmed down the back of his neck and

she hooked her arms around him, he spun her until her back pressed against the door. The moan that escaped between them filled him with more desire for her.

She gasped as he pressed his body to hers, undoubtedly letting her know how aroused he was having her in his arms.

Spencer worked the kiss they shared, eased to her jaw, and down that tender neck he loved to admire when her hair was pulled back, just as it was now.

Her hands slid down his chest and the warmth of her fingertips penetrated right thought the fabric of his shirt.

What was that he heard as he skimmed his lips over her collarbone? Her moan, yes, her moan.

No. He sucked in air, and eased back realizing his phone buzzed in his pocket.

He rested his head in the crook of her neck as they both caught their breath.

"It's my timer. I have a meeting."

She groaned as she wrapped her arms around his neck and pulled him tighter to her.

"Tell me you're not angry for me doing this again," she said on a pant. "Tell me it wasn't a mistake."

He chuckled, but it only groaned out as he gasped for breath. "Not a mistake. Not mad." He sucked in a few more breaths.

Julie rested her head on his shoulder and he breathed her in.

"I have to go." He pulled back but kept his hands on her hips. "Don't leave and run back to Oregon or anywhere else." He sucked in another breath. "Have dinner with me. Promise me you'll have dinner with me."

She nodded.

"Okay." He let his hands drop. "I have to head out to the site later. Are you headed there now?"

She nodded, again, and he knew she was having a hard time catching her breath too.

Spencer leaned in one more time and brushed a soft, needy kiss over her lips.

He walked back to his desk, picked up his files, and gave her one more look. She was beautiful standing there with her cheeks flushed and her lips swollen from his kisses.

Spencer's body buzzed thinking of what could happen next, and hoping he wouldn't have to wait too long to find out.

SPENCER WATCHED Julie walk back to the boardroom, drink down the now cold coffee, then sit down at the big table and simply catch her breath.

If they were lucky, Amber wouldn't happen back by for at least another ten minutes and maybe Julie would be able to function again.

He, on the other hand, needed to get upstairs to the boardroom in his father's office and discuss the production schedule on the new hotel they were working on. Ed was heading it, but Spencer had been working with the cement contractor. Either way, he needed to get his heart rate slowed before he walked into that room.

Spencer walked out of his office and toward the stairwell. At least if he climbed the two floors up to his father's office, it would explain his extra intake of oxygen because he couldn't will his body to calm.

She'd given into him. No, that wasn't correct at all. If that were the case, she'd have continued kissing him yesterday. This was all her. She'd come after him—pushed him up against the door.

It was crazy to want this—to want her—but Spencer simply couldn't help it. He'd seen her work. He'd been studying her for months. Of course, never had he thought it was desire that had him knowing how she sat when she was casual or how tense she got when she was in an argument. He intimately knew the shades of brown her eyes became and now he knew how they clouded when filled with passion. If she wanted to be taken seriously, she wore her hair in that low bun at the base of her neck. And her hair skimmed her shoulders if she was at ease and enjoying herself as she had in the bar with his family.

Even a week ago he could have picked her laugh out in a crowd or even her scent.

"Glad you could join us," Ed made the first jab as Spencer hurried through the door.

"Sorry."

His father pointed to the vacant seat next to the job foreman and the concrete foreman. "I think you know everyone."

Spencer gave them each a nod, but for the life of him he couldn't call them by name. In fact, he'd be surprised if he could answer his own name if someone asked.

Work certainly wasn't on his mind. The adorable, recently divorced—probably on the rebound—blonde two offices below them had him all worked up. And damn if he wasn't enjoying it immensely.

# CHAPTER 28

*A*s quickly as she could, Julie had high-tailed it out of the Riverside building and to her little desk at Hart Estates.

The trailer had been locked, and she had to ask Tiffany for the key. That had been something she'd wanted to avoid. But Tiffany hadn't said anything. Perhaps she and Spencer weren't as good friends as Julie had thought. He hadn't called or texted her right away to say he'd made out with the bitch lawyer.

Okay, she thought as she put her bag and purse in the bottom desk drawer, that wasn't fair. He'd apologized for that, and in truth she was a bitch when she was in Oregon running mergers. She didn't have to be that person anymore.

On her desk were four more folders, which meant four more lots had been sold. She'd have to go in and look at the display to see where these homes would be. After walking through the future model home with design schemes in her mind, she wanted to see what other people would choose. This certainly would be an insightful trip into the minds of other people.

When the door to the trailer opened, Julie looked up expecting to see Chuck walk through the door and curse as it shut behind him. Instead, Tiffany walked in, dressed to the nines again in another pair of shoes that Julie would die for. She had to stand nearly six foot tall in those shoes, and that mass of red hair swung hypnotically. Julie was mesmerized.

"Brought you some coffee," she said handing her a mug and then sitting on the edge of Julies desk with her long slender legs crossed at the knees.

It was no wonder Spencer had wanted this woman. She was stunning, and Julie desperately wanted to hate her—but she didn't.

"Sold four more lots." Tiffany raised her cup in cheers. "Mama is getting a new pair of shoes."

"You must have quite a selection. I love those you're wearing too."

"Oh, these old things?" She looked down at her foot and moved it from side to side. "Spence bought them for me for Christmas years ago. Of course, I had to drag him to the store, try them on, and beg him to do it. But he did."

Julie forced the smile. Okay, maybe she did hate her a little.

"Do you have plans for lunch?" Tiffany continued.

"I have a sandwich I brought."

Tiffany shook her head and the red aura swung again. "No. You and I are going to lunch."

"I don't have funds for lunches out."

"I do." She grinned and sipped her coffee. "My treat. Save your sandwich."

"Thanks."

"Okay, I've made small talk long enough." She playfully raised and lowered her eyebrows. "Spill the beans. You and Spence? You must have had one hot morning in his office."

Julie felt her mouth open, but nothing came out right away. "He called you? He told you?"

Tiffany's eyes lit and her grin widened. "Didn't say a word. I read it in your face. You didn't want to see me this morning. You're afraid of what I'll say."

Julie dropped her shoulders. "How could you possibly know…"

"Aside from the fact that I think you just told me," she said grinning, "I know Spence and I know the effect he has on people. And he's taken by you. Oh, he's got it bad too."

"By me?"

"You might have pushed all the wrong buttons before, but I think that's why he was so irritated by you."

Julie pursed her lips. "This doesn't sound like a man who would be interested."

Tiffany laughed. "Don't you get it? Remember when you were a little girl and a boy would push you or pull your hair?"

"Robby Brickman."

"Okay, so Robby was mean to you?'

"Horrible."

"And he liked you?"

"He wrote it on his notebook, in his math book, and the stall in the boys' bathroom."

Tiffany nodded. "Just like that. Only you were the mean one in this situation."

What a horrible conversation and it was sucking all the glory out of that hot kiss she'd had with *Spence*.

"So you're saying I liked him?"

She shrugged. "I think you were doing your job. I just think he was watching very closely."

Julie felt her skin heat. "What about the two of you?"

Tiffany bounced her foot and admired the shoes Spencer had bought her Christmases ago. "Sex. It's all sex."

"Oh," her voice dropped and the disappointment hung in the air. Not to mention the heaviness in her chest.

"Not recent sex, mind you."

"Oh," she said again a little more enthusiastic.

"We were a couple when, let's see," she said looking up and giving it some thought. "I think I was eighteen—nineteen, something. I was there for him when they found out about the baby his mom gave away and her ex-fiancé trying to kill her."

"Spencer mentioned that. Darcy, right?"

"Yep." She sipped her coffee again. "His brother broke. Couldn't handle it. Took off for three years or so. Traveled the world. Got a grip on people having pasts you can't control."

"From what I understand she gave her away to protect her."

"Right. It still hurt Tyler. Spence, on the other hand, fell in love with Darcy. He was excited for her to be part of their family. He was mad at Tyler for a long time for leaving his family. But Tyler's back and married, and everything is perfect again for the Bensons."

"And you were Spencer's comfort through all of it," Julie asked gauging their involvement.

"Sure. I thought it was true love... that he'd sweep me off my feet and we'd be married by now."

Even though they were talking about the man Julie had just had an incredible kissing experience with, and one she'd like to try that sex thing with, she was intrigued.

"So why aren't you married?"

Tiffany shrugged. "He's not in love with me."

"Who wouldn't be in love with you?"

Tiffany laughed. "I'm not. So it's hard for men to love me too."

"I can't imagine."

"He's deeply family rooted. I'm not. I like the flashy things—like his penthouse. Money isn't an object to him. In fact, he doesn't care much about it. I give that to his upbringing. That family could have anything and everything. But that isn't important."

Julie could see that. Wasn't that a reason to cherish the man right there?

"We realized we were soul mates, but not in the way a man and wife are. I've got his back. And I tell you if you screw him over I'll mess you up."

Julie gasped. "I would never…"

"I know. I just want to make it clear." Tiffany sipped her coffee. "Anyway, now we have sex if neither of us are involved. And we plan sex, but it doesn't always work out. Sometimes pretty blondes who have his mind tied up get in the way." She bore her stare into Julie.

"Me?"

"I think I was supposed to be a distraction. I wasn't."

"We kissed," she blurted it out as if she were telling her dearest friend her deepest secret. "I mean I kissed him in Oregon, the night before they fired me. It was an impulse."

Tiffany smiled. "Those are the best."

"We kissed last night, but I freaked out."

"It happens."

Julie nodded then stood to meet Tiffany eye to eye. "But this morning. Oh," she moaned feeling a flush move over her. "I just had to…you know…I made my move."

Tiffany's grin widened even more. "Lots of tongue? Any grope?"

"What? Oh, no, just…" She could feel it just as she had. "I shouldn't tell you this."

Tiffany climbed down off the desk, rested her hands on the top, and leaned in. "Are you kidding me? I want details. Lots and lots of them."

"It was hot. I think if we were alone in the whole building…"

"Now that's what I'm talking about." She stood erect. "Oh, he's in love."

Julie fell back in her chair. "No. No. It's not that."

"Says who?"

"Says me."

"I'm talking for Spence."

"I just got divorced."

"From a lying, cheating, bastard."

Julie only stared. Then she laughed. The laughter rolled harder and she covered her mouth to keep it in.

"I like him," she said dropping her hands. "I think that's why I'm here. I mean there are a million reasons, but that must have driven me here."

"You'd be crazy to come if you detested him completely."

"You're not jealous?"

Tiffany shrugged. "I'll have good sex again, but not with him. Do you have a brother or a cousin?"

Julie shook her head. "Neither."

"Okay, well just know that as long as you're in the picture I'm not. And that's not just me I'm speaking for. Spence doesn't screw around. If you're important to him, you're the only one."

"I want that." God didn't she. Someone who truly believed in the sanctity of being a couple? That's what she'd always dreamed of.

"I think he does too," Tiffany said as she looked out the window. "Hey, there's your lover now."

Julie was sure the heat in the room shot up. Tiffany moved from the desk to the door and opened it. "Hey, handsome. We're over here."

Julie watched him nod and walk toward the trailer. When he walked through the door, he met eyes with Tiffany, but they didn't travel further. When he looked at Julie, satisfaction radiated on his face.

"Hey," he said easily.

"Hey."

Tiffany picked up her coffee from Julie's desk. "Oh, you two are pathetic. I'm going back to work." She turned for the door, opened it, and looked back at Julie. "Lunch. We have a date. And no boss man gets in the way of that." She gave a curt nod, with a wink to Spencer and disappeared.

"She's already hounding you. I'm so sorry. I should have considered that."

Julie smiled up at him. Oh, he was so handsome. "I'm not sure she hounded. She walked in and told me everything that had happened between us."

Spencer's eyes widened. "I didn't tell her anything. I'm not like that."

"I know. She says she just knows you well enough."

He considered. "True enough."

"She also told me that you two have sex."

His cheeks flushed almost immediately and that gave her some satisfaction. "She told you that?"

"I'd have assumed you had sex the other night the way she was kissing on you in front of me. I mean…"

"We didn't," he quickly interrupted.

"You didn't?"

He moved closer to her desk. "No. I was a bit preoccupied that night."

Julie stood and leaned over the desk as Tiffany had earlier. "You passed up sex with her because of me?"

"Yeah," he said easily as he leaned in over her desk with his hands pressed on the top.

"This isn't going to work with me working for you."

He moved in closer. "I already told you, this is a family tradition."

"I told you I'm not marrying you."

"Isn't going to make me want you any less," he said, and he moved close enough to take her mouth and make her head spin without touching any other part of her.

# CHAPTER 29

*S*pencer pulled back when he heard the familiar shuffle and mumbled curses from Chuck as he opened the trailer door.

He stopped, gave a nod to Spencer, went to his desk and began to toss papers about.

Julie had slid back into her chair and opened the new files for the lots Tiffany had sold.

She studied it. "I think this is the model I liked the most. Not too big, but roomy enough for a family."

"I designed two of the six options. That one is one of mine."

She lifted her eyes to meet his. "You did this?" He nodded. "I'm very impressed."

"Thank you."

Spencer watched her appreciate spec sheets. She shook her head. "They opted for the loft instead of the extra bedroom."

"You'd take the room?"

"Sound gets lost when you have a loft. Don't get me wrong, it's pretty, but you always need a room. They might have people stay, so a guest room is nice. What if they each started a home business?"

"There is an office, just off the family room."

She nodded. "But each of them might like an office. Each of my parents had offices in our home. Of course, I didn't have siblings, so there was plenty of room for that."

He could still hear Chuck cursing over papers and he thought it was time for him to switch his attention from her to him.

Spencer stood and walked over to Chuck's desk and watched him stew over plans.

"What's got ya cursing?" Spencer asked and Chuck's eyes rose from looking at the plans to pierce Spencer's.

"That lumber company you bought to make this easier is late with another shipment. Twice in one week."

"Transition."

Chuck grumbled. "I'm going to have to do something. Tiffany sold four more lots. It's not going to stop."

"I'll look into it," Spencer assured him and it was met with another grumble.

Spencer hadn't planned on making a trip to Oregon for another two weeks. The hope was that the four executives he'd left there to head up the operation would be doing their jobs. But it seemed as though that wasn't the case.

Spencer walked back to Julie's desk, took the notepad and pen she had off to the side, and wrote down his address.

He handed it to her, and she looked back at him with a questioning frown.

"Seven-thirty."

Julie leaned in and whispered, "This is your address?"

He nodded.

"That's moving too fast," she said keeping her voice low.

"It's only dinner." He set the pen down. "I have to head back downtown. Looks like I'll be making a trip back to Oregon sooner than I'd planned. I need to get Amber to set that all up."

"I don't know why you'd have a delay. PLL never had delays."

Spencer nodded again. "I know. I'm going to assume it's just growing pains." He gave her a wink and mouthed the words seven-thirty once more.

This time she smiled, but there was still some fear in her eyes.

He said goodbye to Chuck and received only another grumble as he walked out of the trailer.

* * *

AMBER MET him in his office five minutes after he'd returned. Already in her hands was his itinerary for his trip to Oregon starting Monday morning.

"Hell of a way to say goodbye to being twenty-five," he mumbled.

"You're much older in your maturity. I sometimes forget what a baby you really are," she retorted.

He sat back in his chair. "Dad took me up to the top floor of an unfinished high-rise when I was six. Tyler stayed in the construction trailer shaking like a leaf. Dad never let go of my hand, but I was hooked. I can't imagine not doing this forever."

"It's in your blood and so is the negotiating. And if you want that land just south of Hart Estates you'd better get that negotiation hat on. The farmer is ready to talk."

Spencer sat up and leaned forward on his desk with his elbows. "Are you kidding?"

She shook her head with a grin. "Seems that the first figure you gave him might have made him look at that crop a little different. His kids are over plowing it too."

"He knows he can either keep his house there or we will build him one, right?"

"He knows. I think you sold him."

Spencer could feel the smile widen on his face. He'd stop in and talk to the man tomorrow. That lot would mean another hundred and fifty houses and a string of patio homes. Dinner at seven-thirty just became a celebration, he thought. Even though it wasn't signed, sealed and delivered, it was still good news.

Amber started out of the office, but stopped and shut the door instead.

"Problem?" Spencer asked as he picked up the folder she'd brought him with his travel plans.

"Julie."

He set the folder down. "Why is Julie a problem?"

"She's not," Amber walked toward his desk. "Two days in and I think she'll be a good asset. But she's married."

Amber was sometimes too much of a mother figure, he thought. "Newly divorced."

"Hmmm," she murmured as she folded her arms in front of her.

She was watching out for him. Obviously, they weren't going to be too good at hiding this relationship.

"Husband cheated on her," he defended.

"With Libby Grayson. I know. I hear talk. But he's still working for you."

Spencer sat back in his chair. "Julie's ex-husband works for me?"

"He closed the deal on PLL."

He felt the blood drain from his face. "Steven McDaniels is Julie's ex-husband?"

"You didn't know that?"

"No."

"If I were her, I'd file suit for wrongly being fired. I mean, she was very thorough with the merger, she shouldn't have been let go. She got fired, in my opinion, because her husband was screwing around with Libby."

He nodded slowly. "She said she wouldn't press charges against PLL for wrongful termination."

"Why would she? Things are pretty good for her here. You set her up nice."

Spencer didn't like this tone Amber was taking with him. He understood it, but he didn't like it.

"I trust her," he said.

"I do too. But I don't trust Steven and Libby. I think when you're out there next week you'd better do something about that. PLL is your company too. Contract states you'll keep their employees as long as they are doing satisfactory work."

"What have they done wrong?"

"Fired Julie."

Right. He let out a breath. That was wrong. But he felt as though he'd benefitted from that mistake and so had Julie.

"I'll check on that department when I get there. Let me know if anything comes about before then. And I mean that in the gossip department. Sometimes that seems to be more legit than a spreadsheet."

Amber nodded and let herself out of his office.

Spencer clasped his hands behind his head and rocked back in his chair.

He was going to need to figure out Libby's agenda. She wasn't even on the payroll with the company, but she seemed to be making a lot of ripples in the water at Pacific Line Lumber. The last thing he needed was to lose a company like that because of the heir apparent.

# CHAPTER 30

*L*unch had been an unexpected surprise, Julie thought as she climbed into her car at the end of the day. Tiffany had splurged for a deli sandwich, which hands down did beat the sandwich Julie had brought. Afterward, they toured a lovely shoe store.

Julie was an expert at window shopping, and had been most of her life. Tiffany, on the other hand, was an impulse buyer. That had netted her a pair of scarlet suede Stuart Weitzman Mae platform heels. No doubt Tiffany had a stunning dress to match.

Julie had splurged too. Chuck had seen to it that she got her own key to the construction trailer. She bought a nice keychain with a sparkly pink high heel shoe on it. She figured it was the little victories.

As she pulled out of the parking lot, she looked at the little sticky note she'd placed on the dashboard with Spencer's address on it. It was downtown. It was the first time she'd ever followed directions somewhere that had the word 'penthouse' in the address.

Swallowing backwhatever fear seemed to be rising, she drove back into Nashville to have dinner in the penthouse. But, she reminded herself she'd be sleeping in her own bed. She owed herself that bit of respect, and Spencer too.

When she pulled up to the address and looked up, she wondered what it would be like to live in a building that overlooked the streets of Nashville.

Even though Spencer dressed nicely, drove a beautiful BMW, and hadn't yet cleared three decades on the earth, she couldn't begin to imagine what he was worth. She didn't look at him like that, but she couldn't help but wonder when she knew he lived at the top of the enormous building in front of her.

She parked her outdated car in the visitors lot and hurried into the lobby of the building which was a mix of both office space and residential.

A security guard was positioned near the elevators. She supposed that after work hours only residents could get upstairs. He gave her a nod to let her pass, and she pushed the button to call the elevator.

When one opened, people moved off and she and one other man climbed on.

He pushed his button on the twentieth floor. "Which one for you?"

His British accent gave her chills.

"Top floor, please."

He pushed the button and narrowed his eyes. "You are friends with Tiffany?"

Julie nodded.

"Nice apartment. Clark," he said holding his hand out to shake hers.

"Julie."

"Ah, you are the woman Spencer Benson dumped her for." He laughed, but Julie didn't find humor in the situation.

"I'm not…"

"I am joking." The elevator slowed to the twentieth floor and the door opened. "Tell Tiffany hello for me. And if things do not work out for you and the builder," he gave a shrug, "look me up." He winked as the door closed.

Julie winced. These were the kind of men that Tiffany preferred? No wonder she kept Spencer on a leash.

Then, as the door opened to the top floor, she thought that was disgusting too. How had she played into some love triangle? She should absolutely despise what Tiffany and Spencer had— especially if she thought she ever was going to sleep with him. Maybe she wasn't going to. Maybe kissing was enough. After all, she just got out of a relationship with a man who used sex and didn't believe in the sanctity of marriage. Did she really want to get into another relationship where the man kept friends just to have sex with?

Before she could knock or ring the bell, Spencer pulled open the large front door. "I saw you on the camera. It looked like maybe you were going to turn around and get back in the elevator."

"I was thinking about it."

He took her hand and pulled her into the apartment.

The sight stunned her enough that she didn't pull her arm from his grip. Then again, she didn't feel inclined to do so.

"This is stunning," she said taking in the marble floors and the Art Deco covered walls.

"My dad designed it."

"The interior?"

"The whole building actually, but specifically this apartment. He'd built it for himself before he met my mother."

She turned to him. "You come from a lot of talented people don't you?"

He shrugged. "My family is very supportive when you have a passion. My father's is much like mine. He enjoys the build and the design."

"What is your brother's passion?"

Spencer smiled. "Have you ever heard of the *Diamond Gift*?"

"It's a non-profit. I saw a sign for it in the building when I was in the elevator last Friday. When I came looking for you. When Tiffany…"

"Got it."

"Anyway, I know it said something about supporting women and children."

He nodded. "That's right. They help those who need help finding work and housing to remove them from domestic violence, mostly."

"Your brother started the organization?"

He shook his head. "No. Avery's mother. She saw a need and she filled it. It started with giving a woman in need the diamond earrings right out of her ears."

Julie placed her hand on her chest to ease her heart. "That's precious."

"And that's how things get done. Tyler and his wife work in the organization and put together the gala that brings in most of the funds for the year."

"That's why they called Avery?"

"She has a lot of clout to get big names to give big money."

"But she's into wine?"

Spencer shrugged. "For now. I'm not happy that she jetted off to France. I'm sure her parents aren't either."

"Why?"

"Her mother and grandfather have had a strained relationship for years. Family politics I guess." He took her hand. "C'mon. Let me show you the rest of the place."

Spencer led her to the enormous kitchen and she stopped. "This is the size of my apartment."

"It's too big for one person," he said.

"Looks like you do just fine. And it smells great in here. What are you making?"

"Nothing fancy. Rigatoni. Baked chicken. Tossed salad."

Julie walked over to the pot on the stove. "You made your

own sauce."

"Not hard really. My grandmother taught me."

She lifted the lid and breathed in deep. "Your grandmother is Italian?"

"German, but still a marvelous Italian cook. Can I get you some wine?"

"Yes, thank you."

He poured her a glass of wine from a bottle that breathed on the counter and handed it to her.

She sipped. "Very nice."

"Tester bottle from Avery's vineyard," he said with a bite to his words.

"You don't like this new adventure."

"Not comfortable with it. What does she know about business in France?"

"You learn, right?"

He shrugged and picked up a glass that sat on the counter and sipped. "I worry about her. I always have. We're all a team. Ed, Chris, and Clara are a lot older, but still, the six of us are a team."

"I think that's nice." And her heart ached for just a taste of what it was to have a team. She noticed the balcony just beyond the living room. "Can I go check out your view?"

"Yeah, come on. It's the best time of the day. When the sun is sinking low and the lights on Broadway begin to twinkle."

He took her hand again and walked her through the apartment. She wondered where all of his personal effects were. There were no pictures on tables or shoes lying around. In fact, it was more like a hotel room. Was he so neat and tidy? Was this just because she'd come to visit? Or, was he just living in the space and not living at all?

The warm evening air wrapped around her as they walked outside. She could hear the traffic on the streets. It was—interesting, she thought. She'd much prefer the sound of a lawnmower, children's laughter, or the sound of birds in the trees.

"Did you grow up in the city?" she asked and sipped her wine.

"No. Sprawling Tennessee land, my mother would say. Long dirt road where Tyler and I rode bikes, ATVs, and learned to drive." He smiled and that dimple formed in his cheek. "My grandmother has a stream that goes through her property. On it is an enormous boulder where you could sit for hours, sun yourself, and just forget everything." He closed his eyes. "You can hear the horses in the barn and the trees as they blow in the breeze." He opened his eyes and looked at her. "I get caught up in it."

"I would too." She moved toward him. "Why do you live here?"

Spencer shrugged. "I'm a young exec. Aren't I supposed to? At least until I'm married and have kids?"

The very thought of it made her chest tighten. Steven had never wanted that. "You want that?"

"Always have. You?"

Now she shrugged. "I'm not too good at the marriage thing." But, yes, she had always wanted that.

"That is a two-way street. You might be just fine at it."

She'd give him that. It was hard to have a marriage when the partner wasn't interested.

Spencer reached his hand to her hair which she'd let down when she'd left the office. He pulled his fingers through it and then rested his palm on her cheek.

"You're beautiful, Julie."

Her breath caught. "You think so?"

"Oh, yes. I think that even when you're dressed as the hard ass lawyer, it's sexy."

"My husband—ex-husband," she corrected, "never said those words to me."

"His loss." He moved in closer to her. "I want to be with you, Julie. I need you to know that. And I won't cross any lines until you say it's okay. Marriage and relationships are for real in my world."

She gazed up into his dark eyes and got lost there. "I got hurt, Spencer. I don't want to be hurt again."

"Are you ready to be in another relationship?" He moved in closer. "I'll wait."

She wanted this. She might have been married, but she wasn't cherished or loved. Everything in her gut told her that Spencer would cherish and love her.

"I'm scared," she admitted.

"I am too. I've spent the past five months convincing myself that I don't like you at all. But I think that whole time I was fighting it."

Julie tucked her lips between her teeth and gazed up at him. "If we continue with this, I'm going to quit. You need to know that. I won't be the boss' fling. And I'm not just looking for some rebound because I was hurt."

"It won't be a fling."

To this point in her life, that had to be one of the most romantic things anyone had ever said to her. "I know. But I won't be someone who feeds the gossip. I've done that already, and I didn't even know it."

He brought his face closer and lingered with his lips a breath from hers. "We can talk about that later. Right now, I want to kiss you under that big Tennessee moon that's trying to peek through the cloud over the city lights."

She let her eyes look up and then back into his. "I'll bet the moonlight at the site is fantastic."

"It is. We'll go park out there one night and stargaze. For now, I just want to kiss you."

Julie took a deep breath and closed her eyes letting him move in closer and press that kiss to her mouth, and take away her doubts.

She hadn't come to Nashville looking to fall in love with Spencer Benson, but it looked like that was where she was headed.

# CHAPTER 31

*R*igatoni and chicken had never tasted so good, Julie thought. Spencer was celebrating, he told her. The potential purchase of more land had him making plans behind those dark eyes, which had gazed at her all night.

After an evening of intimate kisses, it would have been easier for Julie to have fallen into his bed and awaken with him. There had been a few moments when his words drew her in and his kisses nearly sealed the deal. But they had mutually fought against it.

That would have started the rumor mill—if it hadn't already started.

The fact that Julie was staring at her ceiling, in her own bed, in her own apartment, meant that they were being responsible.

After all, it had only been a week since she'd attacked him with a kiss in that elevator.

Julie smiled in the dark thinking of it. It had taken her by surprise, she could only assume he was equally as surprised by her actions.

Closing her eyes, she gave into the fantasy of what might

come if she let it. And as she dreamed she found comfort in Spencer's arms.

The next morning her alarm startled her and she was more than a little sad to find she, in fact, wasn't wrapped in his arms.

With Avery out of the house, mornings were quiet. She wasn't sure she enjoyed that nearly as much as being woken by loud music.

Julie showered, picked out a more conservative outfit to work on site in, and left her hair down in natural waves. It certainly made her look more feminine and less hard. She wasn't a lawyer right now. She didn't have to look so hard.

Today there wasn't a need for her to go into the Riverside Building, so she headed to the Hart Estates office, stopping to get Tiffany and herself a coffee.

When she walked through the door, Tiffany was on the phone. She shot her a look and then continued writing notes.

"I seriously don't want to be the one to tell him that," she said writing. "You know I don't like you on those smaller planes. Maybe you should fly commercial like you originally planned." She nodded. "I know. Call me when you get there." Tiffany rubbed between her eyebrows. "Okay, I'll talk to you later. Goodbye."

She hung up the phone and lifted her eyes to Julie.

"I brought you a coffee. I'm thinking I should have brought you something stronger," she said handing Tiffany the coffee.

"Spence is on his way to Oregon."

Julie felt it—the pang of sadness in her chest. "What's wrong? I thought he was going next week."

"Three of our delivery trucks are missing. I have to tell Chuck that we have delays. Benson, Benson, and Hart doesn't go over budget or have delays. They live by that."

Julie sat down in front of Tiffany's desk. "How do you lose three trucks?"

"I have no idea," she snapped out. "Someone is screwing with him."

"Libby," she said under her breath.

"Libby?"

"Grayson. Granddaughter of the founder. Mistress to my ex-husband."

Tiffany inched over her the desk resting on her arms. "Your ex-husband is screwing the founder's granddaughter? And now you're here? You do understand this doesn't look good." She sat back. "Especially since you're moving in on Spence."

The tone in Tiffany's voice struck a nerve—she assumed it was meant to. "I'm not doing anything underhanded. I came here to get away from my ex-husband and to start new. I knew the company. I'm familiar with the industry. I took a chance."

"And now Spencer has a thing for you."

Julie narrowed her eyes. "Are you jealous? You said you'd back off if we were an item." Her words came out as sharply as she'd felt Tiffany's words.

Tiffany stood and Julie followed. "I said I'd back off, but if you're the one screwing him over I'll kick your ass."

"I'm not that kind of person."

"I don't know that. Spencer doesn't know that. All he knows is you're one bitch of a lawyer."

Julie inched in. "Then I did my job right," she said through gritted teeth.

She picked up her coffee and marched out of the office. She didn't need to be accused of anything. Julie Jacobson made her own way. Her relationship, or interest in Spencer Benson, was nothing more than physical attraction. Sexual appetite. Desire. Need. Compassion. Romance. Dammit!

She pulled open the door to the construction trailer, walked to her desk, and set down her coffee and bag. She was falling in love with the man and there was no reason for her to. She came looking to start over and she really hadn't thought it would include the man who detested her, but it did.

Who was Tiffany to tell her she was screwing Spencer over? Fine.

She'd quit.

She'd walk out right now and go get a damn job at that fancy shoe store they went to yesterday. Rent wasn't too expensive. She could live off of packaged noodles if she had to. The bus went right from her neighborhood to downtown. Things would be fine.

Julie sat down behind her desk as Chuck pulled open the door.

"Shit! God dammit!" He threw down the papers. "What the hell?"

Julie figured Tiffany told him about the trucks. Maybe she got the good curses. These ones were weak.

"Hey, Jules, Tiff wants to see you," Chuck growled out the shortened names.

In a huff, Julie pushed back from her desk and marched out of the one trailer and back to the other.

"You need something else?"

Tiffany shot her a glare as she put a pin into the display. Julie watched. It was the best lot Julie thought. The backyard would be plentiful with an amazing view. The front situated on a cul-de-sac and the park would only be a short walk away.

Tiffany closed the glass lid on the display and turned to her.

"First off, I'm sorry." Her words were strained, but one thing Julie understood was anger filtered through words. She'd made a living from it.

Tiffany fisted her hands on her hips and continued, "It still stands that if you screw him over I'll mess you up. But I like you and coincidences happens." She watched Tiffany's shoulders drop. "Spencer needs you to go home, pack a bag, and meet him at the Riverside Building in an hour."

Julie held her breath for a beat. "It'll take me an hour and a half to do all that. It takes thirty minutes from here to get home."

Tiffany shrugged. "Maybe don't pack a bag."

"Where am I going?"

"You're his assistant on this job. Amber can't go."

"I'm going to Oregon?" She shook her head. "No. That's not a good idea. I don't want to do that. You go. You know the job better than me."

"I'm sales. And are you kidding me? You're going to send me with your boyfriend?"

Julie balled her fists at her side. "Does that mean I can't trust you?"

"No, it doesn't mean that. It means get your ass in your car and get over there. This is business now. It just so happens he needs you and you have to go back to where you used to work. Big deal."

But it was a big deal. She'd been fired. Steven would be there. Julie didn't want to deal with that. She didn't want to deal with any of them. It was just going to look bad. God, why had she come to Nashville? They were all going to think she was moving in on the big boss now. Was he going to think that too?

Her stomach churned and she was damn sure she was going to get sick.

"If you puke on my new shoes, I'll still mess you up," Tiffany said walking toward her. "You're not screwing with him, right?"

"No."

"You fell into this relationship, right?"

"Yes."

"Did you sleep with him?"

Julie stared at her. "No. No. I didn't sleep with him."

Tiffany's lips curled into a smile. "What are you waiting for?"

"I'm not jumping into a relationship. I'm not on the rebound. I didn't sleep with him," Julie repeated.

"I didn't think you had. He's too much of a gentleman and you seem to be to goodie-two-shoes to do that in the first week."

"I don't know if that was an insult or not."

Tiffany shrugged. "Take it however, now get your butt out of here."

Julie went back to her desk, grabbed her purse, and headed out to her car. Why hadn't Spencer called her if he was going to demand all of this from her? She had no idea she was going to have to travel.

She climbed into her car, started the engine, and drove out of the development.

Pulling her phone out of her purse, she noticed he had called. Six missed calls. Four missed texts. He must have been calling when she'd gone in to get coffee.

As she maneuvered through traffic to get to the highway, she called called him back.

"Ah, you do have your phone," he answered. "I thought I had the wrong number."

"What's going on? Why do I have to go on this trip with you?"

"You're my assistant on this specific build."

"But PLL is your lumber supplier, not just on this project, and has been for years."

"And you have insight into the company. Listen, something is going on in there, and the guys I left to run it don't know why shipments aren't getting across country to us. I need you there."

Julie began to merge into the next lane when she heard a car honk. Quickly she swerved back into her lane.

"I don't have time to pack."

"No worries. Just get here, and when you get to Oregon you can go shopping."

"I don't have any money to do that."

"Consider it a travel expense toward BBH."

Strangely that didn't appeal to her. "I'm not comfortable going back, Spencer. The thought of it is making me sick."

She heard him let out a breath. "I'll talk to you when you get here. Maybe we can work something out."

They said goodbye and she tossed her phone into the passenger seat. Perhaps she could talk him out of her traveling with him. It would be better for everyone if she stayed away for a while, especially since she was seeing Spencer and since her ex-husband still worked for PLL.

The thought crossed her mind briefly. Maybe she should go. There was a matter of him living in the house she owned and she was letting him. Suddenly she thought it might be time to sell it out from under him.

# CHAPTER 32

S pencer paced in his office waiting for Julie to arrive.
They had a car waiting in the garage for them. Ed and
his father were going with him. Something told him he'd need to
let a few of the original employees go if they found out something was going on internally.

The moment she rushed through his office door, Spencer
stood and moved to her.

"You have fifteen minutes to decide whether you're going or
not," he said.

"I'm not. Spencer, I can't just show up there again a week
later. Besides, I don't know anything about this build, really, and
it isn't about the build. It's about your supplier."

He turned from her and paced again raking tunnels into his
hair with his fingers. "I guess I just needed someone there to
comfort me."

He moved to her and took her hands in his, lacing their
fingers together.

"Julie, this has been the craziest week of my life," he said
looking down into her eyes. "When you dropped those papers in
that boardroom, I was a goner." Lifting his hand to her cheek he

caressed. "Maybe you don't have to go. I think I was looking for companionship that wasn't just my father and my cousin."

"They're going too?"

"They have to. Essentially my dad owns PLL, well the company, and he heads that."

"I'll be right here when you get home," she said raising her hands to his chest. "And I'm only a phone call away if you need to know something."

Spencer lifted her hands to his lips and pressed kisses to her knuckles. "I might take you up on that." He waited a moment and thought about asking her about her ex-husband. She'd never mentioned who he was. Why? What was there to hide? Steven's affair was common knowledge, yet she'd never mentioned she was married to another lawyer on the payroll.

Spencer's phone buzzed in his pocket. Pulling it out, he looked at the screen. "That's Ed. I need to go."

Julie hooked her arms around his neck and pulled him in for a long, deep, satisfying kiss.

Spencer sighed. "Remember we talked about parking out at the site and looking at the stars?"

Julie nodded, resting her forehead to his. "I remember."

"Maybe by the time I get back, the other parcel of land will be ours too. We can check out the view from there."

"Let's make a plan to do that when you get home."

He nipped her nose with a kiss. "It's a date."


THE DRIVER OPENED the door for Spencer when he saw him walking toward the car.

Spencer slid into the back next to his father. "You're alone? Where's your assistant?"

"Julie pointed out this is a supplier issue not a build issue," Spencer said.

The thought crossed his mind that he hadn't even introduced Julie to his father, but he was sure Ed had filled him in.

"Julie is the lawyer from PLL," he admitted.

His father nodded. "It was mentioned to me."

"I hired her to work on site. She has a good eye and her background makes her very organized."

His father nodded again. "Are you justifying your employee?"

"No. Maybe," Spencer shrugged. "It wasn't fair of me to ask her to go back there. They fired her a week ago. Though I'd like to know why they did that at the end of negotiations." He'd ponder that later. "She's not ready to walk through the door there again."

Both Ed and his father laughed. Then his father pulled a ten-dollar bill from his pocket and handed it to Ed.

"Thank you, sir." He laughed as he put it in his pocket.

"What was that about?" Spencer asked.

"Your dad has more faith in you. He figured you'd sweet-talk her and she'd come. I thought you were way out of your league and she'd talk you out of it."

"You bet on me?" Spencer looked at his father.

Zach Benson shrugged his shoulders. "I was rooting for you." His father was grinning, and it was a bit unnerving. "I took your mother on a business trip like this once. I figured you were getting serious, even though I haven't officially met her yet."

"I know. You will. I'll bring her to the birthday party and then everyone can meet her officially."

"So I take it she isn't a bitch anymore?" His father asked leaning back against the seat.

Spencer shook his head feeling deflated. "No. I wish I hadn't said that to anyone. I don't think I ever really meant it."

His father patted his knee. "Spence, one thing about this family, we all know you pretty well. I don't think any of us took it to heart."

"Good. Besides, Avery and Tiffany like her. I'd say they'd have been the best judges."

His father nodded. "You're a brave man. You put your new girlfriend under the nose of your keeper."

"Tiffany is not my keeper."

That caused Ed to snort out a laugh. "Whatever. You've kept Tiffany on a leash for years just like Avery has with Pete."

He didn't like the term *on a leash*. "Tiffany has always done what she wants. She's even been married. She wasn't mine to have."

"Maybe not, but I think that was because she's not your type. You like someone a little more like-minded, who goes after what she wants. Grounded, but courageous. You know, the kind that will pick a fight—because she's a lawyer. And someone who would leave where she lived and cross the country to start all over again under the watchful eye of a man who despised her. That's gutsy."

Spencer threw his head back against the seat. He supposed it was gutsy of her. And she had stood up to him. Julie was sure she didn't want to make this trip with him. Who could have blamed her?

He thought while they drove through the streets of Nashville on their way to the municipal airport, without her there, he could do some prying. He could see what Steven McDaniels was all about.

# CHAPTER 33

$\mathcal{I}$t was a wonder that such a bad day could actually get worse.

Julie sat at her desk with the file for the perfect house on the perfect lot in front of her. It was to be a corporate house, and they wanted her to design it. She'd never heard of the company before, and she was sure if they had execs moving into a full house for a family she would have heard of the company. Regardless, there was a little pang of sadness that Spencer's house design, on that lot with a view, wouldn't be personal to someone.

She closed the file. It wasn't the house, and she knew it. It was that lonely feeling when someone was missing, and that someone was Spencer.

It wasn't just that he was missing from her afternoon either. It was that he was in Oregon where her life had been a mere week ago. Only Spencer had been there too. But so were Steven and Libby.

Julie hadn't told Spencer who her husband was. What if something was said? Steven had a temper. She was sure Spencer did too, but he was professional enough to keep it tucked away.

The door to the trailer opened and Tiffany stepped inside. "Are you done brooding for the day?"

"I'm not brooding."

Tiffany gave a deliberate roll of her eyes. "You haven't left your desk since you got back here. You should have gone to Oregon with him. Who cares if you run into your lying, cheating, sack of shit ex-husband."

Julie wanted to laugh, but she couldn't. Not yet.

Tiffany sat down in the chair in front of Julie's desk, crossed her legs, and admired those shoes Spencer had once bought her. The pang of jealousy that ripped through Julie was enough to make her sick.

It was interesting, she hadn't trusted her own husband—of course his track record wasn't stellar. But she trusted Tiffany and Spencer. If they said they were just friends with benefits, then they were. If they said they'd not partake in those benefits, she believed them. The interesting part about that was Julie didn't tend to usually believe people. She was a lawyer. She always wanted proof.

"Do you want to go home and change?" Tiffany asked standing from her chair.

Julie stared at her, unsure of why she was asking. "Change for what?"

"We're going out."

She shook her head. "Oh, I don't think so."

"I don't care what you think. Mr. Accent from Spencer's building called and wants us to meet him at Tootsie's."

Julie gave that some thought. "The British guy? Are you kidding me? Tiffany, he made a pass at me when I went to Spencer's the other night. You can't be serious about going out with him."

Tiffany tossed her hands up in the air and let them fall. "What is it with you getting in the way of me going to bed with a hot man? First you take Spencer and now Clark?"

There was a humorous tone in her voice, but Julie didn't like it all the same.

"I haven't slept with Spencer."

Tiffany gave her another eye roll and mimicked her sentence. "Your loss. And because you seem like the kind of girl who focuses on one relationship at a time, I know you're not going for Clark. And I'm only going because I have to hear his pillow talk." She shook her body and smiled. "That gives me chills just thinking about it."

Julie certainly wasn't up for a night out. Then again, maybe it would take her mind off Spencer. Okay, that wasn't going to happen. But for a few hours she could worry about it less.

\* \* \*

SHIPMENTS OF LUMBER were now en route to Nashville. How the trucking company could claim that their funds hadn't been good was beyond Spencer. The financials of PLL were solid, that was why he'd sought it out as the company to buy, that and the reputation for quality manufacturing.

Spencer, Ed, and his father sat at a small table in the hotel, each with a drink in their hands. The three of them were silent.

Ed had called Darcy to check on her. His father had called his mother. Spencer itched to call Julie, but after the ride to the airport that morning, he didn't want to seem desperate. He'd make the call back in his room.

"I think we need to do an internal audit," Ed said looking down into his drink. "I know what all the paperwork said when they presented it to us. I know our auditing of the company before purchase showed the company was financially stable, but I just still can't get over the fact that the trucking company nearly cut loose a contract of that size. BBH doesn't have a bad reputation anywhere."

His father nodded. "It wouldn't be the first company I'd taken over where things got sloppy after I took ownership. It's hard to let go when something has been in the family for generations."

"Why sell it then?"

Spencer gripped the arms of the chairs. "Maybe to keep it from an heir."

His father focused on him, gave him a long hard stare, and then nodded with a cluck of his tongue. "Simone's father was like that. He'd have sold off every oil rig to make sure she paid for her indiscretions."

"Avery isn't an indiscretion," Spencer argued.

"You don't have to tell me twice. And likewise, I think his purchase of this vineyard is playing the opposite game."

Ed motioned to Spencer with his glass in his hand. "You think one of Grayson's kids had something to do with this?"

He shrugged. "The granddaughter."

"She's not even involved with the company, is she?"

Spencer shook his head. "She's having an affair with one of the lawyers."

"That's a nasty word," his father said picking up his glass and sipping.

Spencer stood. "I'm exhausted. I'm going to head up."

"You're staying a few more days?" Ed asked.

"Just a few. I think the internal audit is necessary, but let's see what happens if I'm just here."

"You'll be home by next weekend?"

Spencer smiled. "Yes. I hear I have a pink and black birthday cake ordered."

His father laughed. "That girl has tried to outdo you every year since you were born."

"It's a damn good thing I love her like I do."

He held out his hand to his father who shook it, then stood and pulled him in for a hug. "Keep us posted."

"I will."

Ed stood and shook his hand. "Don't doubt yourself. This was still a good buy."

He gave him a nod and headed out of the room and toward the elevator with that thought still in his mind. It was a good buy. It would net them a near fortune—in time. But first, Spencer had to find the leak.

# CHAPTER 34

*H*e rode the elevator up to his room. Leaning back against the rail, he closed his eyes and thought of the ride a week ago. Never would he have thought Julie Jacobson would have kissed him like she had.

The kisses after that had only grown in intensity and now he realized he was longing for them—needing them.

He hated not being with her, and wasn't that funny, because a week ago he'd hoped to never see her again.

Spencer tunneled his fingers through his hair. It was more than kisses. Even once he did get to make love to her, which he was hoping to seduce her into soon, it wasn't going to satisfy him. He came from family and there was something about Julie that made him think about it more and more.

The failure of her marriage wasn't hers. He was sure she was a good wife. The very thought gave him a jolt. A week ago he hadn't considered a wife for many more years. But now it was in his head.

There was a lot of time to mull it over. Sure he had relatives that jumped into marriage and it had worked. Heck, Clara and

Warner had even eloped. That wasn't his style, but neither was jumping into things that weren't thoroughly thought through.

As the door to the elevator opened, and he walked toward his room, he thought about the merger. Julie obviously wasn't the person to let things go too fast either. That was evident by the amount of time the negotiations took.

Sliding the keycard into the lock, he thought about how her face would flush when he'd question her. Her eyes were deep brown when she was presenting something, but when contradicted they flashed.

They got even darker when she was aroused. The thought crossed his mind. She enjoyed her job as a lawyer, when she was working to make a change, as much as she enjoyed the affection Spencer gave her.

He kicked off his shoes and pulled his tie off from around his neck. Throwing it on the bed, he took his phone from his pocket.

Maybe she should take that bar and work in Tennessee. His legal department could use someone as passionate as Julie.

Then again, maybe that was just his wanting her near. She'd be working on the same floor of the Riverside Building then.

Spencer sat down on the bed and pulled up her number. He placed the call and waited.

"Hello." Her voice was so familiar to him now. It only made the need for her grow.

"Hey," he said feeling the pang of sadness now that he heard her voice. It was crazy, but he was missing her. "How was your day?"

"You know, it was horrible. But I'm bigger than that, and I'm moving forward. How was yours?"

"Sounds like we had similar days. Looks like I'll be here at least the rest of the week. But it might go into next week."

"Oh," her voice dipped. "Well, you'll get what you need out of it. Anything I can do here on this end?"

Spencer smiled. That was just like her. Making sure everything was covered. "I'll let you know. So what happened in your day?"

"You're gone," she said and that made the pang deepen. "Chuck was in a rage over the lumber, of course. Got my heel stuck in the stair grate of the trailer, and yes, I know I shouldn't wear them on site. It's habit." She laughed. "And now I'm getting dressed so I can go out with Tiffany to Tootsies."

"You're going out?"

"Accent man wants to meet her. I guess I'm her keeper? Watchful eye? I don't know. I don't like that guy. He made a pass at me the other night."

Spencer stood and paced the floor. "You didn't tell me that."

"Didn't seem important at the moment when it happened. I'm just not in the mood to go out."

"Tell her no."

There was a sigh that softened his spine. "No. I can't always just focus on my job or on you," she said nearly inaudibly, and that twisted inside him. "I'll go for a few hours. See the sights."

"You can stay at my place when you're done. It's closer."

"No. If I haven't stayed with you, I'm not going to stay without you."

He sat back down again. "While I'm gone, think about staying when I get back."

"Spencer..."

"I know. You're not ready for a rebound. It's not going to be one. And we haven't been friends for months, and now I want you to stay."

"I want to stay. Let's just see how it goes."

He pressed his fingers to his eyes. "Let's do that."


JULIE SAID her goodbyes and disconnected the call. With one final look in the mirror, she decided she looked good enough to have a beer in a bar, and that was when she heard a knock at the door.

Tiffany was early.

Julie walked through the apartment and pulled open the door. There in the dark stairwell stood a man and a gasp instantly jumped from her throat.

"I'm sorry. I didn't mean to startle you. We need to fix this light out here. I didn't know it burnt out," he said

"It was on earlier," she countered and now wished she'd looked out the peephole.

"I'm John Forrester. Spencer and Avery's uncle."

"Oh." She stuck out her hand. "It's nice to meet you."

John shook her hand and smiled. "I didn't mean to startle you. Avery wasn't home or I would have had her introduce us."

Julie nodded. "She's not due back until…" she paused. "Well, before next weekend."

John's brows furrowed. "Where is she?"

"France."

His lips tightened and even in the dark stairwell Julie could see that wasn't a welcomed answer. But the look was only a flash and he smiled again.

"I take care of the property and usually I check it out before they rent it. Just to make sure everything is okay. Do you mind if I look around? I can come back sometime when you have someone else here. I understand that."

And she figured he really did. Why did she feel he was completely safe? Julie wasn't one to rely on someone's word as a judgment of their own character. The lawyer in her needed proof, but she supposed Spencer had already given her that. This man was part of his family and from what she'd already learned that family was tight.

"I don't mind if you look around. Can I get you anything to drink?"

"Nah, I'll only be a minute. You look like you're heading out."

"Tiffany, Spencer's friend," she said as if she needed to clarify, "and I are going out."

"Tiffany?" There was a bit of humor in his voice as he looked around the room. "She keeping a close eye on you?"

"Why is that?"

"She's always been in love with Spencer." He walked down the hallway, turned on the bathroom light, and stepped in. "Ed might have mentioned to me you and Spence have an interest in each other."

"Well, we're getting to know each other."

John stepped out of the bathroom. "Looks like the shower head could use a tightening." He turned off the lights and headed toward her bedroom then stopped. "May I?"

He had to be the most courteous man she'd ever met. "Of course."

John turned on the light and stepped it. "You couldn't do better," he said from inside the room.

"I beg your pardon?"

He stepped out and turned off the light. "Spence. You couldn't do better. Those are some fine boys Zach and Regan have."

"Oh. He's very kind. He gave me a job and found me a place to live."

John nodded as his eyes wandered along the walls and floors. "You've stumbled into a family who works that way." He headed toward the kitchen and Julie followed. "How's the ice maker in the freezer?"

"Fine I guess."

"Good. I just replaced it last year. Let me know if anything happens." He turned on and off the water and the same with the oven and stove. "Everything looks okay. I'll come by this weekend and fix that shower head before it does become a problem."

"Thank you. I really appreciate the place to live."

He nodded. "My wife bought this place years ago. I think almost everyone in the family has lived in it."

"Your wife is the actress?"

There was a flash in his eyes again, but this time they sparkled. "That's her. She hasn't been on stage in quite a few years, but she still directs. You've seen her work?"

"No. Spencer told me about her."

"His mother is my wife's blood sister. Let me tell you, the bond between sisters is tight. They don't even have to talk to speak. Do you have sisters?"

She shook her head. "Only child. Only everything now," she said quietly.

"Your parents?"

"Passed a few years ago. They were older when I was born."

John nodded slowly. "Spencer is in Oregon?"

"Yes."

"Why don't you plan on dinner with the family on Sunday. I can arrange to pick you up if you'd like."

Julie felt her throat close off. She couldn't go if Spencer wasn't back. And he did say he might not be back.

"That's very generous of you. But…"

"Think about it," he said. "I'm sure it won't be the first invitation you get." He smiled as he headed for the door. "It was nice to meet you. I'll try to call before I come back over."

"It's no problem. Thank you."

He gave her a nod and headed up the steps twisting the bulb along the way. It flickered and turned on.

"Ah, loose. That's better. Goodnight."

Julie closed the door and leaned up against it. What had she gotten herself into? A job, a house, a man, and a family? Her heart thudded in her chest and she rested her hand over it. Disappointment would surely follow because she found herself wanting it all so desperately.

# CHAPTER 35

Keeping an eye on his watch, Spencer had waited until he knew Julie was in her office before he called.

"Hello," the soft voice said on the other end and a smile formed on his lips. Five months ago he'd never have imagined that hard shelled lawyer could be just that—a shell.

"Good morning."

"You're getting an early start," she said.

"I'm headed out to the factory to make sure that the trucks headed to Nashville are loaded. We have three more trucks heading out today and I don't want any delays. As it looks right now, I won't be home until Tuesday or Wednesday."

She sighed into the phone, and though it should have brought him sadness, it filled him with relief. A few days into this new relationship—as he was considering it—she obviously missed him.

"I'm sure it will be well worth your time to be there," she said convincingly.

"Is Avery home yet?"

"No. Pete said next week. He's talked to her a few times."

Spencer fixed his tie in the mirror. "When did you talk to Pete?"

"Last night. He came to the bar."

"Right." Now that warmth from her missing him was a cold poke in the chest. What was Pete doing? "Did Tiffany go home with Clark?"

"He stood her up. Thank goodness too. That was the last thing I wanted to do last night. I'm glad Pete came. At least I had someone to talk to while she brooded."

Spencer slipped his arms into his suit jacket and gave himself another look in the mirror. "I'll take you out when I get back to make up for the nights you'll have to deal with her."

She laughed easily. "And where do you plan to take me to make up for that?"

"I have a place. Do you like barbecue?"

"Who doesn't?"

Now he laughed. "It's a date then. What are you doing this weekend?"

"I had a very nice dinner invitation, though I'm sure I won't be going."

Spencer's jaw tightened. "Who invited you to dinner?"

"Your Uncle John."

He felt the hairs on the back of his neck rise. "My family invited you to dinner?"

"Well, he did. He said I'd probably get more than one invitation. I'm not comfortable with someone's family if they aren't there."

Spencer knew that wouldn't be the case with his family. If she went to a family dinner without him, she'd never feel alone again. But he wanted to be there to take her. He wanted to walk in with her on his arm.

Spencer bit back the oath he wanted to let free. He didn't want to be in Oregon all weekend. Instead, he wanted to be in

Nashville with her trying to get a grip on these new feelings he was having for someone he thought made his stomach ache.

"Hold on," she said and he could hear her muffle the phone. "Hey, I have to go. Tiffany has an office full of people."

"On a Thursday morning?"

"I guess. I'll talk to you later."

He'd wanted to say goodbye and pull her in for just a few more minutes of conversation, but the connection went dead and he was alone in his hotel room holding his phone.

All the better he decided. He needed to be focused on the tasks at hand. Why were loads getting to Nashville late, and who decided that BBH doing business with PLL was suddenly a bad idea?

AN HOUR LATER, Spencer was at the mill watching trees become the lumber that would build the houses in his development. He had a call into the farmer who owned the land behind the development. The eldest son had said they'd like to talk it over as a family and with their lawyer, but Spencer was sure his offer was good enough. However, he could wait on it. PLL needed his attention now.

The factory manager, Marcus DeLuca, gave him an extensive tour of the facility, with the executives he'd left in Oregon. They'd been through the factory numerous times, but had they missed something?

"We've used that same trucking company for nearly thirty years. I can't think of a thing that has changed to make them refuse loads," he told them. "Maybe some computer glitch?"

It could have been, Spencer thought. But he was going to be thorough in finding out.

The milling of the wood was fascinating, Spencer thought as they walked back through the facility. A tree in the forest would become someone's home. It was like seeing a small lot of land

and a year later seeing the building that stood on that footprint. What would, or could, they build in a hundred years, he wondered.

As the driver took them back to the office of Pacific Line Lumber, Spencer watched the scenery outside his window. The lush green didn't hold his attention as it had for the past year. Now he just wanted to get home.

He rested his head back against the seat and wondered if Julie would someday miss Oregon. Could the wonder that was Tennessee hold her heart for the long term? West coast and southern lifestyles were certainly different.

Raking his hands through his hair, he let out a breath. Why was he thinking of at all? They had shared a few kisses and still lingering was the fact that for the past year he'd cursed her name.

Oh, how he wished he hadn't.

He cranked his neck from side to side.

Tomorrow he was going to spend some time in legal getting to know the staff better—including Steven McDaniels.

# CHAPTER 36

*S*leep had eluded him. Friday morning was fueled by coffee and anxiety.

Spencer walked through the front doors of PLL and up to his office only to find Libby Grayson seated on his desk.

Every muscle in his body stiffened, and he stopped short of entering the office completely.

She sat cross-legged. Her skirt rose high on her thighs and the blouse she wore was cut low. Long dark hair cascaded down her back and when she licked her lips, Spencer thought he would be sick.

He gripped the foam coffee mug as tightly as he could without crushing it. "Can I help you with something, Ms. Grayson?"

"Oh, you certainly don't need the pleasantries, Spencer. Call my Libby."

Still standing at the threshold, he watched as she slid from his desk and sauntered toward him. "I hadn't expected to see you back in Oregon so soon."

Her perfume filled his nose and he gritted his teeth. "I had more business."

She reached out a long, manicured finger and ran it down the buttons on his shirt. "Don't trust your employees?"

Spencer grabbed her hand with his free one. "I trust them more than most people I know. What can I do for you?"

Her painted red lips curled into a smile. "I want to have dinner with you."

"I don't think so," he said firmly as he let go of her hand and walked past her.

She turned and walked back to his desk as he skirted around the backside and set down his semi-crushed cup.

"People don't turn me down." Her tone was cool. He was sure she was correct and no one turned her down. He was different.

"Looks like I just did that."

A moment later she was seated on his desk again. "I think if you got to know me you'd reconsider."

Spencer bit down on the inside of his cheek hard enough he could taste blood. "I was under the impression you were dating someone in legal." The words were nearly inaudible as he pushed them out through tight lips.

She brushed away his words with a flick of her hand. "I date many men. I keep the important ones," she said with her eyes fixed on him.

"And he isn't important?"

She shrugged. "Was married now divorced. Needy. Not really my type, but I'll give him some credit. Wife is a bitch."

That had Spencer grabbing the edge of his desk. "I have things to do. I'd really appreciate you leaving."

Libby gave him a wink, stood, and then placed her hands flat on his desk so that the view right in front of him led down the V of her shirt.

"I'll be around, Spence. So will you. Mark my word."

She puckered her lips and blew him a noisy kiss before she turned and with her hips swaying, walked out of his office.

Spencer fell back in his chair and sat there for a long moment with his hands flat on the top of his desk. It wouldn't jeopardize anything to have security keep Libby out of the building. She wasn't on the payroll. She didn't have a job title. There was no reason for her to be near him or his employees.

He pushed back from his desk and headed toward the legal department. He was going to have a conversation with Steven McDaniels.

\* \* \*

JULIE RUBBED her temples to ward away the headache forming behind her eyes. She'd been looking at her computer screen all morning. For the past two hours, she'd been on the phone ordering supplies and going over the specs for the corporate house.

Why Spencer had put her in charge of that didn't make any sense to her. But she'd do her best and he'd be proud to turn over the key to the owners. However, there was a moment when she was picking out the flooring in the kitchen she wanted to go with something just disgusting and write in to have the walls painted orange and find an avocado-green oven.

The thought made her chuckle as the door to the trailer opened.

There wasn't a slew of curses that followed it shutting, so she looked around the small wall and her breath caught in her chest and held there.

Steven stood in the doorway with his arms crossed and his brows furrowed behind dark sunglasses.

Julie was quick to her feet. "Why are you here?" And where was Chuck she wondered? She'd like to have him in the room just to be there.

"This is where you came? Six figure income and you left what you had for this?" He gestured up with his hands. "Are you insane?"

Julie clenched her jaw and placed her hands on her desk. "Seriously why are you here? I don't have ties to you anymore."

He chuckled. "That hurt." He moved in closer to her desk. "Do you want me to say I'm sorry? I made a mistake."

That had her head popping up. "A? One?"

"Now, Jules."

"Don't Jules me." Fire pumped through her. "I walked into my bedroom, in my house, and found you with Libby. That was enough for me. I never should have taken you back after the other times."

"Now, none of them..."

"Meant anything to you. I know the speech." Her voice was loud and strained. Every ounce of anger had poured into those words.

He took his sunglasses off and those eyes, which had once held power over her, didn't. In fact, when she looked at them, she didn't remember what it was she'd seen in them before at all. They weren't soft and kind like Spencer's. They didn't hold honesty in them or kindness. Not like Spencer's.

"Sugar, can I sit down?" he asked pulling the chair back and sitting before she'd given him an answer.

"Why are you here? Seriously do you have a valid reason?"

The trailer door opened. Tiffany and Chuck both strolled in casually. Chuck muttered under his breath. Tiffany smiled, looking much too gorgeous to be working on a construction site.

Steven stood up and adjusted his jacket when Tiffany took in a long look of him. "Sorry, Julie. Didn't know you had company."

"No trouble," he answered for her and shot out his hand toward her. "Steven McDaniels. I'm Julie's husband."

"Ex," she quickly spewed back.

She saw the surprise move over Tiffany's face. She noted some anger too.

Chuck flashed her a look and she knew there would need to

be a discussion on it. Obviously he knew something was going on with Spencer.

"It's nice to meet you," Tiffany said through gritted teeth, but Julie wasn't sure Steven noticed. "Julie," she shifted her glance to her. "I'll come back in a bit. I just have some things to talk about."

Julie wondered if the pleading stare she was giving her wasn't working. His charms certainly couldn't be winning could they?

"I'll let her get back to work," Steven said. "I just wanted to drop by. Say hi. And," now he turned fully toward Julie, "to let you know that I'll pick you up here at five-thirty for dinner."

She opened her mouth to speak, but nothing came out before he gave Tiffany a nod and walked out the door.

Julie's hands shook as she sat back in her chair, deflated.

Tiffany watched from the window, and Julie could hear his tires on the gravel as he drove away.

"What in the hell was he doing here?" Tiffany spun back to her.

"I don't know. I don't know." Her voice shook as much as her hands.

"Did you tell him where you were?"

Julie lifted her head to look at her. "No. I didn't." That made her stomach tense even tighter. "I didn't tell him anything."

Tiffany sat down in the chair in front of Julie's desk. "You don't think Spencer..."

"Why would he?"

Tiffany shrugged. "He wouldn't." She moved in over the desk. "Is he dangerous? I mean are you scared? You can stay with me. We can put you up at Spencer's too." Tiffany nodded at her own comment. "We should do that. There's security there."

"He's not dangerous. He's just stupid."

"He's a lawyer."

"A stupid one."

"But I'll bet he's convincing."

Julie dropped her shoulders and let out a sigh. "He is."

Tiffany stood. "You're not meeting him. Not alone anyway."

Tiffany sat back down and Chuck finally walked out of the trailer.

"You're a lawyer. Can't you file for something to make him stay away?"

"He's never harmed me. There's no reason. Someone's ego isn't something that needs protection."

"Do you suppose he knows what's going on at PLL?"

"Maybe," Julie said as she thought about it. "Why else would he come this far to talk to me?"

Tiffany sat back in the chair. "I don't like you going alone."

"I'll be okay. I'll call him and tell him I'll meet him. I won't go with him in his car. Is that better?"

"Where are you going to meet him?"

"I don't know."

"When you call him you set the place. Make it very public. And you call me so I know where you are at all times."

Julie smiled. "When I first saw you I despised you."

Tiffany acted shocked. "Me? Why?"

"You're pretty. You're sexy. And you were pawing all over Spencer."

"You ruined my sure thing that night," Tiffany reminded out.

"Sorry," she said on a laugh. "When I saw you here, and he was going to make me work with you, I was sure he was torturing me for those five long months."

"Maybe he was," Tiffany said as her mouth curled into a smile.

"Maybe. But I never thought we'd be lunching, shoe buying, friends."

"I have your back."

"I know you do."

"Spencer does too. His whole family will."

Julie knew that. She'd only met a few members of his family and, she knew nothing was going to happen to her. Steven didn't know just how un-alone Julie really was.

# CHAPTER 37

The fog was thick and rain slicked the runway. Spencer sat in the terminal of the small airport and glared out the window. There was no going back to Tennessee tonight, and he needed to get back.

His heart was racing and it drummed in his ears as he grew angrier. The day certainly hadn't turned out the way he'd anticipated.

Finding Libby perched on his desk had sickened him. Walking into the legal department only to find Steven McDaniels had been asked to leave the company by the Graysons—that didn't make sense either. Where was he? It was that question that had Spencer waiting out a storm to get back to Nashville. What if McDaniels had gone after Julie. What if he hurt her?

The thought only made him angrier.

He had called her four times already, but she hadn't answered. Finally, he'd called Tiffany, who had answered, but her voice was muffled and he couldn't hear her. Hell, he'd even called Pete and asked him to stop by the house, but all he could do was leave a message. What was the use of having technology if you couldn't get anyone on it?

He plopped down into a seat and let his head fall back. If this wasn't bad enough, he thought about the report that had been dropped on his desk before he left. Accounting seemed to have found a monetary leak that had been going on for nearly six months. Thousands in revenue was missing. It was no wonder things weren't getting paid. Funds seemed to be funneling out through transportation, most recently. Interestingly enough none of this showed when they'd prospected the company.

Spencer pressed his fingers to his eyes. To hell with the company. There were lots of lumber companies they could use or buy. If it all fell apart, that was monetary. The feelings he had for Julie—those were real.

His phone buzzed in his hand and he looked down to see a text from Pete.

*I'm with her. All OK.*

That was supposed to be soothing? After Pete had asked to take Julie out, Spencer didn't like the thought of them together either.

He set his phone in the seat next to him and raked his fingers through his hair to calm himself—not that it ever worked. Pete was the least of his worries. What he needed to worry about was getting home to Julie. He had some very strong feelings for the woman. Damn, he never thought he'd think that, but he did and they weren't new.

For the past five months he'd convinced himself he didn't like the woman, but he'd only been fooling his heart into not caring. When you disliked someone, you didn't know how they took their coffee or how they wore their hair with each outfit. When someone disgusted you, you didn't know how their eyes shimmered when they were in conversation and how they darkened when they were proving a point. You certainly didn't let them kiss you, as Julie had, and then pull her into you so you could taste her.

Spencer let out a breath. He thought of the look on her face in

185

that elevator. The pain that resonated through her. No one ever deserved to be treated like her husband had treated her. If a man married a woman, he should be true to her and vice versa. Marriage wasn't just a word. It was a promise.

His thoughts shifted from Julie to his mother and Darcy. In his chest, there was a heaviness. What had his mother really endured when she'd run from that man that tried to kill her? Had she been as broken as Julie was when she'd come to his office? More so, he thought. To Spencer it was unimaginable—to his father it was probably something he suppressed.

Why did men play with women like that? Why did they marry one and sleep with others?

What he had with Tiffany might not be true love in the sense of marriage, but they knew going in what they were doing. And never—ever—would either of them make a play for the other when they were involved.

He knew now his days with Tiffany were over.

And the more he thought about Steven McDaniels, and what he'd done to Julie, the more he wanted to help her get that new start she'd been looking for. If she didn't love him, that was okay. If her place wasn't in Nashville with him, he'd deal with that. What he couldn't deal with was a man pledging to one woman and making his rounds with others.

Spencer's fingers balled into fists, and his teeth ground together as he thought of it.

"Sir, we're able to take off now," the flight attendant for the private flight had come near him.

He did all he could to breathe in and out to appear calm.

"Thank you."

He'd be there as soon as he could. All he wanted to do was wrap Julie in his arms.

Spencer stood from his seat and carried his bag toward the jetway. Only a few more hours, he told himself as he walked toward the plane. A few more hours and he'd be with her. He'd decided he had a lot to tell her.

# CHAPTER 38

*W*ith a quick text message, Julie had instructed Steven to meet her at a diner not far from the site.

One frantic hour later, Tiffany had settled down and informed her that she'd be in a booth not far from her. If that ex-husband of hers tried anything Tiffany would stab him with the stiletto she was going to wear.

Though they'd laughed about it, Julie was sure Tiffany would do just that.

Julie's nerves were more rattled when Pete showed up in her office and said he'd be there too. Really, did no one trust her?

She'd been calling Spencer for nearly an hour, but his phone went right to voicemail. He'd have to hear about her estranged husband's visit when she talked to him again.

Now she sat and waited in a corner booth at the diner hoping that the man she'd once married would be decent.

Julie knew the moment he'd strolled in. The waitress had looked toward someone walking their way, and a very satisfied smile formed on her lips.

"Hey, doll," his voice pierced through the sounds of the restaurant.

Julie was surprised when she looked up he was actually speaking to her and not the waitress.

He ordered a cup of coffee and sat down across from her.

"Why are you here? How did you find me?" She dove right into the conversation.

His expression changed and now he looked scared. No matter what he'd done to her, she didn't like to see him look like that.

"Libby told me where you were."

"Libby? I didn't tell anyone."

He nodded as if he'd known that. "She says you're sleeping with Spencer Benson." His voice matched his expression.

She shook her head. In all honesty, she could answer him. "I'm not."

He nodded again. "I was sure you weren't. I figured you were just trying to get your job back."

"I don't want it back. I can't go back there. I can't work with you. I..."

"I was let go."

The muscles in her body stiffened. "Spencer fired you?"

He shook his head. "The Grayson family asked me to leave."

"Steven..."

He held up his hand. "I screwed up. I lost you. I lost my job." He ran his hand over his chin, which was unshaven and that was uncharacteristic of him. "How involved are you in BBH?" He lifted his eyes to her.

"I work for them."

He nodded. "I know that. Why?"

Julie clasped her hands in her lap and pushed back her shoulders. "I needed a job. I needed a new start. I took a chance."

"Lots of places to go. Lots of other companies to work for that hadn't bought out a company you negotiated the deal on."

"Sure. So."

"So what do you gain?"

Her fingers tightened around each other in her lap, under the table. "Gain? Some self worth. Something for myself. Something…"

"How much did you steal from PLL before you left?"

She felt the air rush from her lungs as he asked it. It felt as though a hand had jabbed into her chest and squeezed at her heart. Every muscle ached, and when she did breathe it came as a gasp of air. "What did you say?"

"I know what you did. Is that what you're doing here too?"

Julie placed her hands atop the table to keep them still. "Are you accusing me of embezzling?"

"They'll find out. Whatever you have going on with Spencer Benson is going to crash down around you."

He scooted out of his side of the booth.

Julie moved from the booth and stood. "Steven, I don't know what you're talking about. I never…"

"There's a trail, Julie. And it leads to you." He took an envelope out of his back pocket and placed it on the table. "Here, this is yours. I can't be part of anything you're part of." He rested his hands on her shoulders and kissed her cheek. "Goodbye."

All she could do was stand there and watch him walk away. A moment later both Tiffany and Pete were standing next to her.

"Did he hurt you?" Tiffany looked her over from head to toe? "Why was he here? What did he want?"

"God," Pete interrupted. "Give her a chance to talk. Let's all sit down."

Julie shook her head. "I don't want to sit. I want to go. I just want to go."

Tiffany took Julie's hands in her own. "I want to take you back to Spencer's. I don't trust your ex-husband."

Julie picked up the envelope and opened it.

"What is it?" Tiffany looked over her shoulder.

"The house. He gave me the house." She shook her head. "I'm the one that paid for it. I guess his sense of decency kicked in to sign over his half."

"This is good, right? This is all he wanted to talk about?"

"No." Julie forced a smile.

"What else." She studied her. "Are you okay?"

"Yeah, I just have a lot on my mind. That's all." She wasn't about to tell them what Steven had said. She had no idea what he was talking about, and until she did she wasn't saying anything.

"Let's go."

Pete threw a few dollars on the table and escorted them both out. "Where are you headed?"

Tiffany gave Julie a stern look. "I want her at Spencer's. There's security there."

Pete nodded. "That's a good idea. I'll follow you downtown. Let me know when you're in the building."

# CHAPTER 39

*J*ulie unlocked her car and Tiffany opened the passenger door. "You're riding with me?"

"Pete brought me and you're not leaving my sight."

Julie slid in behind the steering wheel and closed the door as Tiffany climbed in the other side. She didn't need to be protected from Steven, though she had to admit, having people look out for her was nice.

"He's not dangerous," she said as she backed out of the parking space."

"He seemed genuine enough when he looked me over today and when he did the same thing to the waitress."

Julie shrugged. "It's just how he is."

"And how did you end up with him?"

The very thought stuck in Julie's chest. She'd been lonely.

Friends had come and gone over the years. Never had she really bonded with anyone. Then her parents passed on and she was alone. What young woman wouldn't buy into an older, successful man telling them what they needed to hear?

The threat of tears stung her throat, but she swallowed that back. She was woman enough to admit she'd made a mistake.

"I'm not the first lonely woman to fall for a man who dressed nice or said nice things."

Tiffany quickly turned her head to look at her and Julie could feel the stare burn through her. "Tell me that's not what's going on with you and Spencer."

"Don't accuse me of using him," she said, her tone resonating her irritation at the accusation.

"Tell me you're not."

"I'm not."

"What is this then? What is it between the two of you?"

Julie gripped the steering wheel tighter. "I don't know what it is or what it'll become, but I care deeply for him. I think I always have." Those tears she'd swallowed down forced themselves back up. "I know he hated me. I don't blame him. I put through the wringer. But he is one of the only people—men," she corrected, "that was ever decent to me."

Tiffany laced her fingers in her lap. "I hate that I'm going to tell you this." She let out a grunt. "About three months ago, when he took me out to dinner, I called him out because he was preoccupied. He wouldn't pay attention to me, and it was pissing me off."

"Spencer always has something on his mind," she said.

"Yes, well that night it was you."

Julie slowed the car at a stoplight and turned to look at Tiffany. "Me?"

She nodded. "The words *I hate that bitch* slipped through when I quizzed him about what was consuming him, but it didn't hold."

"Well," she coughed back those tears again. "Doesn't that sound charming?"

"Let me finish."

Julie eased through the green light and headed toward Spencer's building.

Tiffany tossed her hair over her shoulder. "The reason he hated you was because he couldn't identify the cause of his frustration. Mergers take time. And no one appreciates a thorough agenda more than Spencer. He never questioned the things you brought up. He might have been irritated, but he never questioned them."

"Then why hate me?"

"Because you brought something out in him that he couldn't lasso. I didn't satisfy his need anymore. I have no intention of marrying him, and he has no intention of marrying me. Spencer needs someone who can meld into his family and become his family. He needs someone who will love unconditionally, and without fail. He needs you."

Julie pulled into the visitor parking at Spencer's building and threw the car into park.

"Are you kidding me? You tell me he hates me. Then you tell me he's just looking for some wife?"

"No. That's not what I'm saying." She tossed her hair again. "His problem is, he's been attracted to you since the day he met you. You go after what you want—so does he. You were standing up for the Graysons because you believed in them. He stands up for his family in the same way. You were already married."

"He hates me because I wasn't single."

"He hated that he never got the chance."

Julie opened the door and got out of the car. "This is the stupidest thing I've ever heard."

"Why?" Tiffany argued as she climbed out of the car and they both slammed the doors. "You can't believe he's been attracted to you that long?"

"No. I can't believe it."

"I knew who you were the second I laid eyes on you. I would have known you in a crowd."

"How?"

"Because he'd described you to me a million times. I knew the shade of your hair and the color of your eyes. I know that when you smile you have a dimple, and when you're mad your cheeks turn just a certain shade of crimson, like they are now."

"You're making this up."

"I'm not. He watched you for five months. He obsessed about you for five months. Now you're here and he's still obsessing."

Julie stood there and stared at the woman in front of her with her perfect body and wavy red hair. Why would she make it all up if she could have Spencer at any time?

"I think I'm falling in love with him," Julie said, the words just falling out of her mouth as if someone else had put them there.

"You seem surprised by that."

She was. She felt it in her chest and it resonated through her entire body. "I've never had anyone treat me like he does."

Tiffany moved toward her. "I'm very sure he feels the same way. Now, tell me what Steven said to you."

"He was let go from PLL."

"Spencer fired him?"

"No. I just don't know what's going on."

There was more, but she didn't want to share that. She didn't really understand the rest of what Steven had said to her. Until she knew what was going on, that was going to remain her secret.

Tiffany laced her arm around Julie's waist and they walked toward the building.

JULIE FOLLOWED Tiffany into Spencer's penthouse while she spoke to Pete on the phone.

When they entered, Tiffany found a pair of sweatpants and a T-shirt for Julie to change into, and then she poured them each a glass of wine.

Curled up on the couch, as if they were old friends, Julie and

Tiffany talked over glasses of wine and pizza rolls they'd found in the freezer.

As the wine crept through Julie, she felt her eyes grow heavy, and she couldn't be sure if Tiffany was actually still talking to her.

The couch beneath her was so comfortable. Wouldn't it be nice to relax right there in Spencer's arms?

Spencer.

She smiled. She knew she loved him. Was there any one reason? No—she just knew she did.

# CHAPTER 40

*S*pencer looked down at Julie asleep on his couch. Her eyes moved behind her eyelids and a smile stayed on her lips.

"How much did she drink?" Spencer asked.

Tiffany held up the glass she picked up from the table. "I'd say four sips."

"She's just worn out," he said wanting to touch her.

"Your ex-husband coming for you will do that."

Spencer turned toward Tiffany and he could feel the angry heat ball in his gut. "He what?"

"Shhh," Tiffany said pressing her finger to her lips. "Let's talk in the kitchen."

She stood from the couch and walked toward the kitchen and he followed.

"He was here? You saw him?" Spencer tried to keep his voice hushed, but he was finding it hard to do.

"He signed over the house to her."

Spencer wanted to feel relieved by that, so why didn't he? "That's all? He found her and signed over the house?"

Tiffany shrugged. "She said he did. I don't even know if she looked. He met her at a diner, they were there maybe ten minutes, and then he looked as though he got scared and left."

Spencer eased his hip against the counter. "The Grayson family asked him to leave PLL."

Tiffany moved toward him. "He left?"

Spencer nodded. "I don't know what's going on there, but I think it's time to ask the Graysons to move on. Perhaps easing them out isn't necessary."

"Do you think it has anything to do with Libby?"

Spencer nodded as he rubbed his hand over his unshaven cheek. "She came on to me this morning."

Tiffany's eyes grew wide. "You didn't…"

"Don't even go there," he threatened. "You of all people know me better than that."

"I know." She sipped her wine. "That woman is trouble."

"Something tells me she's going to cause more if I don't get her family out of there." He held out his hand for Tiffany to hand him her wine. When she did, he took a long sip and handed it back. "I need to talk to my father."

Spencer looked down at his watch and realized it was too late to call him. Nothing would happen overnight. He'd talk to him in the morning. For now, he wanted to carry Julie to his bed and wrap his arms around her.

When Tiffany laughed behind her glass, he looked up.

"Give me your keys. I left my car at the site. I need to get home," she said.

"You're okay to drive?"

"I'm okay." She moved in and kissed him on the cheek as he pulled his keys from his pocket. "You've been my best friend most of my life. I finally feel as though you'll be taken care of now."

Those words hit Spencer straight in the chest. "You think so?"

Tiffany nodded. "She's the one, Spence. Who would know that better than me?"

He looked out into the living room and his entire body warmed as Julie stirred on the couch.

"Make me something."

Tiffany's eyebrows rose. "Make you what?"

"Design me something special for her. I want to give her something special."

The smile that formed on Tiffany's mouth was wide and as glorious as the sparkle in her eyes.

"How much do you want to spend?"

He looked back at Julie and then at Tiffany. "No price is too steep."

She touched his cheek, flipped his keys on her finger, and left without another word.

Spencer stood in his kitchen and smiled. There had been a day, many years ago, when he couldn't imagine not marrying Tiffany. Now when she kissed him, he thought it felt sisterly. The thought struck him that if they had made it to bed the other night, things might have been awkward.

Tiffany would always have his back, and he'd have hers. He'd love her for the rest of his life, but it was a love just like the love he had for Darcy.

When he looked at Julie, on the other hand, his heart rate quickened and his body temperature rose significantly. If she'd have him, he was hers. And to think he'd wasted so much time convincing himself he hated her.

As Spencer moved through the kitchen toward her, he stopped when he saw the manila envelope on the counter. Reaching his hand out, he touched it as if all the answers to the universe's unsolved questions might instantly come to him. It would be wrong to look inside, but he wasn't sure he was strong enough not to.

He lifted it from the counter as Julie stirred on the couch again. Watching her, wanting her, he pinched open the silver clasp at the back of the envelope. He hesitated, took a deep breath, and laid it back down.

When Julie was ready, she'd show him what was inside.

Spencer moved toward the couch. Kneeling down beside her, he gently moved a strand of hair from her face and brushed it aside with his finger.

She stirred and then her eyes batted open, and she looked up at him.

"You're sleeping on my couch," he said softly as he traced a finger over the curve of her cheek.

"Why are you home?" Her voice was soft with sleep.

"Couldn't stay away," he said on an almost truth. "I want to carry you to my bed."

Her eyes came open fully and he saw in them something he'd seen before—that night in the elevator. Need. Desire. Wanting.

Julie pushed up on her elbow and reached her hand out to his cheek. The touch of her soft fingertips on his skin made something inside of him burst, and he knew she wouldn't only sleep in his arms tonight.

# CHAPTER 41

$S$ pencer moved in, and without softness, without finesse, he took her mouth with his as her arms encircled his neck.

Tucking his arm up under her legs, he lifted her from the couch as their tongues met in maddening pace.

The thought that he should have kept her on the couch crossed his mind as he tried to remember the path to his room with his eyes shut and this woman—whom he couldn't wait to touch and taste—in his arms was making mush of his brain.

As if they'd made that walk a million times, he made it to his bedroom, and eased Julie and himself down on the bed. Her mouth was still on his—heated and devouring everything he had to offer.

Her fingers moved up his neck and into his hair as he pressed his body to hers.

Every curve of her beneath him fit as if they were always supposed to. Spencer ran his hand up her side, carrying the fabric of his old T-shirt with it. Her skin beneath his hands made parts of him ache and forced him to control everything.

Spencer eased back to look down at her.

"Julie, I can't stop this if I start." His voice was low and heavy with the desire that pulsed through him. "I already think it might kill me."

She smiled looking up at him. "Don't stop. Don't ever stop."

"You're mine?"

"I'm yours," she said as she pulled him back down to her and took control of his mouth again.

\* \* \*

IT HAD BEEN NEARLY a year since Julie had been under a man—including her husband. It certainly had never felt special or exciting, she thought, as Spencer pulled the T-shirt over her head and looked down at her.

"You're beautiful."

She sucked in a breath and moistened her lips with her tongue. "I want this, Spencer."

His eyes were dark now and she knew they were both feeling the same thing. "I'll make it worth it. I promise."

And so he did.

Touching her in every intimate place that longed to be touched. Kissing and tasting her skin. Every movement was made with a passionate and loving touch. Every gasp had been worth the wait.

When Julie lay there spent, naked in his arms with his heartbeat hammering next to hers, she knew for sure she had tumbled into that place you don't come out of unscathed. She'd fallen in love with Spencer lock, stock, and barrel. Suddenly she couldn't wait to go to that dinner she'd been invited to and meet the people he came from. If this man could be so passionate about so many things, what did he offer for the long haul?

He might give up on her, and she'd head back to Oregon, but

for this moment, naked in his arms while he stroked her hair and caught his breath, she wanted to dream about the what ifs. She was finding she liked the possibilities.

# CHAPTER 42

Spencer wasn't sure how much sleep he'd gotten. The sun was streaming in through the blinds of his bedroom, and Julie was still wrapped in his arms, and in his sheets.

Nothing—nothing had ever made him feel so alive as last night had. It wasn't all the lovemaking, though they'd done that enough times in the bed, shower, couch, and kitchen to satisfy any man for a long time. It was the passion between them. The soft kisses and words. The shared moments, and even the tears she'd spilled on his shoulder when she told him how happy she was.

That part still pulled at him.

Julie deserved happiness. She deserved to be on a pedestal and looked upon as the work of beauty she was. Why did his soft words and kisses make her cry?

She stirred against him and he pressed a kiss to her head.

Looking up at him through sleep-hazed eyes, she smiled. "Good morning."

"Good morning, beautiful," he said. "I was going to make coffee, but didn't want to disturb you."

"Coffee. I'd like coffee."

He kissed her head again. "I'll make some."

She rolled from him and let out a sigh. "I'll freshen up. Any chance you have a guest set of toothbrushes?"

He chuckled. "It might come as a bad time to bring it up, but Tiffany keeps some travel ones in the bathroom. Right hand drawer. She brings the free one from the dentist each time."

"If it's any consolation, I don't mind that you used to sleep with her."

Spencer crawled out of the bed, opened a drawer in the closet, and pulled on a pair of sweat pants.

"I'll never sleep with her again. Not with anyone else," he promised.

Julie's eyes filled with worry and he could see the gentle change on her face. Spencer moved back to the bed and sat down.

"You said it. You're mine," he reminded her. "And if you're mine, then I'm yours, Julie. I take that very seriously."

She nodded and a faintly smiled. "I know. It'll take some getting used to."

He brushed back her hair with his fingers. "I'll give you as much time as you need. I'm never going anywhere." He chuckled. "Except to make coffee. I'm going to make coffee."

Julie nodded. He left her there in his bed and thought it had to be the most beautiful sight he'd ever seen.

JULIE ROLLED FROM THE BED, put on the borrowed clothes, which were on the floor, and walked toward his bathroom. In the drawer, just as he'd said, were at least six toothbrushes in wrappers with a dentist's name on them. The fact that there were six, and most people went to the dentist twice a year, made her wonder if Tiffany was either sleeping with the dentist or she and Spencer hadn't spent as much time together as Julie had thought.

She'd go with the latter because it calmed her nerves.

The smell of coffee filled the penthouse as she looked into the mirror. Her hair was tousled and her makeup smeared, but aside from that, she saw someone there she'd long ago forgotten. A woman with love in her heart.

"I haven't decided if I like you better in an uptight lawyer's suit or in my clothes," Spencer said from the doorway holding two mugs of coffee. "I'm actually thinking my favorite is you out of both."

He moved into the bathroom and pressed a kiss to her neck as he held out both mugs on either side of her.

"You don't regret last night do you?" she asked, and he eased back from her.

Spencer handed her a mug and looked at her. "What have I done that would give you that thought?"

"You haven't done anything. I'm just too happy, and that worries me."

He stepped closer to her and cupped her chin in his hand. "You deserve to always be happy."

How had she fallen into this, she wondered as he gave her a wink and backed away.

"I'm out of eggs, bacon, hash browns and most everything else. Interested in taking a shower with me and going to breakfast?"

"I'd love that."

"I have to go down to the site. Tiffany took my car, would you mind giving me a ride?"

She smiled until her cheeks nearly hurt. "I could do that."

"Maybe you can walk me through that corporate build. They said they started framing."

"They did. I hope you like what I've done for them."

"I can't imagine I wouldn't."

She shrugged. "Nicest lot on the site. It's a little sad that a family won't always live there."

"Corporate houses sometimes sell in a few years. You never know who might move in then."

That did give her some peace. "Why don't you start that shower," she said setting her coffee on the counter. "I'm going to brush my teeth and then," she stopped, pulled the T-shirt off and dropped it to the floor. "I'll join you."

She watched his eyes glaze over before he moved toward the shower. He was putty in her hands. It might be fun to enjoy a man of power who could melt just by looking at her.

# CHAPTER 43

$\mathcal{J}$ ulie woke in her own bed in Spencer's arms Sunday morning. She was afraid to breathe or move. She was so content.

They had spent every moment of Saturday together and it had moved into Sunday morning.

Spencer had been pleased with her work on the corporate house. He'd complimented her numerous times on her organization skills in keeping the other builds in order.

They'd walked to the property just behind where they were building and met with the man whom Spencer was negotiating with. There was no talk of business, and Julie had seen how that eased the man who was sure Spencer had come to rattle him. But that wasn't how Spencer worked. If the man decided to live there forever, Spencer would make sure his build didn't bother the man.

It was Spencer's thoughtful manner that had her easing more in love with him. And it was her luck, with everything, that kept her from telling him.

After a quiet dinner, they'd gone back to her place, and there they'd made love and fallen asleep in each other's arms. She thought if she was quiet long enough, the fairy tale she was living could go on just a bit longer.

The tranquil calm of the quiet house was disrupted by the loud beat of music from upstairs, and Spencer sat straight up in bed nearly rolling Julie from it.

"What in the hell…" He winced at the sound.

"I think she's home," Julie laughed.

"Jesus, she's crazy." Spencer fell back on the bed. "You're moving out."

Julie snuggled back against him and nuzzled her face against his neck. "Am I?"

"How could you possibly live with that? She's absolutely inconsiderate."

"I've yet to meet anyone related to you that is inconsiderate."

Spencer kissed the top of her head. "You're going to meet them all tonight. Are you ready for that?"

She let out a satisfied sigh. "I think I am. Although I'm worried what your parents are going to think."

"Need I remind you again that my father married his assistant?"

"Right." She ran her fingers through the small tuft of hair on his chest. "And everything was fine for them after they started seeing each other?"

Spencer shifted to look down at her. "What do you mean?"

"Rumors fly. People get nasty when intraoffice relationships start. How did they handle it?"

"Like professionals. Are you worried they won't like you?"

She shrugged. "I know it looks sketchy. I made you miserable, got fired, showed up here and begged for a job. Now here you are wrapped up in my sheets…"

"Right where I want to be."

"But it's sketchy, and I see that. And now my ex has been let go."

"I didn't do that either," he assured her.

Julie looked up at him and narrowed her gaze. "I'm an older woman," she said grinning.

"Right. That might be the deal breaker. But as of next Sunday you'll only be a year older," he said on a laugh.

"Your birthday, that's right. Big party."

"Actually there won't be too many more than you'll meet tonight."

She bit down on her lip and listened to Metallica blare through the vents. "I've never been around family. It was always just my parents and I. I had one grandmother who died when I was seven. I don't know how to handle family."

Spencer rolled on his side to face her. He lifted his hand to her cheek and held it there. "What's to handle? You've met most of my cousins, and you did just fine."

"I want them all to like me."

"I adore you, that should satisfy them."

"But you didn't always."

That made him sit up and drag her with him. "I can't apologize for that enough. I just couldn't wrap my head around what I felt for you. I…"

She pressed her fingers to his lips. "Tiffany told me."

His shoulders dropped. "Meet them. Then decide if I'm wrong about how you'll feel around them. If you want to know what family is, then you're about to get a crash course. If you want to be accepted at first sight, this is the family that will do that. I promise you, you will belong."

She could feel the tears well in her eyes. "What if things don't work out between us?"

"Don't say what if. I don't live on what ifs. I'm not going anywhere. I meant it when I said I was yours."

He pulled her into his arms and held her there. In that moment, she believed it. Forever she was Spencer Benson's.

Spencer moved back and looked at the ceiling. "I'm going to go shoot that stereo."

Julie laughed. "In her defense, she hasn't had a housemate for a long time."

"She's spoiled." He swung his legs over the edge of the bed and slid on his jeans. "Hell, I'll invite her to breakfast."

"That would be nice of you."

He gave her a grunt and headed for the inside stairs.

THERE WAS a moment when Spencer thanked God for his cousin's thoughtfulness to at least be dressed. He wasn't sure how he would handle finding her dancing in her living room naked.

When she saw him, she didn't even seem startled that there was someone there.

"Ah, I thought you were down there," she said grinning. "Sleeping with my neighbor are you?"

"Trust me there is no sleeping going on with that noise." He moved to the stereo and turned down the sound. "When did you get back?"

"Yesterday. Pete picked me up."

"You could afford a cab. You use him."

"I do not. We're friends and that's what friends do for each other." She moved to the stereo and turned it up just a little. "So, give me the scoop. I was away long enough for you to start an affair with the bitch lawyer."

Spencer moved right to her and held up his finger. "Don't ever say that again. I'm sorry I said it in the first place."

Without even a wince, Avery lowered his hand. "I didn't believe it then either. You're together?"

He couldn't help the smile he felt form on his lips. "We're together."

Now she smiled. "You love her."

That took the air out of his lungs and he simply stared at his cousin. "A part of me thinks I always did, but I thought she wasn't mine to have."

"I like her, Spence. I think she'll be good for you."

He kissed Avery on the cheek. "We'll see how it goes tonight. You're going to dinner, right?"

Now her smile faded. "I don't know. I didn't tell anyone I was home yet."

"What are you hiding from?"

"Don't be like that."

Spencer merely raised his eyebrows.

She turned and shut off the stereo. "I'm leaving."

"Going shopping?"

"No, Spence." She turned to him. "I'm moving to France."

Now his smile was gone too and he moved to her and took her arms in his hands. "Avery, what are you doing?"

"The vineyard is beautiful."

"You don't know your grandfather. You can't just leave everyone and move to France."

She moved from him. "I'm not some kid. I can do this."

"You don't want to hear what your mother has to say about it?"

She shook her head.

Spencer moved to her. "Don't you suppose you're worried about that for a reason? I mean if this was the right thing to do you'd be happy to tell everyone."

Avery turned her eyes up to him and they were filled with tears that threatened to spill. "I have to do this. I need this —for me."

He wasn't sure about that. He kissed her cheek and pulled her to him. "I'm always here. We all are. You're not alone, you know that."

"I know."

"Don't you ever forget it."

# CHAPTER 44

*J*ulie had always been a quick study of people. She could read their moods to meet her needs. It was a very handy tool, which had helped in her career.

And now, as she watched Spencer drive through town, she knew something had transpired that morning with Avery. He simply hadn't been the same the rest of the day.

This happened with important people, she knew. Spencer had high-rise builds, his neighborhood build, and the daunting transportation troubles with PLL on his mind. Not to mention, he'd spent time with her all weekend that he'd planned on using in Oregon. But that wasn't all of it. There was something under the surface eating at him, and she couldn't quite put her finger on it.

She reached for him and took his hand in hers. "Are you sure you want me to go with you tonight? You seem a million miles away."

Spencer shifted her a glance. "I'm sorry. I guess I have a lot on my mind."

"That's normal, but are you sure everything is okay?"

He smiled a tight smile and lifted her fingers to his lips and pressed a kiss to them. "Everything's okay, especially with you here."

He turned down a residential street. She followed his gaze when he looked up at the house with the American flag flying off the front porch.

"Whose house is this?"

Spencer smiled. "Right now it belongs to Darcy and Ed. But it was my grandparent's house. This is where my mom grew up."

"That's very cool," she said feeling the respect for family just by living in their homes. "How many of these cars are your family's?"

He let out a chuckle. "Most of them. The house isn't that big, but there's a lot of room when it's needed. And I suppose its just tradition. Sometimes you just don't mess with tradition."

Spencer found a space to park, turned off the engine, and they both opened their doors.

They stepped out of the car, and before they walked up to the house he pulled her to him. "I'm sorry about my attitude. I've been entrusted with a secret and it's killing me."

Though she wanted to ask, she was sure he wouldn't tell, so she said nothing.

"And the conversation I have to have with my dad tomorrow is weighing heavily on my mind," he added.

"Anything I can help with?"

"How are you with accounting?"

She shook her head. "That was never my strongest subject."

He brushed a kiss over her lips. "Knowing you'll be beside me when we figure out what's going on with PLL, that's all the help I need."

As he took her hand and began to lead her to the house, she felt her chest tighten. *When we figure out what's going on with PLL,* resonated in her mind. And then Steven's words, *There's a trail, Julie and it leads to you,* had her stopping at the base of the steps.

Spencer turned and looked at her. "Are you okay? You're shaking."

"Am I?"

"I promise this isn't going to be bad."

"No. I mean…I know." She tried to catch her breath. "I guess I'm nervous."

But there wasn't another moment to think about it. The door opened and a very pregnant woman looked down at them.

"Tell me you brought some air with you. It is stuffy in here."

Spencer laughed as he moved up the three little steps and kissed the woman on the cheek.

"Julie, this is my sister Darcy."

Julie pushed back any worry, and any thought that something bad would happen. She smiled at Darcy, and moved in to shake her hand.

"It's very nice to meet you," she said, but Darcy didn't take her hand. Instead, she pulled her to her and enveloped her in a hug.

"And it is very nice to meet you. Ed told me you might be coming. I'm glad you're here. C'mon, let's introduce you around."

She took Julie's arm and led her away from Spencer.

They hadn't gotten but a few feet into the house when people moved toward the door. At that moment, she knew Darcy was right. It was very stuffy in that small house.

A woman who looked just like Avery walked toward her.

"So you are my daughter's new roommate," she said. Her French accent was thick, and Julie knew this was Avery's mother.

"Yes. I'm Julie," she said holding out her hand.

"It is very nice to meet you. I am Simone and this," she said pulling a man toward her, "is Avery's father, Curtis."

Julie shook his hand and they moved further into the house. As the crowd moved in, she realized she'd been moved far away from Spencer. She was on her own. Whatever he'd told these people about her it was now up to her to face it.

Julie shook hands with Christian, Spencer's cousin, who then introduced her to his wife Victoria and their children.

It hadn't gone unnoticed that every woman who was married to, or was one of Spencer's cousins, was pregnant and due at any time. There must be something in that thick air, she thought as she was introduced to Tyler, Spencer's brother.

"So, you're Julie? I've heard a lot about you."

And for the first time, as she shook hands with one of his relatives, she felt as though she were being judged.

She must not have been the only one who thought so. Spencer's arm came protectively around her waist. "So you've met my brother. Nothing impressive here. It's his better half that is more impressive."

"I won't argue with that," Tyler said as he moved to a woman who had her back toward them. She took his arm and he led her toward them. "Julie, this is my better half, Courtney."

Courtney extended her hand toward Julie and only at that moment did Julie notice that Courtney was blind.

Julie took her hand. "It's nice to meet you."

"Likewise," Courtney said pleasantly. "How are you enjoying Nashville?"

"It's very lively."

Courtney laughed. "It is. I heard you were already down at Tim, Tim, and Tom's?"

"Avery took me."

"They let me help with planning the layout. Could you hear everything okay?"

Julie couldn't help but smile at this woman still holding her hand. "It was perfect."

"I like that word," she said. "C'mon, you have to come into the kitchen and meet grandma, Madeline, Arianna, and I think Spencer's mother is hiding in there too."

Courtney adjusted her grip from Julie's hand to her elbow and together they began walking toward the kitchen.

$\mathcal{A}$s Julie was escorted away by Courtney, Tyler took hold of Spencer's arm.

"That's her? She's that lawyer you've been complaining about all year?"

Spencer yanked back his arm. "Would you be quiet?"

"Everyone knows what you think of her."

"It's not like that." He raked his fingers through his hair. "She's not like that."

The smile on his brother's face had him wanting to knock it clear off. They all thought they knew him better than he knew himself. Then again, maybe they were all right.

"You have a protective stance about you. No one here is going to say anything to her to make her uncomfortable."

Spencer nodded. He knew that. "It's just that..."

"You're seeing her. As in you're involved. As in you're..."

"Right," he said stopping him. "She's not just here to be social."

"We knew that the moment you said you hired her."

A hand was placed on his shoulder and Spencer turned to see his father standing behind him. "Your mother's been waiting for today. She was hoping you'd bring her."

"Perhaps I should have introduced you all earlier."

His father shrugged. "You needed some time. She's quite a catch," his father raised his eyebrows and Spencer could feel his cheeks fill with heat. "I can see why you didn't like her."

Would that ever go away? Why had he done that to himself and to her? It was putting him in a very awkward position—that was until he heard her laugh from the kitchen.

"Well, my guess is Grandma Emily said something non-characteristic of a ninety-something woman."

Spencer laughed and followed the commotion into the kitchen where he found his grandmother holding hands with Julie and laughing at the table.

JULIE LOOKED up at Spencer as he walked through the door with a man she knew for sure was his father, and his brother. Weren't they a sight, she thought as she sat among his family feeling as if she'd known them her entire life.

"I think grandma might have shocked your girlfriend," Spencer's mother patted his arm.

Girlfriend. His mother had let it roll off her tongue as if there hadn't been a history of ill will. And that was just like her. He wrapped his arm around her shoulders and gave her a squeeze.

"It looks like she's fitting in just fine," he said watching his aunt Arianna engage both his girlfriend and his grandmother in something else that had them laughing. The sound was soothing.

"I think she'll do just fine. Why don't you help me set the table," his mother said as a command and not a question.

He kissed her cheek. Wouldn't it figure he'd always get suckered into that job?

. . .

Julie wasn't sure when Spencer had walked out of the kitchen. She hadn't had time to notice. She was embraced in the noise and the people.

Julie could only assume this was what it was like for most families at Thanksgiving, but this was only Sunday dinner.

Grandma Emily, as she'd told Julie to call her, was at the stove with Avery's mother. Madeline, whom Julie found equally as entertaining, had taken a seat at the table. She bounced a little girl on her knee who giggled with delight.

"Who is this?" Julie asked holding onto one of the little girl's hands.

"Little Emily. She's named after Grandma Emily. She's Ed and Darcy's daughter," Madeline beamed with pride.

Quickly, in her head, Julie did the trail down Spencer's family tree. So little Emily would be Spencer's niece, his mother's granddaughter, and his aunt's granddaughter. The thought alone brought a smile to her face that she could feel in her heart.

"Madeline, will you help me a sec?" The man who had been introduced to Julie as Carlos waved to Madeline by the backdoor.

Madeline gave him a nod. "Here, would you mind holding her for a few minutes?" she asked, but proceeded to hand Julie the little girl. As she did, Madeline leaned in closer. "He thinks he's being sneaky. He's going to ask for help with the cooler, but he's going to drag me out to the garage to make out."

The humored gasp from Julie had her slapping a hand over her mouth.

Madeline laughed. "Men are always the same. Only their hair gets thinner and grayer." She winked at Julie and kissed little Emily on the top of the head as she scooted away from the table and toward her husband who Julie witnessed give her a slap to the rear.

How silly was it that it made her want to laugh and cry all at the same time.

Little Emily laid her head on Julie's shoulder, and for the first time ever, she thought her heart might actually melt. She batted away tears that stung her eyes. It was foolish to be so overwhelmed with such emotion. These were just people having dinner.

Julie looked up toward the doorway as if she could feel Spencer's eyes on her. There was a look that came from him and now those tears were going to spill.

He was in love with her.

He didn't have to say the words. She'd never seen anyone look at her as he did, but she recognized it.

Spencer's father had looked at his mother like that. His uncle looked at his aunt the same. Even Grandma Emily had looked like that when she talked about Grandpa Alan, who was in the other room.

The pace of her heart ramped up as the little girl on her shoulder began to breath heavier and Julie realized she'd fallen asleep in her arms among the noise of family.

Family.

Julie batted the tears away and wiped the one that had fallen as Spencer moved to her.

"Do you want me to go lay her down?"

Julie stiffly shook her head. "No. I really want to keep her right here if it's okay."

He took the seat his aunt had vacated and put an arm around her. He kissed the top of Emily's head gently. When those dark eyes shifted to her, the words she was feeling simply fell from her lips. "I love you, Spencer."

She'd expected him to blink hard or pull away. Instead, he leaned over Emily and pressed a kiss to her lips.

"C'mon, c'mon," Courtney said standing next to the table. "Dinner's ready. No making out at the table."

Spencer laughed. "I'm telling you, she says she's blind, but the woman sees everything."

Courtney laughed. "It's soul vision, Spence. Don't think I can't see into it."

Spencer laughed again as Courtney walked away and he helped Julie up as she held on to Emily.

Darcy waddled into the kitchen, both hands on her stomach, and looked toward Julie. "Oh, I can put her down. She gets so much grandma love on Sundays it puts her to sleep."

She reached out her hands toward Julie, but Julie held the baby against her. "Would it be okay if I held her through dinner? I've never held a sleeping baby and it seems to be doing a lot for my soul right now."

Spencer rubbed her back and Darcy smiled. "It's like medicine isn't it?"

Julie nodded. "I don't have brothers or sisters or cousins. This is so overwhelming, and comforting all at the same time."

"I remember the feeling," Darcy said as she escorted them to the dining room, which had a table that extended into the living room to seat them all.

Dinner took hours. Laughter and abundant love encircled the Kellers and the Bensons—and Julie.

They talked to her as if she mattered.

They included her as if she belonged.

They loved her, and that resonated through her.

Perhaps Spencer hadn't hated her as she thought he had.

When he slipped his hand under the table and folded his fingers around hers, she knew that what she'd told him in the kitchen was absolute truth. She loved this man with all her heart. She loved his family. What she wouldn't give to be a part of all of it forever.

# CHAPTER 46

*S*itting behind his desk on Monday morning, Spencer felt a sense of renewed spirit. Julie hadn't stopped talking about his family all night. She'd held Emily through dinner and fed her when she'd awakened. Clara had let her feel her baby kick, and had promised to let Julie hold him the moment he was born.

His mother sat and talked to Julie for nearly an hour in the corner of the living room. Julie hadn't said what they'd talked about, but what Spencer saw between them only made him more sure that the path they were headed down was the right one.

But they still had a lot of obstacles in their way.

Julie had let him see the papers Steven had brought her. She would need to go back to Oregon and move her belongings to Nashville. There was also the time it was going to take to get the house sold.

A bit of him worried that when she got back home, unattached from Steven, she'd want to stay. But he'd deal with that if the time arose.

Now, as the timer on his cell phone rang, he was headed to his father's office with the accounting report. They still needed to find the leak in PLL before it got any bigger.

* * *

JULIE FINALIZED the plans on the corporate house, and she was genuinely pleased with how it was going to look. She arranged everything for the three houses Tiffany had sold on Saturday, and brewed a new pot of coffee for Chuck when he walked back in after dealing with inspectors.

Everything was brighter today. Everything made her happier today. For the first time in her life, she felt part of something. How could meeting someone's family do that?

Julie didn't know, but it had happened to her.

When the door opened to the trailer, Julie looked up expecting that Tiffany had sold another house. She cleared the files from her desk and smiled up. But the smile fell away when she saw Libby Grayson standing before her.

The room went absolutely cold.

Libby looked around. "So this is what it looks like when you fall from grace?"

Julie wanted to stand. She wanted to look the woman in the eye, but her body was frozen in place.

Libby looked down at her. "I guess sleeping with your new boss doesn't get you a cushy job. It's dusty and messy in here."

"Why are you here?" Those were the only words that would come out.

"I came for what's mine. I think it's time to hand it over."

Julie felt the blood rush from her head. "I have no idea what you're talking about."

Libby's red painted lips turned up at the corners. "I don't believe you. Your husband came to you. He thinks he's being sneaky, but I know his moves. Now, you need to give it to me."

Fear and anger balled up in her stomach and gave her the strength to push to her feet. "I'll tell you again. I don't know what you're talking about. I don't have anything that belongs to you."

Libby set her hands down on Julie's desk. "You'd better find that husband of yours…"

"Ex-husband."

Libby pursed her lips. "Find him. Get what is mine or that precious project you're working on will be a pile of ash once it's framed. Do I make myself clear?"

Julie swallowed hard. "What do I have?"

Libby stood and the smile grew. "I'm not going to tell you. I think it will be much better if your lover finds it first."

She spun, walked out of the trailer, climbed into the taxi that waited out front, and drove away.

Julie fell back into her chair and looked at her hands. They shook. She needed to find out what Libby was talking about before Spencer did. She tried to gather her thoughts. Julie didn't have anything that belonged to Libby. What could she possibly have?

Her stomach clenched and she thought she might vomit. Sweat beaded on her brow.

The door opened again and she snapped her head up as Tiffany walked in. Her eyes grew wide. "Are you feeling okay?"

"No. No, I'm not. I think I should go home."

Tiffany nodded in agreement. "I can get a ride for you. Maybe you shouldn't be driving."

"I'll be fine," she said as anger pumped through her.

"I'll call Spencer and…"

"Don't," she bit the words out harshly. "Don't call him. Don't tell him anything. I'll be back in the morning. Just put my work on my desk."

She pulled her purse and bag out of the drawer in her desk and walked past Tiffany.

"Hey," Tiffany called after her. "Are you sure you'll be okay? Are you and Spencer okay?"

She didn't even know how to answer that. At that very moment, she didn't know anything—let alone what Spencer might think if he found out first—whatever it was.

# CHAPTER 47

S pencer watched his father flip back and forth through the pages of the report he'd brought him.

"What do you think?" Spencer asked.

"I think sixty-thousand dollars is a lot of money."

Spencer stood from his seat and paced in front of the large bank of windows in his father's office. "What do we do? This impacted our business, but happened before we took ownership."

His father leaned back in his chair and steepled his fingers in thought.

"Someone must have been very desperate to do something like this."

Leave it to his father to consider that someone was in some kind of trouble and not just vindictive.

"Fine, but our trucks aren't on the roads when they're supposed to be because someone was desperate." Spencer shoved his hands in his pockets. "If this person is still employed by us, then we need to plug that leak."

His father nodded. "So we need to go through the personnel records and find out who worked in areas they could get to information like this. And then find out who has been let go in the last six months. Chances are it isn't someone who's been fired or the leak would have stopped."

Spencer loosened his tie. "I was hoping not to fly back this soon."

His father smiled. "You're a man with his hands in many things. This new venture is one of them."

"Do you think I could pass off the high-rise builds to Ed? They're fairly established."

His father gave him a long slow nod. "I don't see a problem with that."

"I think the farmer will decide to sell this week too."

"One more thing on your plate."

Spencer raked his hands through his hair. "What did I get myself into?"

Now his father laughed. "You're a Benson and you're ambitious. You might think of slowing down, but you won't."

Spencer let out a long breath. "Right."

"But I learned from my father's death that you can be ambitious, and you can enjoy what's there. Don't forget to live a little too."

"When is there time?"

"Make time." His father's eyes locked with his. "If she's important to you, then don't lose her to work."

Well, he could cut right to the chase couldn't he, even when Spencer hadn't brought her up.

Spencer bit down on his lip, diverted his eyes away, and then back to his father. "She's recently divorced."

His father stood from his chair and walked to him. "And your mother was running from a man who tried to kill her. She kept her secrets."

"It doesn't bother you then?"

"Is Julie the person you think she is?"

"Yes."

"You care for her?"

Now Spencer nodded. "I do."

"Do you think you love her?"

He'd expected to have this conversation with his mother, not his father, but he knew the answer. "I do. I haven't told her, but I do."

His father rested his hands on Spencer's shoulders. "Let her know how you feel. One thing I've learned over the years is that relationships are built on trust, not time. You've known her long enough to know her character. You thought enough of her to bring her to your family, and they all seemed to take to her."

"Mom?"

"Loved her," his father clarified. "Take her to Oregon with you this time. Not only can you bond away from all of this, but maybe she knows things that will help."

"Knows things? Like what?"

"She was there a long time. She'd know people who came and went. She could be a valuable source to you. And, some time alone in a hotel room is always well spent."

The heat under Spencer's collar was nearly unbearable now.

"I'll let you know what plans are made," he said moving from under his father's protective hands and toward the door.

"I'll be here."

Spencer turned and looked at the man he most admired. "Thanks, Dad. I appreciate the trust."

"If you can't trust those you love most, who can you trust?"

His father was right on so many levels. It was time to make plans to travel with Julie—even if it was to only use the hotel room.

As he walked toward the elevator, his cell phone buzzed in his pocket. Amber's text displayed on the screen.

*Carson Grayson is here to see you.*

* * *

JULIE HAD COME to Nashville with only a suitcase and her car. Whatever Libby Grayson was looking for, Julie didn't have. That only meant one thing. She needed to head back to Oregon on the next flight and go through her house.

She'd thought Steven was being very genuine when he'd come to her, but she should have known better.

Julie began piling clothes into her suitcase. If she could figure out what was going on, then Spencer would understand her leaving on the spur of the moment. And if her ex-husband was doing something to hurt Spencer, she wanted to stop it.

The thought of the corporate house going up in flames didn't appeal to her either. She knew that was just a threat of words, but all the same, it made her anxious.

Just as she turned off the lights in the little apartment, there was a knock at the door. Julie stopped and stood there. Who could possibly be on the other side? Fear paralyzed her.

There was another knock. "Julie, are you in there? Are you okay?"

Avery's voice echoed in the outside stairwell.

Julie opened the door. "Hi. I'm fine."

"Tiffany called and said you were headed home. I just wondered if you needed anything."

Her brain scrambled. She wished she could come up with something, but there was only one thing she needed right at the moment. "I could use a ride to the airport."

Avery's brows drew in. "Where are you going?"

"It seems as though there is some unfinished business in Oregon I need to take care of. I should be back by tomorrow. But I could really use a lift."

Avery nodded her head slowly. "Sure. Let me get my things. I'll meet you out front."

He'd know now, she thought as she closed the apartment door behind her. Damn Tiffany for saying anything, even though it was out of friendship and love that she'd done so. Regardless, it would give her a day to find out what Libby was talking about.

Julie looked down at her phone and turned it off.

It was for the best, she thought. As soon as she knew what was going on, she'd call Spencer.

# CHAPTER 48

*P*erhaps luck was on Julie's side. There was a standby
seat to Denver where there would be a connecting
flight to Portland. She'd made a few phone calls and secured a
ride from there to her house.

A mere twelve hours later Claudia was waiting for Julie at the
airport.

"I can't thank you enough," Julie said as she loaded her suitcase into the back of Claudia's Subaru.

"Sure, I owe you one after you helped me with that identity
fraud. I mean I could be in jail or something."

"Why would you be in jail?"

"Well, you know, if they'd done something illegal with my
name." Claudia pulled away from the curb. "It's totally cool what
you can do as a lawyer."

Julie wanted to laugh. She knew Claudia wasn't much
younger than she was, but her lifestyle might have been less
mature than Julie's.

She wore a stocking cap over her dreadlocked blonde hair,
and a hoop shimmered in her nose.

Claudia had always been a good friend and that was what Julie needed, especially at one o'clock in the morning.

"So where have you been? Like no one has seen you around for like a month."

"I'm living in Nashville now," Julie confirmed

"No way. You went country?"

Julie laughed. "I'm embracing Blake Shelton."

"That dude from the voice? I'm so team Adam."

And Julie knew she was too. "I needed a change of scenery."

"Did your husband go with you?"

Julie shook her head. "He's my ex-husband now."

"No way!" Claudia snapped a look at her. "You ditched the old dude?"

"He wasn't that old."

"Right," she said on a laugh. "His hair was gray."

"Silver, and not all of it."

"Weird that you both left PLL. I mean what was with that?"

Now Julie knew she had her foot in the door. Claudia worked the mailroom in the corporate office. She'd know the ins and outs of what was going on around there.

"I was let go before the merger finished. I guess the Grayson family didn't like my work."

Claudia snarled her lip up, which was also pierced with a hoop. "Are you kidding me? You were their best attorney. Why fire you?"

That was a good question. "I was asked to leave, so I did."

"That don't make sense," Claudia said pulling into the driveway of Julie's dark, hillside home. "I heard a rumor that your husband was seeing Libby, but I put a kibosh on that."

"He was," she said matter-of-factly. "I caught them in my bedroom." She pointed to the window.

"Really? Couldn't she splurge for a room? She's a Grayson."

"Not a Grayson on the payroll."

That made Claudia laugh. "Her and her sexy brother. Why not let them take over the company? Why sell it?"

And that had Julie's radar going off. "Good question. I don't know Carson Grayson very well. He didn't seem to be a player like his sister."

That caused Claudia to laugh again. "Hey, can I come in and pee? I had a Big Gulp waiting for you at the airport."

Julie held in the laugh. "Of course. Maybe the ex left a beer."

"Cool."

Julie pulled her things from Claudia's car and walked up the front steps. She unlocked the door, pushed it in, and reached her hand in to turn on some light.

"The bathroom is the first room down the hall on the right."

"Did you take everything with you?" Claudia asked as she walked in.

That had Julie stepping in carefully. Son-of-a-bitch had taken all the furniture out of the house. So much for that letter he'd written saying she could have everything. There was nothing left.

She heard the toilet flush and a moment later Claudia was walking toward her. "You wanna stay with me? Do you have a bed?"

"I have no idea," she said. "This isn't what I expected."

"Not to sound mean, but I never liked your husband."

"Ex."

"Good," Claudia said. "Hey, I can wait for you to look around."

"Thanks."

Julie did just that. She lit up the house turning on every light. It wasn't much of a surprise to find the entire house empty. The only thing left was a pile of mail on the counter.

"He takes everything that belongs to me, and leaves me the bills," she growled through clenched teeth. "I guess I'll take you up on that place to stay."

# CHAPTER 49

$S$pencer stood with the fire chief and watched the frame of the house burn in the early morning light. His gut twisted with anger as water shot at the fire that consumed the house he'd designed, and Julie was to fill with her colorful touch.

It was just the frame. It was just wood. In a few weeks, it could be rebuilt and everything would start over.

He rubbed his hand over the back of his neck as he watched Tiffany walking toward him in a pair of sweatpants, her hair piled atop her head, with bottles of water in her hands, and a pair of athletic shoes on her feet. The contrast to her normal attire should have lightened his mood. But it did nothing of the sort.

"Have you heard from her?" she asked, her voice cracking in the early hour.

He shook his head as she handed him a bottle of water.

Tiffany took a sip from her bottle of water. "Don't go jumping to conclusions. You don't know why she did it."

He felt the twitching in his jaw and anger boiled in his chest.

Spencer grabbed Tiffany's arm and pulled her far enough away from the chaos of the fire to have a word without everyone hearing him.

"Sixty-thousand. That's a lot of conclusions to jump to don't you think?" he spat out the words.

"And where is it? She lives in your aunt's house in the basement. Have you seen how old her car is?"

"And she sleeps in my penthouse."

Tiffany's eyes narrowed on him. "Spencer, this is bigger than her. I don't believe for a minute that those papers Carson Grayson brought you are real."

Spencer pulled his fingers through his hair and then again. He did find it very interesting that Libby was sitting on his desk only a few days ago trying to seduce him. Then she shows up in Nashville, and so did her brother.

But it was all too convenient for Julie's ex-husband to show up too—right before she disappeared and Avery of all people drove her to the airport.

He'd have thought perhaps Julie had been kidnapped if Avery hadn't called him.

She'd left on her own. "In a big hurry to get back to Oregon," Avery had said. No calls or texts from her and when he called her he got her voice mail.

Tiffany placed a hand on his arm. "You love her."

"I thought I did, but..."

"You love her." She bore those blue eyes into him. "Something is wrong. Don't you see that? Why do you think she left there to begin with? She's not running now. She was running then."

"And you of all people believe in her why?"

"Because she's my friend," she said with determination and he knew in his heart Tiffany believed in Julie's innocence.

Spencer shoved his hands into his pockets.

Tiffany was never the voice of logic. In fact, if he'd met anyone more illogical, it was her. But even though, watching the flames engulf this house, this all too important house, had his insides tied in knots, he somehow knew there was more.

Julie had the money. He'd seen the records Carson had

brought to him where she'd funneled it out bit by bit. And yet, he didn't feel it.

He was filled with anger at the thought of the embezzlement, her running away, and the fire. But he'd seen her eyes that night she'd kissed him in the elevator. Those weren't the eyes of a woman who was screwing him over for his money. He'd touched her, kissed her, made love to her. There wasn't anything vengeful in her.

The bitch lawyer was her shell. Julie was more than that. She was a lonely soul who needed love. He'd given her that love. His family—his friends—gave her that love.

There was more to it, he thought again. God, for the first time since he'd known her, he thought Tiffany might be right.

"Call my dad. Get him down here."

Her eyes widened. "Are you kidding me? I'm not calling…"

"Do it. I have to figure out what the hell is going on."

He started toward the trailer when she called to him. "Spencer, they're going to want to talk to you."

"I'm a phone call away. I have a deep rooted feeling that when they go looking they're going to want to arrest someone for arson."

His father's advice ran through his head as he headed for his car, *If you can't trust those you love most, who can you trust?*

* * *

JULIE HAD CLEANED out the mailbox before reloading her suitcase in Claudia's car. A notice from the post office that her mail was being held because the box was too full only made her more infuriated. Steven had left Oregon shortly after she had, according to the dates on the last pieces of mail delivered.

By the time she'd laid down to sleep on Claudia's worn out futon, it was past three o'clock in the morning.

. . .

AT NINE-THIRTY, Julie stepped out of Claudia's borrowed car at the post office. Fifteen minutes later she was back in the car looking at the pile of junk mail, bills, and an enormous envelope from a bank where she'd never had an account.

Her fingers trembled as she opened the envelope with her name on it.

It was a quarterly statement of an account. Deposits had been made on a weekly basis for almost a year. None of the deposit amounts were the same, and there were no withdrawals.

She flipped through the pages. Why was her name on this account? There was nearly sixty thousand dollars in the account.

Throwing the papers into the passenger seat, she started the car and headed back to the corporate offices of PLL where she'd dropped Claudia off earlier.

She parked the car out back, where Claudia would park, and with Claudia's door pass, she entered through the back. Julie needed to get up to the legal department. Maybe there was something in her office files, or in Steven's, that would give her some kind of information as to where the account came from.

Julie had worked at PLL long enough, she knew how to avoid people. After her ex-husband's first indiscretion, she'd been successful enough to talk to nearly no one for a month. This was a skill that had certainly come in handy.

The only person who noticed her was a janitor who gave her a nod. Chances were he never knew her enough to know she'd been fired nearly a month ago.

Julie slipped into her old office and closed the door behind her. It seemed so foreign now. How could she feel so removed from somewhere she'd spent so many years? At that moment, she longed to be back listening to Chuck curse.

She needed to go through her files. Julie knew she was being set up. This was what Steven had been talking about. The paper trail led to her. Well, this wasn't how it was going to happen. No one screwed over Spencer and his family. No one.

Julie went about looking through the drawers of her file cabinet. Files from negotiations she'd managed were right where she'd left them. Everything was color-coded and alphabetized. Drawer after drawer was just as she'd left it.

She sat in the chair at her desk and looked around. All she needed to do was take the information to Spencer and he'd believe her. Why wouldn't he? She'd told him she loved him and she meant it.

That's what she'd do. He'd understand.

# CHAPTER 50

*J*ulie pulled her phone from her pocket and turned it back on. It had been nearly twenty-four hours since she'd left Nashville. Perhaps it was wrong, but she sincerely hoped Spencer had texted and called numerous times looking for her.

She silenced the ringer as text after text filtered in.

As she scrolled through the messages, without reading them, she realized she'd gotten what she'd wished for. Spencer had been texting her, from what she assumed, was the moment Tiffany had told her she'd gone home sick until midnight. However, there were no texts from him that morning.

Surely he was mad. After all, she'd…

She stopped thinking at all.

An Oregon number had caught her attention and she'd opened the text.

Tears instantly filled her eyes as she saw the pictures of the house she'd put so much planning into going up in flames.

The final text from that number simply said, *I warned you.*

Julie needed to call the police. This had gone too far. She was innocent, absolutely innocent.

Julie opened the middle drawer on her desk to pull out a pen and a pad of paper. In the middle drawer was another manila envelope, which she hadn't put there.

Slowly, with unsteady hands, Julie pulled the envelope from the drawer. There were photographs inside along with a note.

She dumped out the contents and sifted through them. They were pictures of her and Spencer.

Her heart lodged in her throat.

They weren't even just pictures of her and Spencer in the past few weeks. They were from the past five months.

Someone who had been in on the negotiations took a lot of time to snap pictures in exactly the right times.

She'd walked through the door with him, and ten others, but they weren't seen. He'd told her something nice and she'd looked up at him and smiled. They'd caught that.

At a luncheon where Mr. Grayson addressed the employees, Spencer had sat next to her. As they'd applauded his speech, she'd leaned in reach for her water. Spencer had put his arm around the back of her chair to talk to the person on the other side of her. But in that very brief moment it looked as though he'd put his arm around her.

There were at least twenty different shots where she and Spencer looked intimate or engaged with each other during the course of the merger.

They had spent a lot of time near each other.

She studied the pictures with a different set of eyes now.

He had gazed at her, joked with her, and touched her gently on the arm.

Her breath grew more rapid. They'd had a few nights where they argued points of the merger in her office. She sat where she did now, and he in the chair across from her.

Just him and her.

Just a few late nights.

Oh, she'd been blind.

The letter caught her attention.

*Give her what she wants. It will only get worse for you.*

It was Steven's handwriting. Was he blackmailing her? And for what? She hadn't done anything with Spencer until the papers were signed. Why were they doing this?

Panic and fear paralyzed her as she saw a shadow walk in front of her office window. The blinds were closed. They couldn't...

Then the doorknob twisted and the door pushed open.

Carson Grayson stood there in a dark gray suit, arms crossed, and eyes narrowed on her.

"Funny thing. I just got a phone call that said you'd be here."

She was absolutely speechless. No one knew she was there. Though looking at the pictures scattered on her desk, someone knew she'd be coming.

Julie stood as Carson walked in and shut the door behind him.

"Sit down, Ms. Jacobson," he demanded as he walked toward the desk. "We're going to talk."

"I don't have anything to say to you. I need to..."

"Sit!" His voice echoed through he room.

Julie did as she was commanded to do.

Carson Grayson paced in front of the desk. "You're breaking and entering, Ms. Jacobson. Not a good position for a lawyer."

And it was that lawyer part of her that kept her completely quiet.

As he turned to pace the room again, she reached for her phone, which was atop the desk. The man fuming in front of her was big and mad. She'd never known a Grayson to be violent, but then again she'd seen what Libby had done to her marriage and to Spencer's corporate build.

Someone needed to know where she was—just in case. There was no telling what this man would do to her if he was anything like his sister.

As far as she knew he wasn't on the payroll. Why was he even in the office?

From under the desk Julie turned down the volume on the phone. Next she needed to figure out who to call. The police? No, she was the one who entered the building with Claudia's pass.

Spencer? What if he was so mad at her he didn't answer?

Tiffany. Even if Tiffany was mad at her, she was sure she'd answer. She'd be looking for a good fight. What she hoped was she'd get what she needed.

Aware that Carson was fueling up to lash out, she discreetly pressed Tiffany's name on the phone and watched as the timer began on the phone call.

"Carson, I just came back for a few of my things. I don't know who told you I was here…"

"Shut up! You think you can manipulate me and my family like this?"

"I don't understand."

He moved toward the desk in such a fury that Julie stood to protect herself if needed and dropped the phone to the floor.

She wasn't going to acknowledge it. All she could do was hope it was still on and Tiffany was on the other end.

Carson slapped his hands down on the top of her desk and looked at the photos that were scattered across it. "You've been a busy girl."

"I found these. Someone is trying to blackmail me."

That caught his attention. "You're sleeping with the boss and now someone wants something. Is this a family trait?" His voice rose.

"I never had anything to do with Spencer Benson before the merger. These pictures are out of context."

"And I'm going to believe you?"

Julie kept her lawyer cool intact, even if her womanly instincts were to shudder and nearly cry.

"I don't exactly know what is going on. So I myself don't know what to believe."

He leaned in closer. "Here's what I believe. I think you screwed my family over. You negotiated a merger that was to be cut and dry and you dragged it out. Then you ran off and started sleeping with the new boss all the while you were embezzling from the company. Does that about sum it up?"

It summed it up. It sounded horrible. And only part of it was true.

Julie pushed her shoulders back and looked Carson in the eye. "The merger was thoroughly negotiated to get the most worth out of the company for the Benson family and the best sale price for the Grayson family."

"It was a cut and dried deal."

Julie nodded. "Your sister asked me to look into a few things during the negotiations. I was very thorough."

He ran his tongue over his teeth. "My sister has nothing to do with this company."

"I was under the impression you didn't either."

He narrowed his eyes again. "That changed."

She wondered if Spencer knew that. "That's news to me," And she assumed completely untrue. "But, regardless of who is involved, I looked out for the Graysons on behalf of your sister."

His lips turned up at the corner. "What would make you do anything for my sister after your husband hit on her?"

Julie's jaw tightened. "Hit on her? Carson, your sister and my husband were having an affair. I caught them myself."

There was a slight flash in his eyes, but they darkened quickly as they bore into her.

"Libby isn't like that. People only make her out to be like that."

This man was dense.

"Carson, I think we should call Spencer and even your grandfather and talk this out. I've never done anything to harm this company. My job was to protect it."

Now he moved around the desk toward her and she backed away as he came at her.

"You want me to believe you're the innocent one here?"

Julie continued to back around the desk. "I just want to sit down and talk."

"Where is the sixty-grand you stole from us?"

"I didn't steal it."

"It's in a bank in your name."

"How do you know that?"

Her head was spinning. There was so much in that one sentence that shocked her and incriminated her.

Carson came at her full force now, his hands grabbing hold of her shoulders as he slammed her back against the wall. Julie's head rammed against it, and her eyes clouded before she could blink them clear.

"You took what was ours," his voice was demonic.

"I didn't," the words were now weak and came out with panic filling them. "I didn't do that."

"The money is in your name. You're a goddamned liar."

He slammed her back again.

"No." Now she was sobbing and her head throbbed. "I didn't do anything. I'm innocent."

"You're a liar!"

She watched as his large hand swung up in the air and started toward her, but the door opened again. Carson let go of her and stepped back, letting her wobbly legs give out beneath her, sending her to the floor.

# CHAPTER 51

Spencer and Mr. Grayson stood in the doorway.

Spencer had his phone to his ear. "I found her," was all she heard him say before he moved to her.

Behind Mr. Grayson, two armed security guards moved in. With one bony finger Mr. Grayson gave a direction to Carson to sit, and he did.

"Are you okay?" Spencer's voice was soft against her cheek.

"My head. Throbbing." Even her sentences weren't full ones.

"Can you get up?"

She wasn't sure she could. Everything pounded in her skull and all she could do was blink heavily.

"Just sit a moment," he said with his hand on her back.

Mr. Grayson moved into the room and Spencer stood. "She's hurt," he said and Mr. Grayson gave him a slow nod.

He moved toward his grandson who stood at least six-foot-four, Spencer presumed, but sulked in a chair like a little boy.

"Why?" Mr. Grayson's voice was low.

"She stole from us," he said weakly. "Look."

Carson pointed to the pictures on the desk.

The elder Grayson walked around the desk and looked at the photographs.

Spencer wondered what they were and where they'd come from. Mr. Grayson moved them around with his hand and then picked up a note.

His eyes narrowed as he read the note and directed his attention to Carson. "Where is your sister?"

Carson lifted his head. "She was in Nashville the last time I saw her," he cowered from the man who was decades older, but obviously had control over him.

Spencer balled his fists ready to lean in on the attack against Carson. He stopped as his phone buzzed in his pocket where he'd tucked it when he'd knelt down by Julie. He pulled it out and looked at the screen.

*Julie's phone is still on. Libby Grayson is in custody for arson.*

He smiled at the text message. Tiffany was a good friend, and Julie was a genius.

Spencer had flown to Oregon to hopefully get some answers. Her house was empty and his leads stopped there. Only by chance had he gone to his office at PLL and Tiffany had called to tell him Julie had called, but all she could hear was people arguing. Spencer was sure that was exactly what Tiffany was supposed to hear.

Until the room was clear, he'd leave her phone connected without anyone knowing.

"Sir, I just received notice that your granddaughter is in custody for an arson fire on one of my build sites."

Both sets of Grayson eyes turned to him, but the elder set turned sad.

Mr. Grayson shook his head. "I wish I were surprised."

"This isn't Libby's fault," Carson defended.

Mr. Grayson's head rose as he looked at his grandson. "I'm sure your explanation is better?"

Carson stood, but each security guard placed a hand on his shoulder pushing him back down in his seat.

"Grandfather, please."

"I'm waiting to hear from you," Mr. Grayson said.

"It's not Libby. It's Julie. You have to believe me."

"I haven't believed much of anything you or your sister has said for the past fifteen years," the old man's voice shook with anger.

"Look at the pictures. She's been having an affair with Benson."

Mr. Grayson looked down at the pictures again. "These are very interesting," he said. "You know what's interesting? I was there the whole time." He picked up one of the pictures and threw it at his grandson. "I'm old. I'm very old, but I'm not stupid." He walked around the desk until he stood in front of his grandson.

"Do you think I'd sell my company to a man with no ethics?" His voice rose and the large man before him sunk down in his seat. "I have known the Bensons and the Harts for years. I trust them, Carson."

"Grandfather, they played you."

"No, not him. Not Spencer Benson."

"Julie and her husband," Carson retorted quickly. "They're the ones not to be trusted. You need to do something."

Mr. Grayson leaned against the desk. "If the problem is with my law staff, then why is your sister in custody for arson?" Again the old man's voice rose.

Spencer moved toward the desk. "Sir, I need to get her to a hospital and have her looked at."

The protest came from behind him. "Spencer, I'm fine."

He turned to see Julie on her hands and knees pushing herself up.

Spencer hurried to her side and wrapped a protective arm around her waist. "You should sit."

"I'll be fine."

He held Julie in place as she reached for the back of her head. "Sir, I have an account in my name with over sixty-thousand dollars in it."

"Julie," her name slipped from Spencer's lips in nearly a disappointed sigh.

She looked at him and then back to the elder Grayson.

"I didn't expect that," Mr. Grayson said.

"I didn't either," she replied. "The paperwork was in my mailbox when I arrived back in Oregon. Sir," she said making sure his attention was directed at her, "I didn't open that account."

"How do you open an account and fill it with money like that, Ms. Jacobson, and know nothing about it?"

"When it's fraud, sir."

Spencer watched Carson sink deeper into his chair and he was sure that Mr. Grayson noticed.

# CHAPTER 52

$S$ ilence had engulfed the room as Julie waited for Mr. Grayson to acknowledge her.

"I'd like to talk to Ms. Jacobson alone," he said steely as the security guards each took an arm of his grandson. "Escort my grandson to my office." He turned his gaze to Spencer. "You may wait in your office," he told him.

Julie watched Spencer's face contort as he tried to control himself.

She gave Spencer a nod, and his lips pressed together in a thin line.

"Julie, I don't…"

"Spencer, I've worked for Mr. Grayson for many years. I'll be fine."

He kept a cool eye on her before he leaned in close to her ear and whispered, "Don't turn off your phone."

She agreed with a nod and he walked slowly out of the room.

As the door closed, Julie turned toward Mr. Grayson. Her head throbbed, and it hurt to focus her eyes, but she was going be strong. She'd done nothing wrong, and Mr. Grayson knew it.

"Ms. Jacobson, sit," he commanded just as he had with his grandson.

Julie did as she was told.

"You've worked for me in a capacity of trust for many years. There isn't anyone in this organization that knows more about me and my family than you do."

"With all due respect, sir. I don't work for you anymore."

He nodded slowly. "I guess none of us really do."

"You fired me," she quickly added.

His eyes widened. "I did what?"

Julie swallowed hard. "The day before the merger was finalized, I was asked to leave the company. I was handed a signed letter, by you, and told to vacate the premises immediately. Security guards saw me out with nothing but my purse and my bag."

That obviously had surprised him. He sat down in the seat next to her.

"Julie, dear Julie, why would I do that?"

"Sir, there were a lot of things going on. I just assumed I'd gotten in the way. I know it wouldn't be the first time."

He reached for her hand and held it in his. "You've never gotten in the way."

"I know you gave me this job as a favor to my father. I'll never forget that."

"You proved to be worthy of that favor."

She smiled as she fought off the tears caused by the pain of her throbbing head, and the emotions over her father's conversation with Mr. Grayson when he asked him to take care of his little girl.

"Sir, I would never steal from you, but I do, in fact, have an account with sixty-thousand dollars in it."

"Why? Julie, I would have helped you if you were in trouble."

She shook her head. "I didn't put the money there." Julie took a deep breath. "My husband has been having an affair with Libby."

He let out a long slow breath. "Oh, Julie. I'm so sorry."

"I didn't want to tell you that. She's your granddaughter and…"

"You can't choose your relatives," he reminded her and patted her hand. "I love Libby and Carson, but there is a reason I never put them on the payroll. I can't say my son chose wisely in his first wife. She didn't do right by those kids, and even as adults, I can't control them."

For whatever reasons, that seemed to comfort her. This was why she'd been so loyal to them. Since her parents had died, Mr. Grayson had always taken care of her and protected her as she assumed her father would have. He'd paid off her law school tuition, given her the job at PLL, and not just a job behind a desk pushing papers. He'd let her negotiate deals and handle suits from disgruntled employees. She'd been in charge of the merger between PLL and BBH since Spencer and Mr. Grayson first met.

She'd drawn up Mr. Grayson's will, and changed it when it needed to be changed.

And at that moment of realization, she knew why she'd been targeted.

"Julie, do you feel alright?" Mr. Grayson moved closer to her.

"Your will. I changed your will for you."

"Yes, we did that last year," he said and gripped her hand. "What does this have to do with that?"

She looked up into his aged eyes which always reminded her so much of her father's. "You were very specific to not leave anything but the trust funds that had been established to your grandchildren. All of them."

"Yes, but that was between you and me."

"And Steven, my husband," she said as if reminding him that he'd been part of that conversation.

Mr. Grayson sat back in the chair and folded his hands together. "I'd forgotten about that. And you just told me he and Libby…"

"Yes."

He let out a deep groan.

"I'll be honest, sir, I don't think my ex-husband was in on the fraud, but I think he was a gateway. That's how they got my information. And just a few days ago, he too was let go from the company."

Mr. Grayson sat forward and rested his elbows on his legs. "I worked so hard to build something that would go on forever."

"You've done that."

"But I had to sell it away from my family. When you can't trust your family who can you trust?"

Julie reached for the man's hand. Some families were just different, she supposed. Her family was very small. She'd never truly understood the dynamics of family until she'd met Spencer's.

Though the Graysons and Bensons were both built on wealth, she knew that Spencer's family roots went deeper than a financial bottom line. Unfortunately, she didn't think the Grayson family's did.

"Mr. Grayson, I would never have stolen from you, personally or from your company. I need to turn the account over to the authorities. They'll have to investigate, but in the end, they're going to find that I wasn't the person who opened that account. They're going to have to prosecute Libby and perhaps Carson."

He nodded slowly. "My wife would be devastated, rest her soul."

She knew it was the right thing to do, to turn it over to the authorities. It broke her heart to think she'd have to put Mr. Grayson through that, but it had to be done. Libby had to pay for the fraud against Julie and PLL. The thought of the corporate house being destroyed socked into Julie's gut.

How could Spencer ever trust her?

Mr. Grayson lifted his head. "I'm sorry my granddaughter

moved in on your marriage, and I'm sorry my grandson hurt you. I should let Mr. Benson take you to the hospital."

Julie's ears were still ringing and the throbbing continued. She nodded.

Mr. Grayson stood. "Perhaps it's time for the Grayson family to turn all of PLL over to the Bensons. I don't want to cause them, or you, any further grief."

Julie stood and then sat back down when her head spun. "Thank you, sir, for everything you've done for me. You've taken good care of me."

His eyes averted. "This doesn't feel like taking care of some-one." He patted her shoulder. "I'm going to talk to Mr. Benson about getting your job back. He'd be a fool to not keep you on here. You're the best lawyer I know."

Julie watched the man walk out of her office broken. How could his own family have caused him so much pain?

She finally managed to stand, after a few tries, and walked around the desk. Wincing at the pain in her head, she bent over to pick up the phone. Blood rushed to her head and the ringing in her ears grew louder.

The room around her began to spin and grow dark.

# CHAPTER 53

Spencer paced behind the desk. The bank of windows, which looked out over the Willamette River made him miss his view in Nashville. When he looked up, Mr. Grayson stood in the doorway.

"Mr. Benson, I've come to let you know that the Grayson family will be stepping away gracefully from PLL. I think in light of what has happened, it is time."

"Mr. Grayson, I appreciate that." He walked toward him and held out his hand.

As the older man shook his, he could feel the regret tingle through their hands, but Mr. Grayson didn't let go.

"Julie Jacobson is innocent. I'm sure that'll be proven, but I also know this in my heart. Look into it. She's not the type of person to steal from anyone." He took a breath. "And I'm sincerely sorry for the loss of your property back in Tennessee."

"It was only a frame. It'll be rebuilt."

Mr. Grayson dropped Spencer's hand. "I've learned that Julie was let go under my orders." He frowned. "I would never have done that. I'd like to see her reinstated here. She's an asset you can't be without. She's a fine lawyer. I think of her as a daughter."

"Will you sit for a moment?" Spencer asked and walked back into his office. He motioned to the chair in front to the desk and he took the other.

Mr. Grayson sat and Spencer followed.

"I didn't realize Julie was close to the family." When the words were out, he felt the deceit in them. There had been a layer of uncertainty, and now he was questioning his feelings for the woman who had taken his heart by surprise.

Mr. Grayson folded his hands in his lap and puckered his lips. "I think of you as a good man. I'd be very disappointed if you held that against her."

Perhaps he needed to come clean. Though he wasn't sure why he'd need to. He owned PLL. He could have thrown Mr. Grayson and any member of his family out of the building a month ago. But in his heart he'd thought it was best for them to stay during the transition. He had a soft spot for the man.

"Mr. Grayson, I hired Julie Jacobson to oversee one of my builds in Nashville. Since you let her go, she's been working for me."

The man's eyes shifted and Spencer could see the tension in his jaw. "Does that mean you did have something going on with her?"

Spencer shook his head. "I didn't then. I can honestly say, I didn't like her at all."

"She's got a hard exterior," the man grinned and conceded.

"I know that now." Spencer thought for a moment. "You said she was like a daughter to you."

"I was very close to her father. No one knows that."

"Why?"

Mr. Grayson considered. "I wouldn't hire my own family, but I hired her."

"As a favor?"

"In the beginning. But she proved to be very valuable."

Spencer clasped his own hands and rested his arms on his

thighs. "Do you think they found out? Why would your family do this to her?"

Mr. Grayson furrowed his brow and tucked in his lips as he thought. "I wrote them out of my will. Julie made the changes, but her husband was involved. They found out."

"Ex-husband."

Mr. Grayson nodded. "She'll be okay without him."

Spencer wanted to tell him he could ensure it, but he'd let that go for now. When his phone rang on the desk, he reached for it.

"It's my office."

Mr. Grayson gave him a nod. "I'll be escorting the family out by Friday. You can take over my office then." He held out a hand to Spencer. "It's been a pleasure doing business with your family. I know PLL is in good hands."

"I appreciate that sir."

"I'll let you get to your call," he said as he walked out of Spencer's office.

Spencer hit the button on his phone. "Spencer Benson."

"Spencer, her phone is still on. I can't get a response. She was talking to someone and then there was a big thud. No one is talking, but the phone is still on."

His heart began to pound in his chest in a painful rhythm listening to Tiffany's rapid fire of words. He had no idea where Carson had gone when Mr. Grayson had come to him.

Running down the hall he burst through her office, but she wasn't there. "Tiffany, she's not..."

But he noticed her leg extending out from behind the desk.

"Christ! Julie!" He dropped the phone to the floor and ran to her. "Julie."

He rolled her to her back and her eyes fluttered behind her lids as she began to moan. "Honey, wake up."

She groaned as her eyes opened and closed again. Then slowly opened as if she'd been asleep.

"I got dizzy. The room was spinning."

She pushed up on her elbows and Spencer moved in to cradle her. "Ow," she winced, lifting her hand to the back of her head.

"You're bleeding," he said as she pulled her hand away from her head.

"I'm tired."

"Don't go to sleep." He looked around and could see blood on the leg of the desk. "I think he rattled you, and when you fell you cut open your head. This certainly isn't your day."

She let out what he thought was a laugh.

Spencer picked up her phone, which was lying next to her and disconnected the now thirty-seven minute call which Tiffany had been monitoring. He'd have to consider buying her some diamonds and other assorted gems to make more jewelry. She deserved it.

He helped Julie up and into the chair. "I'm going to find you something to put on that."

She began to point toward a file cabinet. "T-shirt. Bottom drawer."

Spencer opened the drawer and took out the shirt. She certainly had left quickly he thought.

As he passed by his own phone, he picked it back up. "Okay, I have her. She's safe and with me."

"What happened?"

Spencer moved to Julie and pressed the shirt to her head. "Carson Grayson decided to bang her head into the wall a few times. It made her dizzy and when she fell she cut it open."

"Oh, Spencer," Tiffany said and he could hear the tears in her voice.

"I have one woman to deal with. Don't start crying."

"Take care of her."

"I think I always will. Goodbye."

He disconnected the call and put his phone back into his pocket.

Julie looked up at him, her eyes clearer now. "Did Tiffany get my call?"

He couldn't help but smile at her. "Genius idea."

"I was afraid he'd hurt me. Someone needed to know where I was. I was afraid you wouldn't answer the call if you were mad at me."

He took hold of the T-shirt and looked at her head. "I'd still have answered. You're going to need stitches."

"Great. I don't have insurance at the moment."

Spencer smiled. "I think your boss will take care of the expenses."

# CHAPTER 54

Spencer helped Julie to her feet.

"Mr. Grayson says I should hire you back on here."

"I guess he wasn't behind firing me," she said as he walked her from the office.

"No. I didn't know he was a family friend either." Julie turned to look at him and he raised his brows. "You were in deeper with the Graysons than I knew."

Julie batted back tears that had risen in her eyes. "We agreed to never discuss it. If his family knew he'd hired the daughter of his friend and not them…"

"I know. They'd blackmail you and hurt you."

"Right," she said on a weak laugh. "What are you doing here? And the house. She burnt the house. She said she was going to."

"You certainly have a lot of information," Spencer said opening the door to the outside and leading Julie to his rented car.

"Libby. She came to the trailer and demanded the money. I didn't know what she was talking about. She said she'd burn down your build if I didn't give it to her. And she did. She burnt it down."

Spencer reached for the door and pulled it open. He lifted a hand to her cheek before she could climb in. "You talk a lot when you have a head injury."

"I didn't steal the money. I didn't," she said wincing, the T-shirt pressed to her head.

"I know that now."

"You thought I had?"

Spencer brushed away the tears that began to stream down her cheek. "I did. I had no proof otherwise and you'd disappeared. What was I to think?"

"Right." She ducked her head into the car and slid into the seat. "Maybe, if you'd consider it, I should move back here. I mean how can you trust me if you didn't. I'll always wonder and so would you. I could take back my job. Mr. Grayson said he'd tell you. I'm good at it," she pleaded.

"You are."

Spencer shut the car door. He didn't like that she'd want to move back. They were going to work through this. They'd been played, but justice was still being dished out. Libby would pay for what she'd done in Nashville, and Carson was absolutely going to pay for what he'd done to Julie.

And Spencer would be damned if she left him for Oregon again.

He pulled open his door and slid in behind the steering wheel. "You have a house here, right?" he asked as he started the engine and backed out of the parking lot.

"Yes. Steven signed over his part to me. Though he emptied everything out of it."

"We can replace it," he said as he drove away from the PLL offices. "Now's a good time for you to redecorate it. It seems to be a skill you posses."

She turned to look out the window. "I could do that."

Spencer navigated his way through town. "Where is the hospital?"

"Keep heading this way about three miles. Then you'll see the signs."

He nodded. "Chuck said the fire inspector thought we could tear out the old framing in a week or so. They think they have what they need to press formal charges against Libby."

"Good."

"Are you sure you want stained wood in that house? Don't you like the white painted doors?"

Julie batted her eyes as she turned to look at him, still holding the T-shirt to the back of her head. "You want to discuss that now?"

"Why not? It's still a project we're working on together."

He tried to send her a sly smile, but the knot on her head must have been messing with his sarcasm where she was concerned.

"I was seriously thinking that if a corporation moved people in and out of there, they'd want it to always look clean. White painted doors aren't going to look clean after a few years, or a few moves."

He let out a deep breath and reached for her hand. "Considering I'm the corporation moving people in there, I would think you'd want what you liked best."

Julie lowered the T-shirt from her head.

"Rental car," he reminded her. "Don't get blood on the seat." He smiled, but her eyes were wide as she stared at him, lifting the shirt back to her head.

"You're the corporation that's going to use that house? Why are you doing that? I mean who are you going…"

He gave her hand a squeeze. "The house was for us, Julie."

"I don't understand."

"After you moved to Nashville, I realized I didn't want that bachelor life anymore. My apartment wasn't a home. I miss family waiting for you at the end of a long day."

"That does sound nice."

"I thought it would be fun if you designed it, and then I could surprise you with it in a few months. But now that we have to start over..."

He looked at her and the tears fell freely now.

"You don't want that house?" he asked watching her sob without a free hand to wipe away tears.

"It's the best house in the neighborhood."

Spencer nodded again. "It is, isn't it? Right by the park."

The sign ahead pointed toward the hospital and Spencer turned. A few moments later he was parking and turning off the car.

"I have another proposition for you," he said turning toward her. "BBH would like to buy your house here. I'm going to have to make a lot of trips to Oregon and it would just be easier if I had a place to stay when I was here."

She nodded. "You could stay there."

"With you, Julie. You understand that don't you? I want you to be part of PLL, BBH, and the Hart Estates. I want to live in that perfect house—home," he corrected, "with you by the park and fly here and live in your house when we need to."

She winced as she cried. "I think I need to get this looked at."

"C'mon." Spencer opened his door and stepped out. He hurried to the other side and opened her door. "Maybe when the pain isn't in the way, we can have a discussion you'll understand."

FOUR STAPLES LATER, Julie was released into Spencer's care. She'd never had a cut or an injury that needed special care before. And to think, they stapled her head.

She needed to not think about it since it made her knees weak.

"Do you feel okay?" Spencer asked as he climbed into the car next to her.

"I'm exhausted. Since the moment Libby Grayson walked into the trailer, I haven't been thinking straight."

He took her hand in his and kissed her fingers. "I'll second that. You should have come straight to me."

That made more sense now that she had a knot on her head and had given the police the report on what Carson had done.

"I don't think I believed it, Spencer. I wanted to prove to you that I'd never do that."

"Your leaving, and then admitting you had the account, didn't prove that."

She nodded. "I see that now. I think my logical thinking lawyer side is on vacation."

Spencer turned in his seat and looked at her. "My birthday is Saturday, and I want a gift from you."

Julie laughed. "Just because I have a checking account with sixty-thousand dollars in it, doesn't mean I can actually buy you anything."

He smiled. "I'll cover the expense, but will you go away with me? My dad says that we should."

Her mouth fell open. "Your dad says that?"

"He's fairly open minded. He says there's a lot you can do in a hotel room."

Her cheeks instantly heated. "After all of this, you still want to be with me?"

Spencer cupped her face in his hands and gazed at her. "You forget, I've been poorly working this angle for months. I couldn't make a pass at a married woman."

"You didn't like me."

He chuckled. "I didn't think I did. But looking back at it, we sure spent a lot of time together, just the two of us."

"Where are you going to take me?"

"I'm going to tell you a secret. You can't tell anyone yet."

She nodded. "I won't."

"Avery is moving to France. It's going to kill her parents, but she wants to do this."

"You're kidding?"

Spencer shook his head and let his hands slide down her neck and over her shoulders. "There is a guest house at the winery. She wants us to visit."

"France?" The word came on a gasp. "I don't have a passport."

He laughed. "Well then, we'll have to wait a few weeks until you do."

Pulling her to him, he pressed a kiss to her lips. "Why don't you direct me to your house. We can assess a few things, and then go buy a few pieces of furniture. We'll head back to Nashville tomorrow."

"My boss is going to begin to wonder where I've gone," she said lingering close to him, their lips only a breath apart.

Spencer moved his mouth to hers, urging the thoughts and worry from the past few weeks ooze out of her.

He leaned his forehead to hers. "I'm thinking your boss isn't going to worry about that anymore. He's going to keep you very close."

"I'll make it worth his while."

Spencer raised his eyebrows and smiled as he pulled back from her and drove them toward her home in the hills.

# CHAPTER 55

*S*pencer had deflated when he and Julie walked into the back room at Steve's Barbecue Pit and Beer hand in hand. Amongst the decor amassed from garage sales and auctions, the room was specifically decorated in pink and black.

He let out a large sigh as Avery ran to him and wrapped her arms around his neck. She planted a noisy kiss on his cheek. "Did you think I'd let you have a birthday party without pink and black?"

"I so hoped."

"C'mon, you have to see the cake."

"Do I?"

She took his hand and dragged him across the room leaving Julie at the door next to his brother.

"She's done this to him every year," Tyler said to Julie as she watched Spencer shake his head again.

"I think he secretly loves it," she said.

"I think you're right."

Courtney pushed Tyler aside and reached for Julie's arm.

"Would you mind escorting me to the bathroom?" She then turned to Tyler. "I know. I know my way, before you get lippy."

Julie watched as he grinned. "Yes, ma'am."

With Courtney's direction, Julie moved through the eclectically decorated restaurant. "This place is crazy."

"Best barbecue around," Courtney said as they walked down the hallway to the bathroom.

Julie pushed open the door and they both walked in. "This bathroom is huge. You don't see bathrooms like this in restaurants. Hotels maybe."

"That's why I came in here. I really just wanted to talk to you away from everyone else."

The very thought that Courtney, the one who could see everything without vision, wanted to talk to her made her a little nervous. What did she think? What did she want? Suddenly Julie's stomach tightened with nerves.

"When Spencer came back from Oregon after the merger, I could tell something was very wrong. I know that had something to do with you."

"I didn't make his time there very easy."

Courtney nodded. "I know that. But that wasn't all of it."

Julie grinned and caught a glimpse of herself—her very happy self—in the mirror. "I'd jumped him in the elevator and planted one humdinger of a kiss on him. I think it might have startled him."

A smile formed on Courtney's lips. "That would be it. I knew he had a secret in there." She reached out and touched Julie's arm. "He loves you. You're part of this family now."

Julie quickly pushed back the emotions that statement brought to her. What more could she ever have wanted?

Courtney pushed back her shoulders and turned fully to Julie. "How do I look? Tell me my lipstick is perfect and my shirt is on right."

Julie chuckled. "You look radiant."

"Good. I'm about to go out there and tell my husband a secret which will totally distract from that pink and black cake."

The smile that radiated from Courtney was infectious and Julie knew exactly what was about to happen. She didn't ask or say another word. She simply escorted Courtney back to the room where the celebration of Spencer and Avery's birth commenced.

When Julie found Spencer, he was standing next to his mother. He reached out his hand for her, and that simple gesture had her heart pounding in her chest.

His mother smiled at her. "I'm so glad you're here. Above all gifts, seeing my son happy is the best one."

Julie's lip trembled as Spencer's mother touched her cheek, and then walked toward another woman who had called her name.

Spencer wrapped his arm around her waist. "I think they like you."

"Oh, I love them. All of them." She turned to him. "I'm glad you appreciate all of them too. Because if you didn't, I'd tell you how important it is. It's like a high every time I'm around one of your relatives."

"I'm glad to hear you say that." He pulled her into his arms. "Of course, tonight, this isn't where I want to be."

She grinned up at him. "Where do you want to be?"

"I have somewhere I want to take you. What do you say we skip out of here early?"

From the corner of her eye, she saw Courtney move in toward Tyler and move him to the side of the room.

"Okay, not yet." She turned and pointed toward his brother. "Watch this."

"What's going on? They're just talking."

"I don't think so."

.  .  .

SPENCER WATCHED his sister-in-law whisper in his brother's ear. Tyler pulled back and looked at his wife. Was he crying? What in the…

But Spencer knew exactly what had happened when Tyler scooped her up and swung her around.

"They're having a baby, aren't they?" he asked dumbfounded by what he'd watched.

Julie beamed. "I think so. She didn't tell me specifics, but that's what I thought she meant too."

Spencer reached for her hand and intertwined their fingers. He gave her hand a squeeze and she looked up at him.

"I want to share all these moments with you."

Her mouth opened, but there wasn't time for words before Tyler took over the party with his announcement that he was going to be a father.

THE PINK and black cake had been cut, and Avery had toasted each guest with a glass of her newest wine. At some point in the past week, she must have come clean with her plans, because no one was too shocked to hear her talk about the vineyard. However, the look on her mother's face told Spencer everything he needed to know. It wasn't completely welcome. But he knew she'd have the support she needed. That was the one thing Spencer was always sure of.

He sipped the fancy wine Avery had poured him from the pink and black bottle, and searched the room. There was an obvious guest missing.

But at that moment, in all her glimmering glory, Tiffany walked through the door.

Wasn't she a brilliant sight? And wasn't it equally as brilliant to see the woman he loved run to her and envelop her in a hug? Who'd have thought they'd have ever bonded.

There was a little guilt in his heart when he thought about

that day Julie had asked for a job, and he knew then he'd put her with Tiffany. What transpired hadn't been expected.

With their arms locked at the elbow, both women walked toward him with fascinating smiles.

"Wine seems to be flowing freely here," Tiffany looked around.

"Avery just served us all from her wine collection."

Tiffany nodded. "That does sound fancy."

Spencer looked at Julie. "Would you get Tiffany a glass? I'll get her some cake."

Julie nodded and hurried off after Avery.

Spencer turned his attention back to Tiffany. "Well?"

"You asked for one piece. The second took longer."

"But you have it?"

She smiled and pulled two neatly wrapped boxes out of her purse. "If she doesn't like them I can…"

"She's going to love them."

Tiffany stepped in closer to him so that they were eye to eye. "I love her," she said. "If you hurt her I will mess you up."

Her lips curled into a fantastic smile before she moved in closer and pressed a noisy kiss to his lips, no doubt leaving red lipstick on him.

That was when he heard Julie clear her throat. She handed Tiffany her wine and then looked at him.

"You have a little something…" she pointed to her own lips.

"I figured." He wiped the smudge with the napkin that had been wrapped around the glass in his hand.

"I'm going to go mingle. Pete is looking kinda lonely over there. Maybe I can perk him up."

Spencer shook his head as Tiffany walked away.

"It's a good thing I know you're not sleeping with that woman or I'd be very upset," Julie grinned up at him.

"Never again," he promised.

The room was full of family and dear friends, but Spencer knew this was not where he wanted to be.

"I want to get out of here. How about you?"

Julie's eyes widened. "Are you kidding? Look at all these people. You can't leave."

He took her glass from her and set it on the table behind him with his glass. Then he took her hand. "C'mon. For a little bit. We can come back if they're all still here."

# CHAPTER 56

S pencer had all but pulled Julie out of the party, and no one seemed to notice. They'd climbed into his car, and of all places, he drove them out to the build site.

He didn't park by the trailers. Instead he pulled up in front of the charred remains of the house they'd been planning together.

"Spencer, this isn't where you should be on your birthday."

"I wanted so much to surprise you with that house. I knew you liked it. Tiffany had told me it was your favorite."

"She sure pays a lot of attention to things."

"She's a jewelry designer. Attention to detail."

They sat there in silence for a few more minutes before Julie touched Spencer's arm. "Why don't we go back? This is just depressing."

"I have a better idea," he said as he backed up the car and drove away from the site.

But he didn't drive far. Instead, he drove down the dirt road that led to the farm behind the build site.

"It's late. You don't want to bother him do you?" Julie protested.

"No. I don't plan on bothering him. But there is this barn out here…" his words trailed off as he took a small road through the fields.

The lights of the town seemed to dim the closer they got to the barn, and the sky became brighter with stars.

"You chose tonight to come stargazing?" She laughed.

"My birthday. My choice."

Julie nodded. "I'll give you that."

Spencer parked in front of the barn and turned off the car. He opened his door and looked at her. "C'mon."

Julie stepped out of the car. "Spencer, we shouldn't be out here. This is still his land."

"Yeah, but he agreed to sell it to me," he said as he shone the flashlight of his phone on the barn door.

"That doesn't mean trespass now," she said following him into the barn.

Spencer kept walking and it took her jogging, in her high heels in soft hay, to catch up with him.

"There they are," he said as he shined his phone on the set of stairs that went to the loft.

"Are you serious? You're going up into the loft? Spencer…"

But he'd already taken off.

He was waiting for her at the base of the steps. He reached out his hand and helped her up.

"I couldn't have changed shoes?" she said, but it only caused Spencer to chuckle.

When they reached the loft, the top door was open and the nighttime view was spectacular.

"Oh, Spencer."

With his arm to guide her, he walked them closer to the edge and stopped to take it all in.

"I came up here the other day and just sat here," Spencer said. "It reminded me of my family's house and my grandmother's. All of that charm right here where the country meets the city."

"Just like you."

He nodded. "Sprawling Tennessee land and high-rises," he confirmed. "I was thinking this would be the most spectacular view for a house."

She turned her gaze to him. "You're thinking about your new development?"

Spencer shook his head. "Not this time. I want to show you something else. Close your eyes."

He watched her until she did just that. She could hear him move around, but a moment later he was standing next to her.

"Open them."

When she did, the loft had been transformed. White lights shimmered around her and a small bed had been laid out in the hay.

She turned to him. "How long did you plan this?"

He grinned at her. "Spontaneous. But it pays to have a best friend that will do anything for you."

"Tiffany?"

"I'll owe her a new pair of shoes."

"Her taste is exquisite."

"I know." He took Julie's hand and pulled her toward the little bed that had been laid out. "It occurred to me that you told me you loved me in my sister's kitchen while you held my niece."

Julie fought the sting of tears. "I did."

"You looked so beautiful sitting there with a baby asleep in your arms among my family. I should have told you that."

He pulled her into him and she wrapped her arms around his neck.

"Spencer, I meant it when I said I loved you."

"I know. And I realized I've never told you how I feel."

"When you're ready."

"I'm ready," he said. "I love you. I think I loved you even when I didn't like you."

"I didn't like you either."

"Good," he said smiling as he nipped her lips with a kiss. "I want to give you something." He pulled a box from his jacket pocket. "I asked Tiffany to design this for you."

He handed her the box, but all she could do was stare at him. On his birthday, he was giving her a gift?

"Open it," he urged her.

Julie slipped her finger under the flap of the paper and tore it off, then lifted the lid to reveal the most beautiful necklace she'd ever seen.

"Oh, Spencer, it's beautiful."

"I knew she'd come up with something that was as spectacular as you."

He took the ruby and diamond necklace from the box and moved behind her. Slipping the dainty silver chain around her neck, he clasped it on and then rested his hands on her shoulders. He pressed a kiss to the side of her neck and then let his arms slide around her so that her back was pressed to his chest.

The warmth of the moment would be something she'd go back to forever when she needed a happy place to think about.

"I love you," he whispered in her ear and her eyes closed as she embraced the moment.

"I love you, too." She let the words flow on the whisper of her breath.

She felt him shift and his arm came around her again.

"There's one more."

Julie opened her eyes looked down to the small box in the palm of his hand.

Her breath caught in her lungs as she took the box from him and turned toward him.

"Spencer, I should be giving you gifts."

"You will be. Let me open this one."

He pulled the paper from the box and opened it. For a moment, he studied it before he turned it around.

"This one is for me." He took the solitaire diamond which was set in swirls of silver, from the box and held it under the shimmering white lights. "This one comes with a promise and that's all for me."

Julie swallowed hard trying not to sob as she gazed at him.

"I promise to love you forever. And I keep all the promises I make."

"I know you do."

He took her hand and slid the ring on her finger. "What I ask in return, as a present for my birthday, and for the rest of my life, is your promise to love me forever too."

It was no use. The tears spilled over and down her cheek. "I promise you."

"Julie, will you marry me? Will you be part of my family, and have a family with me?"

The sobs she fought took away her words and all he did was continue to smile at her.

This was what she'd always wanted. A man who loved her and was an honest and good man. She wanted normal. A house. A job. A family.

Spencer Benson was promising it all to her, and she wanted it so badly that she was afraid she'd blink and it would all be gone.

Julie closed her eyes tightly and took a deep breath. When she opened them, he was still there gazing at her, holding the ring on her finger.

"Well? Will you marry me?"

She nodded. It was all she could do. Words wouldn't come to give him a proper answer.

Spencer slid the ring on her finger and then moved in to wipe the tears from her cheeks.

"You talk more when your head is bleeding."

She coughed out a laugh. "I'll marry you. I will. I'll be good to you."

"I know you will. That's who you are."

He turned her so his arms came around her again and his chin rested on her shoulder. They looked out over the view of the beautiful Tennessee land and sky.

"I'm going to build you a house right there," he pointed. "I'm keeping this barn. I love this barn."

That made her laugh. "What about all the other houses?"

"One hundred and fifty will now become seventy-five and they will all be over there," he pointed in the distance. "And we, and our family," he added, "will live here in the middle of it all with Tennessee sprawling all around us."

She turned into his arms and wrapped hers around his neck. "I love you. Happy Birthday."

Rising on her toes, she pressed her mouth to his and let the atmosphere and the love consume her.

"Avery thinks she can trump me by choosing pink and black cakes each year," he said pressing his forehead to hers. "This year I think I win. I think this one will go down in history as the best birthday ever."

# EPILOGUE

$S$ pencer moved Julie toward the bed of blankets and pillows that Tiffany had set up for him. He lowered Julie down beneath him.

She was going to be his wife.

As he moved over her, his lips skimming soft skin, and the low moan resonating from her, he thought about how happy the thought of forever was making him.

He'd watched his father and mother love one another—his grandparents, his aunts and uncles, and his cousins. Now his brother and sister were in relationships that were easily envied. When he'd gone to Oregon the first time, he never could have imagined that it would lead to love an happiness.

Julie looked up at him, her finger lifted into his hair. "We could go back to your party and announce this," Julie said on a breath before she moaned again under his lips.

"They'll find out soon enough. I want you all to myself."

"What if the farmer comes in here," she said as she moved her fingers under his shirt and over his skin.

"He knows I'm here. And we're not going anywhere."

Spencer gathered the skirt of her dress up around her waist as her fingers laced into his hair. "I love you, Spencer," Julie said and Spencer looked into her eyes. He'd always known this was what he wanted—deep inside of him.

"I love you too," he said as he lowered himself down to her just as his phone rang. "Someone has horrible timing."

Julie skimmed a kiss over his jaw. "Are you doing to answer it?"

Spencer growled out his answer realizing it was his mother's ring tone. "What do I tell her?" he asked as he looked down at her.

"I don't suppose you want to tell her what she's interrupted."

"Leave it to my mother to make my engagement feel as if I were being caught doing something like a naughty teenager."

Julie laughed as he shifted to pull his phone from his pocket.

JULIE WATCHED as he absorbed what his mother was saying. He eased back, and soon he was only nodding.

"Okay, we'll be there."

Julie eased herself up on her elbows and waited for him to disconnect the call. "Spencer, what's wrong? Something happened?"

He nodded. "We have to go."

"You're scaring me. Where are we going?"

His lips curled into a smile. "We'll announce this later." He stood up and reached for her, helping her to her feet.

"Spencer, tell me what's going on."

Julie fixed her skirt as he came to her, placed his hands on her cheeks, and pulled her in for a deep and satisfying kiss. "You're going to be my wife."

Julie searched his eyes. "I am. What's going on?"

"We're about to become aunt and uncle." He kissed her again.

"Darcy?"

"Yes. My mother could hardly talk." He kissed her again. "The birthday party is being moved to the hospital."

"Then I guess this will wait." She looked down at her finger. "I guess this has become an epic day. You and Avery were born on the same day, and now you're getting a niece or nephew."

Spencer's phone buzzed again and he looked down at it and blew out a breath.

"Victoria just went into labor too."

Julie began to laugh. "So this is what it's like to be part of a family?"

"This is it."

"And everyone will be there?"

"I can almost guarantee it."

Julie started for the steps. "Then we'd better go. I'm going to be an aunt. I don't want to miss a moment of being part of this family."

We hope you enjoyed Bernadette Marie's
*The Merger.*
Continue the family saga with an excerpt from book ten,
*The Escape Clause.*

# THE ESCAPE CLAUSE

## CHAPTER ONE

*H*ospitals were Avery's least favorite place to be. She had to admire her father for choosing a career that had him bound to them for so many years.

As the day of her birthday slipped away and a new day began, she sat in the waiting room with her family.

She wondered if this was the similar scene twenty-six years ago when she and her cousin Spencer were born. Surely her parents were surrounded by family, and in another room her aunt and uncle were surrounded by the same family.

Spencer was only an hour older than Avery was, and they'd shared every birthday together since that first one. And now, after their celebration, her cousin Christian's wife Victoria was in one room of the hospital in labor, and her cousin Ed and his wife Darcy were in another.

She'd watched as Ed and Christian's parents, her aunt Madeline and uncle Carlos, went from room to room. Ed and Christian's sister Clara sat across from Avery rubbing her very pregnant stomach.

The Keller family was being bombarded with babies, and now her cousin Tyler and his wife Courtney were expecting too.

For a very brief moment, she felt a pang of jealousy rip through her. Would she ever know this moment? Would she ever have that man who would bring her to this moment?

Pete walked up next to her and held out a paper cup of coffee from the vending machine. "Best we can get at one in the morning."

She graciously took it as he sat down. "Thanks. My head is still swimming from all the wine I drank."

He gave her a small nudge. "Lush," he said with a chuckle and then began to blow on his coffee.

For a moment, Avery just watched him. Pete Grant had been her dearest friend her entire life. He'd bowed down and played dress up a few times. He'd taught her how to bounce a soccer ball on her forehead. Thinking back, he'd even canceled his own prom date to take her when her date backed out. He was that kind of friend.

And now here he was, sitting in a hospital at one o'clock in the morning waiting out babies with her and her family.

She rested her head on his shoulder and he pressed his head to hers.

It was nice to be so comfortable around a friend. He was easing that jealousy she'd been feeling. Someday he'd make someone a good husband.

AROUND TWO O'CLOCK, Christian walked out into the waiting area rubbing his eyes. Their aunt Arianna jumped to her feet.

"Well?"

He shook his head. "Her contractions stopped. They're going to let her rest for a little bit and see how it goes. If they need to induce her, they will do that later today. The baby is ready, just not cooperating."

Avery was sure everyone in the room, who was awake, wanted to make some comment to the lack of cooperation and aim it at Christian. However, the look on his face—that look of worry—had them all remaining quiet.

Victoria had lost their first child. As Avery's father had told them, it just happened. But Avery was sure neither of them ever got over it—how could they?

She turned her face into Pete's shoulder so that his shirt caught the few tears that were threatening to spill.

"Are you okay?" His voice was a whisper and so gentle.

"I'm just worried for them."

Pete moved his hand over hers and gave it a squeeze. "Everything is going to be okay. Babies have their own agenda, and it isn't ours."

She supposed he knew what he was talking about. He had four sisters and a brother. His family was as close as her extended family. She, of course, was an only child. It had never felt like that though. There probably wasn't a day in her life where she hadn't seen one of her cousins, aunts, or uncles.

As she turned her hand over in his and locked their fingers, she realized they were both blessed to have that. Now all they had to do was find that right person, for each of them, that could make them happy forever.

A few minutes later, Ed staggered into the waiting room. The clothes he'd worn to Avery's party were now under a paper robe. He had a mask down under his chin and a paper hat over his hair. Darcy had gone into labor at the same time as Victoria. However, their baby was breech and more excited to meet everyone as she was scheduled the following week to have a Caesarean. But, now was a good time too, Avery thought as she looked at her cousin with his enormous grin.

Christian was the first to step to him. "Well?"

"She's here. She's here!"

Christian pulled his brother to him in a hug that had Avery's eyes filling fuller with tears.

"I'm happy for you," Christian said patting his brother's back and looking at him. "She's healthy and Darcy is okay?"

"She's perfect. Oh, she's perfect. And Darcy is wonderful. She's in recovery and Mom and Regan are with her." He looked around the room.

In the corner, Ed found his father asleep in a chair with his daughter Emily asleep on his shoulder.

Avery watched as Ed moved to them. He touched his father's hand, waking him up.

"She's here. A little girl, Dad."

Avery's uncle Carlos smiled a wide smile, careful not to move.

"I know she'll never understand this, but I want to take her to see her sister." He rolled the little girl from his father's shoulder and she stirred. "Hey, big sister. Let's go see your baby sister."

Avery wasn't sure that at ten months little Emily, whom Ed and Darcy had adopted, had a clue as to what was going on, but they'd all remember.

Pete turned to look at Avery.

"You look exhausted. Why don't I take you home for a while? It doesn't sound like Victoria is going to have her baby tonight."

She hated the thought of leaving, but she knew it made sense. She could go home, get a few hours sleep, and be right back there in the morning to wait out another baby.

Avery looked at Clara uncomfortably seated in the chair across from her and Warner rubbing her back to comfort her.

That jealous pang hit her chest again.

"Okay, let me say goodbye to my parents."

# PLEASE REVIEW

We hope you enjoyed *The Merger* by Bernadette Marie. If you did, we would ask that you please rate and review this title. Every review helps our authors.

Rate and Review: The Merger

# ABOUT THE AUTHOR

Bestselling Author Bernadette Marie is known for building families readers want to be part of. Her series The Keller Family has graced bestseller charts since its release in 2011. Since then she has authored and published over fifty books. The married mother of five sons promises romances with a Happily Ever After always…and says she can write it because she lives it.

Obsessed with the art of writing and the business of publishing, chronic entrepreneur Bernadette Marie established her own publishing house, 5 Prince Publishing, in 2011 to bring her own work to market as well as offer an opportunity for fresh voices in fiction to find a home as well.

When not immersed in the writing/publishing world, Bernadette Marie can be found spending time with her family, traveling (mostly to Disney parks), and running multiple businesses. An avid martial artist, Bernadette Marie is a second degree black belt in Tang Soo Do, and loves Tai Chi. She is a retired hockey mom, a lover of a good stout craft beer, and might have an unhealthy addiction to chocolate.